Praise for **Sibella & Sibella**

"Joseph Di Prisco's fearlessness always in[...]
is no exception. Invoking satire and sil[...]
hijinks and hilarity, *Sibella & Sibella* take[...]
narrated through the lens of a young w[...]
at a San Francisco publishing house. Fortunately for readers, Di Prisco
embraces the absurdity, and the result is this wonderfully crafted and
bitingly funny critique that never fails to entertain."

—Lori Ostlund, award-winning author of *After the Parade*

Praise for **Pope of Brooklyn**

"A literary son traces his fugitive father in a pulpy yet cerebral memoir...
This sprawling narrative is punctuated by Di Prisco's reflections
on literature, faith, mortality, and his own tangled romances and
outré experiences, ranging from cocaine addiction to mentoring
adolescents.... Deft, amusing, and tough."

—*Kirkus Reviews*

Praise for **The Alzhammer**

"Part Mafia thriller, part comic farce, part lament about the anguish
of dementia and all hyperkinetic.... Fast-paced and often charming."

—*Kirkus Reviews*

"Di Prisco writes with humor and a great sense of character, poking
fun at things that would leave a lesser author cringing. Think *Cuckoo's
Nest* meets *The Godfather*. He interweaves all these elements with the
skill of a master writer."

—Anne Hillerman, *New York Times* bestselling author of
Spider Woman's Daughter and *Rock with Wings*

"Di Prisco delivers a brilliant portrayal of a wise guy who faces his
biggest arch enemies...time and Alzheimer's. The last tango of power,
fear, loyalty, and love is beautifully danced for us right to the very end."

—Vickie Sciacca, manager of Lafayette Library

"Great, funny lines on every page. Am I recommending *The Alzhammer*? As the protagonist Mikey might say, 'Eggs ackly.'"

—Jack Handey, author of *Deep Thoughts*

Praise for Sightlines from the Cheap Seats

"Musical, muscular, romantic, wise, Joseph Di Prisco's new collection of poems, *Sightlines from the Cheap Seats* offers an expansive view of the landscape, taking us on a curvy trail out of the stadium that leads to our hearts and minds—a poetry adventure that kicks down doors to hidden rooms filled with sunlight."

—Kim Dower, *Last Train to the Missing Planet*

Praise for Subway to California

"A beautiful, heartfelt, sometimes funny, occasionally harrowing story of a man making his way through the minefield of his own family history. Di Prisco has lived more lives than most of us, and managed to get it all down in this riveting book."

—Jerry Stahl, author of *Permanent Midnight* and *Bad Sex On Speed*

"Di Prisco delivers thoughtful contemplation of the human condition and plenty of self-examination that reveals how he made it to where he is, and why he survived when others didn't. His sharp wit and hard-won wisdom make *Subway to California* a story that anyone who's risen out of a hardscrabble life with the odds stacked against them will love and learn from."

—*Foreword Reviews*

"[Di Prisco] can break your heart recalling the most romantic memory of his life or make you laugh out loud when, for example, he defines the Catholic notion of Limbo: 'not a horrible place, not a great place, sort of like parts of Staten Island.'"

—*Kirkus Reviews*

Sibella & Sibella

ALSO BY JOSEPH DI PRISCO

Novels
Confessions of Brother Eli
Sun City
All for Now
The Alzhammer

Memoirs
Subway to California
The Pope of Brooklyn

Poetry
Wit's End
Poems in Which
Sightlines from the Cheap Seats

Nonfiction
Field Guide to the American Teenager (Michael Riera, coauthor)
Right from Wrong (Michael Riera, coauthor)

EDITED BY JOSEPH DI PRISCO

Simpsonistas: Tales from the Simpson Family Literary Project

Sibella & Sibella

a novel by

Joseph Di Prisco

a vireo book \ rare bird books
los angeles, calif.

This is a Genuine Vireo Book

A Vireo Book | Rare Bird Books
453 South Spring Street, Suite 302
Los Angeles, CA 90013
rarebirdbooks.com

First Trade Paperback Original Edition

Set in Dante
Printed in the United States

10 9 8 7 6 5 4 3 2 1

Publisher's Cataloging-in-Publication data
Names: Di Prisco, Joseph, 1950-, author.
Title: Sibella & Sibella : a novel / by Joseph Di Prisco.
Description: First Trade Paperback Original Edition. | A Vireo Book. |
New York, NY; Los Angeles, CA: Rare Bird Books, 2018.
Identifiers: ISBN 9781947856318
Subjects: LCSH Publishers and publishing—Fiction. | Work—Fiction. |
Authors—Fiction. | Women—Fiction. | Humor fiction. | Humorous
stories. | Satire. | BISAC FICTION / Literary. | FICTION /
Humorous. | FICTION / Satire.
Classification: LCC PS3554.I67 S53 2018 | DDC 813.54—dc23

For the Lafayette Library and Learning Center

&

For A Great Good Place for Books

"What country, friends, is this?"
"This is Illyria, lady."
"And what should I do in Illyria?"

—*Twelfth Night, or What You Will*

PART ONE

SIBELLA OF THE BASKERVILLES

D ON'T CALL ME.[1]
Once upon a time, I was the junior editor at my three-ring publishing house answering the fucking office phone because the senior editors were too busy making smooth moves on Mortal Kombat or Tinder to answer the fucking office phone.

You would be wasting your breath on me, however, if you were some hotshot sociopath author, or a big-time smack-talker slash agent hawking a page-turner beach read, or if you were scheming to lock up a blockbuster movie deal over martinis at Chateau Marmont, or if you were bellyaching about our trademark bogus marketing blitzes. *Now* you're going to whine? Bogus marketing blitzes are what made our upstart crow company famous. The publisher himself left no doubt he was all that and wasn't taking your call, so no wonder his house-on-fire success pissed off the book-biz heavyweights otherwise occupied throwing hands during Manhattan fight club nights.

But say you got me, perish the thought. And pretend I got all goosebumpy hearing from the star your publicist tells you that you are. You still needed to get through the wormhole to the publisher. Bon voyage, Einstein. Legend was that Myron Beam hadn't answered the fucking phone since the crash. Not that crash, the one *before* that crash. But he was the publisher and the company

---

1   My one and only footnote, if you're lucky. Something tells me you are going to need more than a rabbit's foot. You're going to need a way bigger boat.

owner, the one you needed to talk to who wasn't going to pick up the fucking phone for whoever you may think you are.

I didn't know to an immoral certainty what a *junior* editor was supposed to do, but I'd been doing my job for a while—at least, when I wasn't answering the fucking phone, I assume I'd been doing whatever may have been the junior editor job. To me it didn't seem all that different from what senior editors did, but I did it faster and cheaper and better, and as far as all those senior editors sneaking off to yoga or spinning classes were concerned, more irritatingly.

I was assured a job description would be on my desk on day one. No such document appeared on that day or any other, but to be fair, neither did a desk upon which it could materialize. Instead, I operated upon a sturdier-than-it-looked LEGO-like construction of interlocking red and blue plastic milk crates. Myron saved a buck wherever and whenever he could. For stability sake, my crates were propped against what seemed to be a bullet-riddled, pockmarked wall, which might have furnished clues as to the fate of my extinguished predecessors. It was also where somebody other than I would have plenty of space for graffiti or for tacking up precious photos of pet pugs and tabbies and significant others. I am pathetic when it comes to photos, but I am a champ when it comes to cultivating insignificant others.

If I may continue.

One ancillary aspect of my junior editor job seemed to be answering, as I may have in passing mentioned, that fucking phone. Suavely, I ferried the snarling pack of snark monsters over to the mineshaft of Myron's voice mail, which in my time had rarely not been full, its need-to-know location in the howling heath that time and Myron continually forgot along with his password. (I hinted to Myron: "Rhymes with *subpoena*... No, not *hyena*, but good try.") Which is why he instructed me to transcribe the messages—including the hysterical sourpuss lawyer legalese— left for him, but why he had a voice mailbox in the first place was another mystery because the same sort of people left the same frantic, threatening messages over and over again.

Then there was *this* call. In a sane publishing house it would have set off warning bells, but in our publishing house it should have been viewed as a harbinger of things to come.

Ring. Ring. Ring. Ring. Ring. Ring. Ring. Ri...

"Hard Rain Publishing, may I help you?"

"Tell'm I sez fuck off en don't wanna talk 'bout it."

I had grown accustomed to the antagonistic tenor and the inscrewtability of messages left for the esteemed publisher. Still, that was an odd way to initiate communication, by saying he was calling so as not to talk, but upon reflection that might have been the counterintuitive winning strategy for dealing with a publisher who would never answer his fucking phone.

"If you would like to leave a voice mail for..."

"Tell Moron that Fig sez I'm through wit duh sonuvabitch. Got that, Missy Sweet Pants?"

Thus I begat. Ms. Sweatpants couldn't forget what the man said or the voice in which he said it. Half frog, half crow. Let's call it a frow. Better yet, a crog.

First opportunity, I handed Myron the note on which I had inscribed the deftly nuanced dispatch. I intuited that the communication had to be of course from none other than Mr. Figgy Fontana, the house's star, a mega-selling author whose latest novel was scheduled for imminent release, the lead title for the season, and orders were pouring in ceaselessly, as expected, and units were rolling out in a flood tide. In case you don't know this, publishers call books *units*. So yes, another Hard Rain hit on the horizon. As for the horizon, if I knew then what I know now, I might have been binge-watching the Weather Channel when I recalled the title of Fontana's forthcoming blockbuster: *Swimming Buck Naked in the Hurricane.*

Myron read the transcribed message over and over, as if it conveyed some secret, coded import, and based on his response, I gather it did.

"That's nice," he said. "Been a while since old Fig reached out."

And Myron Beam's French Foreign Legion of detractors claimed he lacked people skills.

∗∗∗

I AM AN INVISIBLE woman.

Though FYI I get rowdy when startled or provoked.

Like "Don't call me," "invisible woman" constitutes another obvious literary collusion. Literary allusion or literary reference—these namby-pamby terms don't cut it for me. For ease of collusion identification, I was tempted to insert gorgeous, helpful asterisks. I love asterisks almost more than LEGO. To my eye, they sparkle on the page. But even if I did * it, my senior editor colleagues will still thrash about helplessly on the deck of their sinking careers. And if one day I abracadabra my way into an ISBN number, they will Byromaniacally descend like the fucking Assyrians who poetically came down like wolves on the fold and rip my book to shreds anyway. They call me show-offy and babestruse, and I'll endeavor to keep the obscure to a minimum, but no promises.

Whenever anybody probed me during enhanced interrogation and I confessed beneath the naked, swinging lightbulb that I was a junior editor, I reflexively thought of Junior Mints or Junior Leaguer. Not sure which I like less. One is a candy and the other is minty fresh. Tell me, whoever grows up dreaming to become Junior Anything? On this score, I wish I could eradicate one other disturbing association.

My all-through-college boyfriend addressed his darling appendage by the name of Junior, in this sense referring both to the branding opportunity (ouch) as well as, to be blunt, the gone-but-not-forgotten-enough Johnson. And enlighten me, please. Query Nation: What's with guys' pet names for their package? As children did they gnash their teeth and gwail when at Christmas time they were denied the pooches and gerbils they dreamed of?

Why, yes, as a matter of fact I *do* have a black belt in TMI. As far as you may be concerned, Too Much Information has a payoff: you can unconditionally trust me, I have nothing to hide, and if I did, I would conceal it in plain sight.

Speaking of college, I didn't graduate *summa cum laude* and Phi Beta Kappa like Junior's Keeper. I was too busy reading books (when

I wasn't captaining my D1 college basketball team to another sorry season in the Northeastern snow belt) to attend scrupulously to the required courses necessary to grasp the marvels of derivatives and mitosis and the War of the Roses (the historically glorious escapade I mangled into the War *on* the Roses, which sounded quite mean-girlish) and otherwise achieve a well-rounded education, or receive a grade higher than C in any class other than Lit. I myself graduated *magna cum nada* and Phi Beta Mash Kappotatah. Later on, I did pinch a creative writing MFA, about which I am less proud than my dalliance with Junior, and the less said on this topic by this Mistress of the Fine-ish Arts the better.

But speaking of those Juniors idolized by old boyfriends snappily married currently to trust fund snap pea princesses and residing in lah-de-dah Park Slopeshod, this year he actually won the Yale Younger Fucking Poets Prize, which I continue to struggle to believe, and which depressed me more than my apartment's latest punitive rent increase, which was utterly unbelievable. Besides, I was getting older, and it was time to get serious about my life, which was wasting away, though my chances of snagging the Yale Decrepit Poets Prize were perhaps escalating. I was twenty-six already. I had been planning to quit this job as soon as something better came along.

But that's a lie. Not the part about quitting. That's true. But I was not twenty-six, I was twenty-five. I graduated from college at the ripe old age of nineteen. I skipped a bunch of grades on my magnificent journey through the precious deformative high school years, and it was trouble-free for me to be shuttled to the next higher class because I was always by far the tallest girl at an all-girls K-12 school. I was also what the private school counselors labeled "precocious." That insult was margarinely better than others I heard—lanktoid, dork, geek, talltard. I think the counselors meant I had a ridiculous vocabulary from having started reading chapter books while briskly gestating in my sabbaticalized professorial mother's Guggenheimlich Maneuver of a womb. Did they bestuff Mom with that fancy fellowship so she could have her very own baby subject upon whom she could do her groundbreaking research? I have no understanding of Smackademia. Who does? From that embryoyo point forward, I kept reading anything and everything, figuring why stop now? More than any other factor, the high school kept oonching me up the food chain insofar as they needed a lanktard jizzface to play center on the basketball team ASAP because the rest of us girls who suited up resembled gnomes.

***

AT THIS STAGE OF my alleged career, therefore, I was at this publishing house and answering the fucking phone for two years. I was surrounded by non-junior editors, all of whom were getting way, way up there, thirty-ish.

In the case of Hard Rain Publishing where I was ungainly and on the verge of being unemployedly, the publisher's name was, as I said, Myron Beam. To gauge by all the hot shot authors and agents he blew off, you have probably heard of him. He was a very big deal in the book world.

You might speculate that a big kahuna like Myron, who effortlessly enraged A-listers, would cut an intimidating figure. That white noise stillness of crickets would seep like nerve gas into any room he surveyed. That the indigenous book people would run for the hills when he strutted in to claim their village like a fuckwad conquistador. To the contrary, he looked more like the methodical guy in the back room of the jewelry store repairing watches and replacing batteries. Myron dressed in the same undaring fashion every day, using "fashion" loosely. Wrinkled white shirt, sleeves rolled up above the elbow, and a skinny black tie hanging below the untethered top button. Navy blue blazer (draped on the back of his chair) that had seen better decades and was missing the bottom button, which dejected detail spoke volumes as to his threadbare domestic life. He wore gigantic black rectangular glasses, but he hardly used them for their ostensibly intended purpose: to see. They functioned mostly as a prop, and they seemed to be in perpetual motion: sliding down his nose, hoisted high up on his domed forehead, or cast down onto the desk—which I came to discover was a bad sign you didn't want to see: a sign he was pissed. As he often was. Fascinatingly, during the act of reading was the one time his glasses were not on or in the vicinity of his head. Overall, to me, he gave the impression of a man impersonating a book publisher. Which is, I hear, the image most powerful book publishers tend to project.

From the jump ball, I wanted to fit in at my new job, strived to look the part, though fitting in and looking the part were objectives I had successfully failed to achieve at every stage in my dissibellatating life. So from my first day forward I wore a sleeves-rolled-up white shirt and a skinny-snake black tie, too. Myron looked like he belonged, if anybody did, and thus I wanted to pass myself off as a much taller, younger, and femalerish edition of him. Besides, who doesn't love the classic *Blues Brothers* movie uniform? I don't think Myron was impressed, if he noticed at all. But Kelly certainly did.

Kelly was a gosh-and-golly, pretty-as-springtime senior editor who owned more pant suits than Hillary Clinton and who took an instantaneous dislike to me. On my divirginating morn, she craned her head upward and studied me and my gnattily chosen attire.

"Giraffe new girl, I really don't *think* so."

"Giraffe new *girl*? You seriously say *that*?" *Giraffe* hadn't been lobbed into my bunker since middle school. "Look at you. You just sail in on the PMS *Pinafore*?"

"Well, you are unnecessarily tall. Poor thing, do you have some rare, incurable, Elephant Girl–type bone disease?"

"That's an example of what you call *thinking*? They should send out an Amber Alert so we can all go search for your kidnapped brain *function*? Then again, why should I fucking care what you really don't *think*?"

You never get a second chance to make a first impression. Thus commenced Kelly and my fabled association.

One other noteworthy trait of Machine Gum Kelly. As we all would acknowledge, the world is divided between the people like me who are revolted by the sight of anybody chewing gum and the people who should be cast adrift on the high seas minus provisions. And Kelly masticated gum like it was her vocation. I presume she needed some calling to commit to, given her limited editorial acumen. *Chomp chomp chomp chomp chomp chomp chomp*, all the livelong day. Why she couldn't have satisfied her oral fixation like an ordinary person with chewing tobacco or smoking cigarettes or anything comparably salutary is beyond me and, I trust, you as well. If you were wondering whether or not it was possible to chew gum and intelligently edit a book at the same time, the Kelly Girl was all the evidence required to conclude in the negative.

In my little bookish kingdom by the sea, to get to the bottom line, Myron Beam Me Up did sign my checks. In case you were asking yourself what color is your parachute and what you should do for a career, my dad probably has a few copies of that huge-selling book lying around, which you can borrow, from when he went through his two midlife crises. I think it is mathematically impossible to have *two* midlife anythings, but then again I didn't light up the classroom in pre-, post-, or anti-calc. In any event, forget Silicon Valley and rush into the exciting world of publishing, then buy all cash a Park Avenue or Pacific Heights condo, baby. My paycheck was so enormous, a Samoan bodyguard should have accompanied me to the bank. Which reminded me, I needed to sign up for online banking like everybody else between Central and Golden Gate Parks. There were a lot of things I needed to do, like get a new job, like join a gym, like get that stupid tattoo Junior talked me into lasered off.

Muse advertises my electric-blue tat because Junior swore I was that to him and I was gullible and drunk enough one night in the East Village to subscribe to and act upon it. Better than *Junior Editor*, I suppose. And way better than what the drunker, hysterical girl next table over was getting stamped on her rap-star-approved if-and-and butt: USDA CHOICE. Since *Muse* is right above my breast, and therefore I'd have to strip my shirt off for somebody else to see it, there was a solid chance it would never again be viewed by anybody but me in what was shaping up to be my nunnery lifetime. It wasn't like the tat was as big as the logo on my college jersey, and not that it pulsed like a neon beer sign, but *I* knew it was there, and that made me think about Junior every single day, which I wished I could stop doing.

Trouble is I couldn't find time to take care of such business, or to launder my five rotating white shirts as often as I should, because for one thing the washer/dryer was always on the freaking fritz downstairs despite the relentless rent increases supposedly for fictive property upfuckingkeep. I was inundated by manuscripts from the splendidly named slush pile, and I read them all day and night long. When I was not reading manuscripts, I was often reading Proust. Well, trying to read Proust, and you got me how he ever wiggled out of the slush pile. At that time, I was on Volume 1, with—I think—a mere five million mouthwatering pages left to go. Talk about a page-turner beach read. At the rate I was going, I would reach FIN toward the end of Michelle Obama's second term as president. Nonetheless, I hoped something resembling a story not connected to a cookie should kick in one day. As cookies go, his is tasty and very influential, but come on. "For a long time, I went to bed early." As for me, I fell asleep early as well, the instant I turned one of Monsieur Marcel's pages in search of lost time and a human heartbeat. I realize this does not constitute begging the question but: Is there any justification for the French? Their way of life, I mean?

Then again, reading's not what I call a problem. That's what I will always call the best fucking job in the whole world.

Along with Kelly, there were other senior editors. One of them stood out for her knack of expressing more than her fair share of opinions, on a wide range of mysterious subjects, hardly any views of which I comprehended. I say "stood out," but honestly, I have few recollections of her not planted in her chair. Unfortunately, I cannot mimic Murmechka's inimitable accent (but think taffy stuck in your teeth) or identify the country of origin or hazard a guess as to whether that country was in good standing in the United Nations, or if maybe it was a West Texas county and Texas has not yet seceded from the Union. Wherever she hailed from, her ethnic fashion fallback choices were remarkable and idiosyncratic, resembling pastel pup tents. She was plus-plus-plus-plus-size (no disrespect intended), which explained a great deal to her endocrinologist if not me. The other day I had heard her tell somebody, "A dog may blow a whistle but he cannot call himself to the hunt." She often passed along such wisdom to innocent bystanders without prompting or provocation. I knew it was wisdom because the beneficiaries of her insight shook their heads and repaired in a distant port for a private cry or a tequila shooter. Yet the part of the job I liked more than I would have expected was that Murmechka's desk was nearest my multicolored milk crates.

As my colleague liked to say: "A lover may weep for joy but will not swim to the farther shore where the birds serenade her at dusk." My hunch was Murmechka of the North hailed from a landlocked, ice-bound kingdom where denizens doffed patriotic flip-flops the year-round.

That's it for now, Wolf. Junior Editor Sibella reporting from the outermost regions of The People's Democratic Republic of Transurrealia. Now back to you situated in the Situation Room. Wolf?

✳✳✳

SHALL WE GET DOWN to business? It's as good a time as any.

One day—a pretty important day, as it would turn out for everybody, particularly me—I said to Myron Beam, my illustrious boss, "Myron, what fuck the *fuck*? You look like *shit*?"

WUTHERING SIBELLA

BECAUSE HE DID. OUR relationship was like that.
Whoa, do not go there.

Not that we had a *relationship* with stupid air quotes, if you know what I mean. That would have been unprofessional. Also it would have been more probable I'd be whisked off by aliens in their Tesla-look-alike UFO. Antiquarian Myron had to be over fifty, which I deduced from opening his weekly missives from the AARP urging him to enjoy discounted mambo lessons and two-month journeys to destinations like Never-Never Land and Portland, Oregon. To be absolutionly clear, I don't get involved with elderly men. Or, since the Junior, anybody whatsoever. Come on, stop making me think about that sickening subject. If you would be so kind.

"I look like *shit*? Thanks, *Sibella*? But you know *what*? I can *explain*?"

As usual, Murmechka injected herself proverbially: "A man may look like shit, but when the moon..."

I begged her, *"Please?"*

"The day a woman falls silent from a great oak tree, that's when Mr. Coyote..."

"I mean it, Murm, not the right *time?*"

Myron used to say I made him talk like the way he talked to me, like what he termed a "Valley Girl." Such a tic in others Myron considered legitimate grounds for self-defense homicide, but for some reason not in me. Myron said my uptalk was contagious, yet kind of "endearing"—a term that had heretofore never been invoked with reference to anything I said, did, or wore. He contended without any factual basis that when I was a baby I must have been kidnapped by the ferocious Uptalk Tribe, more merciless and cutthroat than any band of savages doing an exsanguinationistic cameo in a McMurtry. Larry McMurtry was a great writer, Myron proclaimed. Therefore, one weekend I rode into *Lonesome Dove*, and that was fucking fantastic, and all the rest of his books turned out to be great, too, and Myron was right about McMurtry, and about many other books until he got screwed up about some con artist or saucy sorceress called Calypso O'Kelly, as you'll see. But I was no dippy Valley Girl. I was an *Island* Girl, as in Manhattan.

He also said I probably had a mild case of Tourette's, and there were mild drugs I should take for that. But I've done more drugs, mild and otherwise, than I care to, by which I mean *can*, remember. X was entirely too much fun on college weekends, its effects disastrously illuminating. I was unaware before being Mollified that everybody was beautiful and that I could really dance, but now, an older and a wizened girl, I realize they aren't and I can't. I'm glad nobody Instagrammed me rocking my go-to ravey moves. I'd also particularly like to forget this one time I swallowed Ritalin. I had the crackbrain notion it would boost my energy and elevate my humble hops before the Big Game against Saint You Don't Got a Goddamn Prayer Tech. Brilliant. I couldn't make a shot. I mean that, not one shot, zero points, goose eggs. It didn't help that the basket looked like it was boinging on a string and was as tiny as the corner pocket on a pool table. The girl I was "guarding" took pity, only going for twenty when she could have had twice that. When we lined up alongside each other on the lane in rebounding position for a free throw attempt, she leaned over: "Hey, Sister Skippy, them rids is bad juju."

So many designer drugs out there, like the current champion of the anxiety-ravaged set, Klonopin. How does Big Farma come up with such *Brave New World*ish names? The brand names seem more suitable to environmentally sensitive, technologically advanced automobiles.

Let's Go Places, Ativan.

Buspar, The Car that Cares.

Zoom Zoom in Your Zoloft.

Shift Expectations: All-New Celexa.

Paxil, Pursuit of Perfection.

Valium—Or Nothing.

Imagine Yourself in an all-new Klonopin.

So, thanks, but no more drugs for me. And let's be clear: I don't have Tourette's, I just have a potty mouth, according to my social scientist mom, who ought to know.

It's kind of entertaining to have an anthroapologist parental unit who tracks your behavior as if you were some exotic species out of Margaret Mead, in my case that rarest of species, *adolescenta aggressiva passiva*. I am the raw, she is the cooked. There is a huge diorama of teenagers in the Museum of Natural Hysteria alongside the Mastodons, or should be, complete with tube tops and miniskirts and iPads and iPods and ankle bracelets and vats of mascara. She and Dad must have whiled away many a happy hour comparing notes of me crawling around in my own individualized Skinner Box. No, I am not serious: no Skinner Boxes permitted by the co-op board in our brownstone. My folks never outgrew the sixties and have the patchouli oil and Birkenstocks and Woodstock reminiscences to prove it. (They are to this day talking about Jimi Hendrix doing the Star Spanglish Banner as if it was Eyegor Stravinsky, but sure, fine, there are parallels.)

Of course, my father is a psychologist who is committed to the talking cure. I myself was betting on the reading cure to do the trick for me someday. Now, everybody who wasn't an anthropologist was a psychologist back in the vainglorious sixties when they weren't a sociopathologist or cinemacriminologist. "Say more, Dad," I often said when I wanted to pull the emergency brake on his runaway train of questions about where I went and what I did last night. Which did not consist of trashing the bowling alley or flashmobbing or tagging the expressway underpass with the rest of us Spence School for Girls Gangbangers, as he might have hoped of a hormonally challenged teenager he had been professionally trained to misapprehend. I was such a disappointment. I was usually at the library with the rest of the New York City deviates. Remember libraries? I miss them now that they have been supplanted by media centers.

Anyway, Myron was trying to be nice with his Tourette's remark, but he didn't type MD after his name. He didn't type anything. Since I showed up, I did all his typing for him when I wasn't, you know, draining the slush pile and answering the fucking phone.

How I got to San Francisco and got a job as a junior editor at Myron's publishing house I don't quite understand. If I may belabor the drug topic, there must be the equivalent of Publishing Rohypnol circulating out there and somebody slipped me a Mickey during some poetry reading. I remember poetry readings like it was yesterday (cue the *bling bling bling bling* sound effects). Such as the reading long ago when my destined-to-be-dumper of a college ex read from his poetry and first made the acquaintance of his trust fund princess, who hung around afterward for way too long near the biohazardous wine and tossed her long blonde locks around like they were lifelines to drowning seamen. I'm tempted to comment on Junior's seamen, but I will resist, as I have gotten over him, a little bit. After I graduated later with that what-was-I-thinking MFA, I sent out my résumé and a cover letter in which I said in twenty different ways how much I loved loved *loved* books, then bought an economy seat on a transcontinental plane next to the portliest guy on any of the seven transcontinents, probably on his way home from some hot-dog-eating contest, and I left New York and Junior and found a studio apartment in San Francisco even a flea band would find claustrophobic, but then it gets fuzzier than that.

This day when the trouble begins wasn't quite as blurry. A screaming comes across the sky.

✳✳✳

"YOU SLEEP AT YOUR *desk*?" Thus spake Sibellathustra.

"I didn't *sleep*?"

If he was right about the uptalk and its being contagious, I decided I would have to do something about that post hasty. I would be willing to volunteer myself to be captured and deprogrammed in Montana or South Dakota or some other state where real bagels are against the goddamn law. If I couldn't manage that, I'd take a class in Uptalk Twelve-Stop Techniques. It was very annoying, no question mark. Funny thing, I never was uptalk-conscious in the moment when I was uptalking, so I couldn't check myself in time before going pointlessly interrogative.

"I read all night this book that came in over the *transom*?"

"Wow, all night, across the transom, must have been *good*?"

"Sibella, do you know what a transom *is*?"

It's where Myron liked to say books came in, that's what I knew. I never found anything that looked remotely like what I imagined a transom to be—yet another arcane Joseph Conrad nautical *device*? I scoured the vicinity of the copier and the fax machine, which perennially had pretty cobwebs and columns of industrious and gleeful ants marching all over it, like they had seized upon a blue-ribbon watermelon at the county fair. So, no, I didn't know what transom meant. I thought all the manuscripts came in through email attachments or via Bud, the postal service guy who liked to whistle a federally happy tune. There ought to be drugs for that whistling affliction. As for transom, however, no problem. Myron told me. What's the use, he could have said, but I never heard him ask a rhetorical question, not once. Evidently a transom has, among other meanings, this one: "the horizontal beam on a cross or gallows."

I am confident you're with me when I admit I was not "following the bouncing ball." In my younger and more vulnerable years, my father gave me some advice that I've been turning over in my mind ever since. (Kelly, you yourself might not miss that Be Latent literary collusion.) My dad often found cause to advise me to "follow the bouncing ball," which, despite being pretty handy with a basketball, I was not always able to do, as you will not always appreciate. That was a choice expression of my dad's, whom I love to pieces, even if he used expressions I didn't understand and asked me to talk about *my* feelings and not the feelings of the Count of Monte Christo or Jude the Obfuckingscure. Another expression he deployed was "loose operation." Which was how he characterized any of my job schemes: a loose operation. I do give him extra credit for never asking me where I saw myself in five years. And don't you try it, either.

"Bingo," said Myron, "transom *is* a word that refers to crucifixions and executions and thus it applies perfectly to my publishing *house?*"

As you can tell, he was exhausted or hungover or something and not making a whole lot of sense. Plus, he was rubbing the top of his head, for lack of a more precise term, nostalgically. I have known guys who lose their hair (not the old boyfriend poet yet, unfortunately), and when they think nobody's looking, they rub the top of their heads, as if one day hair will magically reappear there, that some benevolent force will correct this cosmically cosmetic misunderstanding. The lack of hair that is male-pattern baldness might work like phantom limbs on amputees. Now, that is an inappropriate association, politically incorrect if not inconceivable, which reminds me I will need to get my visa stamped in order to cross the hipster checkpoints that let you pass into Park Slope so you can covertly spike some blonde scheming bitch's non-fat goy decaf latte.

"How long, Sibella, you been working *here?*"

"It's a little after nine, so like about forty-five *minutes?*"

"No, since you started your job at the *house?*"

I told him, and I instantly felt very, very old. If I was a tree and Paul Bunyan stepped out of a Castro Street bar and chopped me down, the number of rings inside me would exponentially explode. That's how old. I felt my shoes curling up around my toes like elfs' booties old. I felt my shirt go right out of fashion on my back. I remembered when I got that ink during the weak moment that was my two years of college old. Ancient.

"Time I give you a new position, Sibella. You've earned a *promotion?* From now on, you're my junior *editor?*"

I counted to ten and gently broke the news to him.

"Oh, I thought you were an *intern?*"

So there I was in San Francisco but it could have also been Los Angeles, it doesn't matter a whole fuck of a lot, as you will see, which is the first and last time you will ever read that the difference between SF and LA is moot, but then again the birthers will find out I'm a New Yorker the way Obama was not Kenyan, so like I fucking care because I will never be a Cali Fornian, and neither will most of them because they never stop name-dropping Brooklyn. (Try to find a book jacket author photo caption these days that doesn't conclude with "and now lives in Brooklyn." This brings up for me an unrelated and equally annoying grievance: the girl. As in *The Girl in Every Fucking Book Title.* I said it was unrelated.) I'm no Raymond Chandler, so I'm not going to try very hard to mask everything and make a Maltese Falcon out of a sow's ear, and I know that's On Dancer On Prancer On Dashiell Hammet, give me a break. Myron's story of his publishing house might end up a mystery in the end, you'll have to wait and see and then tell me.

In any event, I didn't want to burn any bridges in case I needed a job in the industry in the future. It was impossible for me to determine how that career choice would ultimately fit into my hundred-year plan. Anyway, here goes what happened that morning when I got a new promotion to the job I already had. And honestly, trust me, Myron did look like shit.

THE HEART IS A LONELY SIBELLA

Time out. You'll never guess who had written me. I mean, how the fuck could you?

My ex sent me an out-of-the-blue email that morning, before I exercised the duty of astutely advising Myron he looked like shit. The three-hour difference, East Coast and West, often accounted for a bustling inbox when I logged in. I wish the computer had caught on fire and I would have had no choice but to reach out to our tech guy wearing one of his two hundred sweat-stained grimy baseball caps, a guy who chuckles over jokes he tells himself and holds normal people like me (admittedly a weak example) in greatdainful contempt, another story. And why do these guys always wear baseball caps? If they were handed a bat and a glove, I swear they'd try to download a ball.

Here's what Oh Junior My Junior Our Tearful Trip Is Done wrote me:

∗∗∗

Ciao, bella Sibella,

How are you, Sibella sweetheart? I am disappointed we didn't see each other before you peregrinated abruptly for California and publishing stardom at Hard Rain. What a plum job. I am proud of you. I hope we can get together when you're home for the holidays to see your folks or when you have a business meeting in the Big Apple. It will be good to catch up. Let's go to Eataly or to Maialino in Gramercy Park, which you like, or this cool place Carbone in the Village where my agent took me. It's a restaurant straight out of "The Godfather," our favorite movie.

Leave the gun, take the cannoli, Sibella.

Tell Sibella it was only business. I always liked her.

As for me, things have been crazy crazy crazy since the book of poems came out. Reviews, interviews, requests for new work, it's all a little bit dizzying. You know me, how I hate celebrity.

And all along I thought you meant celery!

Nobody knows better than you what it was like for me to write those poems, more than a few of which I began writing, well, in bed with you, my *Muse*, figuratively speaking. If you don't mind my saying so.

No, of course, sweetheartless, your All Mused Up Muse Sibella finds such an observation on this side of amusing and doesn't mind, and then why don't you fuck the fuck off, fuckuratively speaking. The bed you a lewd to was one in which I marked up those early drafts of yours and rewrote every other so-called line. That was also the very same bed where you introduced your Brooklinear Skank to the quaint concept of your Junior while I was out of town and she was on her Latter Day Sluts Mission. How many immortal poems did that cheat bang generate?

Thanks for the kind words you wrote me on that so-you postcard about my little book of poems I sent you. Yale has been great to me, and I am kind of humbled to see my name alongside all the illustrious poets who began their careers as Yale Younger Poets. It makes me happy to know I am on your shelf and that there are no hard feelings anymore. I truly admired the mature way you dealt with our breakup. I wish it could have been easier for all three of us.

All three of us? You mean you, me, and your Junior? Because don't put me and that rich bitch in the same sentence, not if you want your Junior to grow up one day to be Senior. But, ah, I truly doubt you caught the import of my so-me selected postcard. It was of the Vietnam War Memorial, which I unearthed in my peacenik protestor dad's scattered desk drawer. Think about it. You know how to think, don't you? Put your lips together and blow me. And yes, Junior, don't you worry your pretty little Junior. Your book's right here on my office shelf. Indeed, I keep it safe

and warm in an urn, and when I say urn, I mean used illy *coffee can.*
That is the receptacle where I collected its ashes after I torched your prizey
book to a delicious award-winning crisp.

You'll never guess what, Sibella.

Bitch gave you herpes? I warned you.

Remember I told you that I could never imagine writing
fiction, that I was a poet and poetry was my life? Well, things
change, don't they?

They certainly do, you two-timing weasel.

I wrote a novel!

Quick, stop the depresses!

It came fast, in a rush, six weeks, 300+ pages. And I got an
agent in like two minutes, and she loves it. She was about to ship it
off to the usual NY suspects, but I put my foot down, and told her,
Sandy, let's first try Hard Rain Publishing, where my dear college
friend Sibella is an editor. I mean, a big publishing house would
be nice, and a six-figure advance, but money's not that important

Now that you sold your soul and munch bon bons and plagiarize
Gerard Manley Fucking Hopkins all your thirty-minute working day.
My heart in hiding / Stirred for a bird. A bird-brain like you.

and it will be nicer getting close attention from you and your
fantastic cutting-edge publishing operation. I took the liberty of
attaching a file. Hope you will want to read it, and I hope you like
it. My agent sees a great movie in its future.

A movie Sandy sees in its future? Did you ever catch The Departed,
Junior?

But be gentle, I've been hurt before. ☺

Has anybody ever told you how fucking adorable you are? I didn't
think so.

That's all for now. My deets are on the title page with my new
Brooklyn address. Can't wait to hear from you, Sibella. Have you
learned to surf yet?

As Emily D, Belle of Amherst, came oh-so-close to saying, "My life
had Stood a loaded Pun."

Love always,

Me

✳✳✳

Dɪᴅ I ᴊᴇᴛᴛɪsᴏɴ Mᴇ's self-absorbed, tone-death Junior email off into junk mail intergalactic Junior land, where it belonged? You may not know me yet, but you can readily welcome this much: I didn't toss it, which would be unprofessional for a junior editor. In fact, I did open the attached file containing the novel that he and I both supposedly thought he was too sensitive to ever compose, but I could only get as far as the dedication page. Right there, that's all I wanted to see, being a gluten-free for crime and punishment. A sentence was instantly branded onto my cattle-hide brain:

To Chantal, who makes everything possible.

Flagrant foul, two shots and the ball.

But everything? Not so fast, Junior. There was one thing chère Chantal would not make possible, not if I could help it.

Here's what I rashly composed by way of reply:

I would sooner bake LeBron's tennis shoes parmigiana than read your book.

I would sooner moonwalk across the Mojave at high noon.

I would sooner swim with the sharks.

I mean I would sooner you swam with the sharks.

But genile reader, I didn't transmit that email. *Ding.* In flagrante deleted.

As I once heard, publishing as well as junior editing brings out the asshole in everyone. But unlike revenge, contempt is best served flambéed. Junior didn't teach me a whole lot I could use, but he gave me a PhfuckingD in rejection.

SIBELLA THE SCRIVENER

IT WAS A BRIGHT, cold day in April, and the clocks were striking thirteen.

Technically, it was winter in San Francisco, which is a season that reminds me of lovely October in New York, and nowadays clocks don't strike anything anymore.

But that's how 1984 opens, to me an altogether meh book I was assignated in high school. Who are the starchy lab-coated pedephilogogues who cherry-pick those classics for secondary school inmates? Eric Arthur Blair's pennamed book was taught by a Ms. Redburn, a smart, sprightly lady who sincerely urged me to "apply" myself to other academic disciplines if I wanted to attend a good college like hers, which was Sarah Lawrence, Sarah being no apparent relation to D. to the H. Lawrence. ("John Thomas says goodnight to Lady Jane, a little droopingly." Honest to God, the goateed hack wrote "droopingly" of his John Thomas Junior. And again, I must imp lore what's with guys' baptizing their Johnson?) Sarah's institution of higher ed was not the one that recklessly offered me a full basketballian ride, so I never did attend what was to her a good college. Redburn wore cowboy boots and shirts and bolo ties to her run-on-sentence-extermination occupation at the Spence School and she religiously affected British pronunciation. Every week or so she mentioned how she took a "grand" summer school class at Cambridge (CALM-bridge), which could account for how she availed herself of any opportunity to articulate Nicaragua and Jaguar. You would be surprised how frequently she contrived (no con-TROV-er-see here) to reference Ni-Car-Ah-Gyu-Ah (she never was a turista) or Jag-U-Ar. She didn't drive that canonical British automobile or any other, not even a prep school standard-issue Prius. Besides, Spence is on the Upper East Side, where cars seeking parking places go to die.

Nonetheless, it wasn't April and thirteen o'clock the morning that began a new—I suppose I have to say a new link between Myron and me, for reasons that will become medievally oblivious.

Whan that April with his showres soote

The droughte of March hath perced to the roote

That's the day Myron formally fingered me as his confidante.

***

THAT CAME OUT WRONG, but I am on deadline and you get what I mean. Believe it or not, he wanted me to write a book about his favorite subject: himself. He evidently ruled out the editor in chief, whom he called Young Goodman Brown, or YGB for short, for reasons initially puzzling to me. But if you ever chanced upon the spooky stories of Moby Dick's envious buddy, you might hazard a conjecture or two. And "hazard" was Downtown Nathaniel Hawthorne.

(I hope you're enjoying our little collusion pastime, Kelly, while you're getting your weekly mani-pedi. I'd promised Myron to listen to his sad story and take careless notes, and I had to amuse myself somehow.)

To be clear, "Publisher's Confidante" was never bullet-pointed on my job description, which I hasten to remind you (but never reminded Myron because why bother?) had, to that day, not been presented to me. Why did he enlist me? Probably the same reason you should trust me, I would argue.

Perhaps, in the end, I was the one Myron could trust because I believed half of everything he told me and the whole of everything he did not. Hemingway bragged famously about his access to what he called a bullshit detector. Sure, nothing is what it seems to be, including the first part of this sentence. Therefore, doubting everything and believing everything gets you to the same place, that is, nowhere, but if that is so, then nowhere is the place you can make a stand, which is what I am doing in Myron's story, which he believed I would be willing to write, if you can credit that, and to this day I don't.

***

HE OUTLINED HIS PLAN for me to write the book. Then I said, what you must understand I have patiently waited for like fucking forever for the perfect opportunity to tell somebody:

"I prefer not to."

Myron may have never heard anybody voice such a view, or no junior editor at Hard Rain had ever resisted a direct assignment from the boss or ever read Melville's dead letter clerk passive-aggressive genius named Bartleby, whom I quoted. Of course, he may have whiffed on my literary collusion. Which is sort of incredible, because Kelly herself might catch that one. When people don't catch a collusion—I am hypostrophizing here, having never had the experience—they are usually touchy and who can blame them? I can be annoying to people, I realize, when it comes to books. But a tiger can't lose its spots, and good, you are paying attention.

"Bartleby?" I said, trying like a tall Girl Scout to help.

"Whotleby?"

This was not getting off on the right foot. I gently inquired of him as to why he desired a confidante in the first place. He looked shaky, no use making him more self-conscious.

He said I would find out.

I asked him why me.

He said he was a lousy writer and it was agonizing for him to type on account of the Car Pal Tunnel, which did sound like a snappier name for the engineering wonder named after the Tulippicious Land of Holland and is the home of the twenty-four slash seven traffic jam beneath the Hudson River.

I asked him if he wanted me to be his ghostwriter.

No, he said, it would be my book. My book about him. Capitalizing on the material he would generously provide.

I reminded him of the obvious: I had never published anything. I didn't remind him that not everybody had a life story worth telling—or typing. And why would anybody want to read his? If he was conscious of his reasons, he didn't share them.

As for my having no publication history? No problem. He knew people who knew people, he said. (Let's file that under publisher's "humor alert.")

"Myron, are you fucking *drunk*?"

I was the responsible one around here, he observed.

"You are *drunk*?" But he may have had a point.

"Plus, you can type *beautifully*?"

Typing and writing are not the same thing, I told him, which I might also mention to all the writers taking up residence in my slush pile.

But unlike him, I didn't have carpal tunnel, he said.

True enough, I regretted to admit.

And he paid me my salary.

"I rest your *case*?" I said.

That exchange may serve as inadequate explanation for how it was that, in short order, he would be telling me his publishing life story and showing me the book that had been transmitted last night over the Ferris Wheel Transom of Time. The whole affair would get jumbled and garbled fast, and this is my best recollection of the real-time sequence, numbered one through ten for a bean-counter's gaseous convenience.

1. I came into the office in the morning, opened the email from Junior, threw up in my mouth, and contemplated how I could arrange for a hit man like Luca Brasi, and then come up with a rock-solid alibi that passes muster on any of the million indistinguishable episodes of *Law & Order*. (Love that show and all the spin-offs—they are so lusciously predictable—and is there any hour of the day or night when a rerun isn't streaming or playing on cable TV? **DUMM DUMM**...)

2. The editor in chief and I noticed Myron distraught and disheveled.

3. We weighed the idea of dialing 911.

4. Myron closed his office door, casting his editor in chief onto the vanquished plain, and began right then and there to tell me about his company and his life in medias resistible. His business and his biography turned out to be sort of the same thing, and our conversation would ultimately go on and on over the course of months, and he was working hard to enlist me to compose his story. He wanted me to be his amanuensis, he said, a fancy pants word I did not have to look up, but he should have, because it did not mean what he thought, though it is a cool old school word for secretary, which he just said I wasn't going to be. Initially, I suspected he may have meant he wanted me to reshuffle the deck of his mental notes. In any case, he would put me in the middle of the most bizarre contract negotiations in unrecorded history and take me on a spectacularly stupid road trip that judgment-traumatized Jack Kerouac himself would have taken a pass on, all to the end of supposedly giving me a fuller picture, which despite his best efforts at camouflaging the truth, he finally did.

5. "I don't have much time *left*?" he said, at which point I should have funneled toward him all those the-best-is-yet-to-come advertisements from AARP.

6. "You selling the *company*?" That would have meant two things for me: freedom and poverty, never a good hook up.

7. He wasn't planning to, he said. If you read too many books you tend to see real-live human beings as if they were characters in novels, and if you're that way and you think I'm Pippi Fucking Longstocking, we are going to have a major problem. Naturally, I wondered about his motivation. Even junior editors worry about that. But he had made such a strange demand of me, I had to think about who such a man would be to ask such a thing. Was he actually dying or was he merely a drama queen? Either would explain a lot. I have an active fantasy life and a streak of paranoia (thanks, Dad, for sharing your monographs on the fascinating subject). But that doesn't mean I am always wrong.

8. Yet if my worst supposition was on the money, then with your permission let me say Fuck. And may I also add Superfuck.

9. At my first opportunity, I later that day looked at the professed book he received over his fucking transom and read last night, which disturbed him so much, and I threw up in my mouth all over again.

10. There should be a special 911 type number for book people in dire straits (though when are they not?) and somebody should have dialed it forthwith. For him, for his company, for all of us. The fire department would have had to send over a fleet of ambulances.

11. I hate lists that stop at ten, which is barbitrary. There was no way in the world I should write Myron's book. And if I somehow someday did, it would wind up being a fucking Magnum Dopus. Not to bring up a sore subject, but that's a sick name for a Classics major's junk.

✳✳✳

"WHERE SHALL I START, Sibella?" He frisbeed his glasses across his desk to emphasize a point I hoped he was going to elucidate because I had no idea. Like I knew where he should start? Writers say sometimes they are asked the most maddening question in the world: "Have you written something I might have read?" How in the fuck would they know!

However.

Once upon a time, and a very good time it was, there was a moo-cow coming down along the road and this moo-cow that was down along the road met a nicens little boy named baby tuckoo or that was Myron Beam.

In my biz, they call this narrative foreground. This device should be kept to an absolute minimum, like Junior's Junior's foreskin, but I apologize for this unfortunate image and beg your forbearance, please.

Myron had strong views about books. How could he not; he was a fucking publisher. For instance, he was instinctively inclined to hate memoirs because they could be too much like novels, but I hated memoirs that weren't more like novels. In almost every respect, I used to think we were not exactly joined at the hip—though, of course, in terms of uptalk, we were at the lip. In business terms, he gave out miniscule advances with big cash commitments on the back end, invested next-to-nothing on marketing and publicity, and had zero capacity to schmooze with anybody who theoretically had any clout. A loser of a commercial formula, right? Not to Myron and not to Hard Rain Publishing. He unfathomably hit the jackpot time after time. What was the secret of his success?

To answer that question, we need to go back further, way back, to first principles.

You have heard of *books*, haven't you, little children whose glazed eyeballs—once upon a time shiny and bright with wonder— are now permanently glued to your all shiny and bright personal tablets? Yes, I'm talking about books. And later, units.

And what about you, creaking elders hunched over your walkers and reeking of mothballs? You, too, are familiar with books. The quaint content-delivery systems predicated upon an archaic technology, the production, marketing, and distribution of which are contingent upon an obsolete and certifiably wacko business model dating back to a dark age when ogres' knuckles scraped the Middle-Earth floor?

Yes, books, exactly.

And keep on your toes, High Tech Boychick sporting the goofball Google glasses gadget on your pin head, there's a fire hydrant lurking around the corner.

✳✳✳

YOU DON'T KNOW MYRON without you have read a book. Or written one.

That morning, he was going to start to tell me everything. He wanted me to get this right and in the process he cold-turkey strangled to death each and every uptalked sentence ending. That self-control was in and of itself impressive. If a busy man like Myron could achieve that sort of command, there might be hope for me.

He was not drunk. But in the interests of full disclosure, it was early. Any junior editor who finessed his story, he implied and *not* inferred, which would be a usage error, Kelly, will be out on the street looking redundantly for another job in the equivalent of our horse-and-buggy industry. Besides, he told me, publishing books brings out the asshole in everybody, most especially him.

Oh, right, that's when I first heard that.

Despite his ravaged state, he was in an expansive mood. He wanted to shoot for an uplifting, dignified note. He found the thing that should have helped. Consulting the puff-piece Hard Rain catalogue copy right there on his magisterially cluttered desk, he could verify that he owned and ran a small, independent press that specializes *ahem* in *quality literary fiction and nonfiction.* That was one way to put it. But when you talked about his company you were talking about him. In this regard, he mentioned a person he referred to as his "Unlamented Ex-wife": "As I was reminding her newest boy toy, Nicky Narcissus, the other day when I bumped into him at the club—he was waiting for his regular full-body depilation—sometimes it *is* all about me."

Oh, all the things Myron and I had in common—you could count them on the middle finger.

Here's the skinny. Let's not soft-pedal the universal perception slash evaluation of Myron, and I quote: Myron was a scumbag, a liar, a scoundrel, a crook, a sleaze ball, an ambulatory colostomy bag, a blood-sucking, spirit-sapping miserable excuse for a human being. And here I'm cherie-picking, referencing some of the more cherrytable views advanced by his best-selling authors, another term for those ungrateful, wolfish, porn-pawing, lip-smacking, marauding obsessives he kept stocked in boxed wine and smokes and microwavable meals while they desultorily slave over their *quality literary blah blah blah* tales that, despite any of their patented literary drawbacks, he will make turn a profit, you're welcome, very nice. Most of his publishing peers might as well have been selling transistor radios and top hats and typewriters in a digitized hip-hop age. Because he knew something they didn't. He knew how to publish books that people cannot help but buy.

I didn't say *read*, though reading them is hypothetically possible.

"Do you have any concept what goes into bringing out and selling a book, Sibella?"

You probably think you do but you haven't a clue and, not to worry, I didn't, either.

Acquisition, editorial, design, cross marketing, sales, finance, management, distribution, and so on and so forth. Every road to and from the publishing house conceals an IED or leads to a treasure trove, and each step takes you closer to one or both. The minutiae! The technicalities! For instance, Myron would one day talk to me for hours upon hours about paper and binding. I had no idea such considerations would prove so fascinating to him or if my concussion symptoms would one day subside in my brain pan. If I may continue.

Look, there were old-school publishers out there hanging on by their fingernails and there were the new-school publishers equipped with MBAs and shiny object jargon that they impressed themselves with—and who were also hanging on by their fingernails. Myron fell into another category: he was a no-school publisher. That's probably why he said that in the end the success of Hard Rain all boiled down to one thing.

"Me."

When a true genius appears in the world, you may know him by this sign, that the dunces are all in confederacy against him.

Kelly? Kelly, you listening?

✳✳✳

I'm getting ahead of myself, but this is stuff you need to know.

Much like a good book, a little publishing house like his may have been a perfect window into this crazy little thing called life, and for the same reasons. Perfect indeed because his publishing house, successful as it was, was also cause for all the difficulties that complicated his life—and ultimately, therefore, mine. Thanks to the astonishing circumstances I currently find myself in, I have all the time in the world to tell lucky, lucky you all about it—if I ever work up the willpower and swig down a six-pack of Dyspeptic Dismol.

The raft of trouble included but was not restricted to: mayhem, defalcation, betrayal, fumbling three-ways, erectile dysfunction, girl-on-girl-on-boy pornography, higher hair tie utilization (you'll see), ebookapalooza, fraudulent conveyance, insurance fraud, delayed manuscript deliverance, legal malpractice, Hollywood movie and foreign rights negotiation, country living, gun play, guerilla marketing, social media inculcation, right to cure demands (don't you love that legalese: *right to cure?*), Chicken Diavolo, gratuitous bashing of the French but not of the fancy French Laundry bistro, global warming, MFA and Ivy League wisecracks, and Nathaniel Hawthorne.

It was the classic nineteenth-century author Hawthorne—you may blondely recall, Kelly—who infamously derided the most successful authors of his era by labeling them "the damned mob of scribbling women," and who wouldn't wish to have old Nat shambling around today, to see what unpotable beverage he would take to the book launch shindig? And the whole shebang of Myron's was destined to come full circle and end with a gruely smidgeon of more mayhem. All this happened, more or less.

Cue Sound Effects again.

Do you hear that? That's a hush, descending. The tale will now—*whoosh*—darken dot dot dot.

Please wait while we check your account. This may take a few minutes.

THEIR EYES WERE WATCHING SIBELLA

MYRON NORMALLY SLITHERED IN around ten, breezily skimmed emails, deleting most with impunity, forwarding the ones he wanted me to address. Then he threw around his glasses a few times like horseshoes. Usually he carpe diemed the redundant day along with his first opportunity to go to lunch at Avenue Grill downtown, occasionally with an intern or an editor, depending. Never with Young Goodman Brown, Myron's handle for his anointed editor in chief who visibly wilted when he saw Myron passing him over yet again in favor of the company of somebody who looks better in tight jeans (which would exclude me, as I don't wear any sort of jeans, especially mom jeans, which no mom of mine would deign to wear). He could have recommended that YGB use the time to catch up on reading Hawthorne or anybody, but the fact is Myron would sooner eat from the bowl on the floor alongside a pooch than break bread with him, and, no, he didn't have a dog. No disrespect intended toward canines, who are loyal and noble creatures, unlike creatures in the book biz he could and would name.

Gratuitous TMI re: Myron, and I quote him: "Advisory for prospective Query-ists: unless you're the second coming of Willie Goddamn Morris, keep your Saga of Loyal Fido in a locked desk drawer."

Young Goodman Brown had attended the chichi Ivy League institution that shares his surname, happily for Myron if not him. He didn't understand his new appellation, or what Myron was driving at. You see, YGB never read Hawthorne or any other writer born before he was first smacked on the butt by his mom's obstetrician—but I don't think doctors indulge in such routine child abuse anymore. No wonder he looked at Myron with equal parts pity, scorn, and terror. And it is hard to do all three with one set of eyes, but he managed. YGB had tried to undermine Myron ever since, slyly attempting to deflect credit due to Myron onto himself, all the while smoothly scheming to bed the junior editor (yeah, right) and the interns (of whom I was never not one, get it?) when not running up his expense account on fancy lunches with agents and sometimes with bulimic or gluttonous authors.

As I came to discover later, to compensate for his lunatic abuse of YGB, he handsomely remoonerated the round-face gorgeous Catholic school boy with tortoise shell glasses and gym-taut muscles rippling inside the rolled-up sleeves of his precariously buttoned everyday Oxford blue Brooks Brothers professionally laundered and pressed shirt. He was certainly paid better than he would have been at a much larger New York house, and Myron's dividend was the pleasure of rendering him downcast whenever he chose.

I become aware that I am conveying a sadistic impression of the publisher. But don't forget, he named YGB editor in chief. Before the lad was hired, his life had consisted of a string of uninterrupted triumphs. He had been, no fucking kidding, a Rhodes Scholar. Ask me, I think YGB stuck around to find out how the other half lived. I came to see that Myron was his lab rat, he was not Myron's. That, to me, was the spirit of their professional connection. YGB had a lot to learn, and Myron was willing to teach. Somebody had to introduce the boy to Reality.

You wouldn't trust indefatigable Murmechka to illuminate anybody about anything, but that delimitation was no imposition upon her: "On the mountain top every man is a lion, in the valley every boy dreams of the sea."

And look what had just come across my computer, my OED (Oxford English Dictionary) word of the day: *paroemiographer*. A collector or author of proverbs, and a dog-chew-toy of a word I was previously unfamiliar with.

"The hawk is wise that does not take counsel from the swan." Finally, this minor league paroemiographer was making sense for a change.

Then, after lunch, two or five drinks and a few cheap and absolutely unproductive thrills with an acquisitions editor later (biology lesson to follow forthwith), Myron came back to ignore voice mails and slipped out around six for additional cocktails prior to dinner at Carmine's, which is next door to Avenue. Carmine's does in fact wield a wicked veal chop that Myron found irresistible, despite the admonitions of his doctor, who kept hectoring him about his imminent diabetes and heart risk. Afterward he crawled back to his high-rise on Nob Hill (three sparkling bridges in view, eat your heart out) and read a few pages of a book he wanted to publish till he couldn't take it anymore and then turned on the television, which was humming when he woke up at four in the morning.

My personal image of hell: 4:00 a.m. television's radioactive glow.

Wolf? Wolf? Are you on TV 24/7, Wolf? Does CNN ever let you go home, feed the cats, water the plants? Back to you in the studio, Wolf.

＊＊＊

THE DAY WHEN BEGAN this story of his—and what effectively was supposed to be mine someday—was destined to be different. For one thing, no lunch at Avenue. He didn't feel like it. Then it was about five, and he was feeling peckish. His junior editor, yours pecking truly, whom he often believed was an intern, had headed home with her laptop and iPad packed with manuscripts to read, not including the novel Junior wrote (because he hadn't sent it to her yet, but that was okay, because she would have waited for the Rapture in order to read it). And everybody else had left, too. Myron was stuffing his satchel with materials he would not bother to examine during the evening and he steadied himself for his daily exercise—the stroll to Carmine's—when for some reason he would never be able to explain he responded to the Pavlovian *ding* on his computer that indicated the electrifying arrival of a new email that I forced myself to read eventually.

"Dear Publisher," it began, tamely enough. "This is the best book you will read this year, maybe the best book in your thus far wretched, forlorn life. I want a $666K advance, and splits favorable to me, not you. You have 24 hours to offer a contract, which you will want to do. I could self-publish, go the hat-in-hand déclassé route of Print on Demand, because I have access to plenty of capital, but I have my reasons, which you may ultimately understand, not that I particularly care. I read on your amateurish website that I am supposed to send you a synopsis and some bio. I will take a pass on jumping through your hoops. But if this helps you rationalize making an offer, think *Da Vinci Code* meets *Fifty Shades of Grey* meets *Gone With the Wind* meets *Harry Potter* meets *Great Expectations* meets The Bible."

For reasons Myron or a sensible person was simply too obtuse to understand, the one monster book the writer neglected to mention was *The Joy of Cooking*.

"Anybody could break this book out and make it a bestseller, even you. Consider yourself lucky. Tick tock, Myron. And one more thing, Myron. You owe me."

That email wasn't a pitch, it was the equivalent of a crayoned ransom note drafted by a circus clown.

The message was delivered by somebody improbably named Calypso O'Kelly and a file was attached: an eponymously titled manuscript. He opened the file. How could a publisher, especially one with a groaning stomach, resist biting on such a certifiably loopy communication? He had never met a person named Calypso before—and now that I think about it, neither had I. He was in the mood for a good chuckle. It might stimulate his appetite for dinner. The book was titled *Adventures of Calypso O'Kelly*, and it was just under three hundred thousand words long. Once he stopped chuckling, he started reading; what the hell.

***

NEXT THING MYRON KNEW it was nine in the morning and his editors (along with his junior editor) were stumbling in to work

wearing trademark Gen-X standard issue wraparound what-the-
fuck-you-looking-at shades. Wait till they exit their thirties, he was
thinking—they will not know what hit them. That constituted a
half-viayeayeable naval premise for a bestselling self-help book,
but he would not publish self-help, because he had a microscopic
shred of integrity, as he liked to boast without justification.

YGB was standing over the publisher's desk and he was asking
Myron with some earnestness if not solicitude if he was feeling all
right. His glassy eyes and tousled appearance must have prompted
his editor in chief to inquire. His had been a dark and stormy night.
Mine had been a dark and stormy morning after Junior's email.

"Myron, you hear me? Something wrong, Myron?" said YGB.

"Myron, what fuck the *fuck*? You look like *shit*?" I said—
as you recall.

Yes, something was obviously terribly wrong. Something had
happened that had never happened before to him with a book.
It was love at first sight.

✳✳✳

"You get what I'm saying, *Sibella*?"

I fucking did not.

"*Yes*?" I said.

It wouldn't be long before I perused the manuscript that had
knocked him senseless. I would have to await my opportunity to
tell him that he had lost his fucking mind.

This was not going to work out as Myron planned, of that
much I was Surebella. And back then I was thinking that if a
book about him ever saw the light of day, I had the perfect title:
Sibella Seeks New Employment.

SIBELLA WITH THE DRAGON TATTOO

Hang in with me, please. You need to understand Myron in order to appreciate the chaos about to confound us—which had everything to do with a certain manuscript.

He prided himself on the artfulness of his wicked rejection notes. But as he instructed his acquisition editors, be as harsh as you wish with an author you think he should publish. If it's somebody he would not publish on a bet, be sweet as pie. Isn't it pretty to think so? These were the sage, courteous, professional instructions he himself failed to heed. This is why he delighted in composing rejection letters and emails that perfectly spoke his mind. Actually, I was the one who took his chair and did the typing—again, on account of his alleged carpal tunnel—about which, between you and me, I had my *accent grave* doubts. Maybe he simply liked having me nearby, or maybe he wanted me to admyron his handiwork.

Your love scenes made me stab myself in the legs with a letter opener.

The Wall Street Journal *reports that your narration may well drive the blow job industry into Chapter 11.*

If you mail me another manuscript, I will tell Whitey Bulger where to find you.

Stick to your double-entry accounting or Uber-driving or bagging and tagging at the morgue.

I've heard snappier dialogue at the bottom of the pool.

I can't tell who I despise more—your overcoddled cats or your overpampered kids.

Enclosed is a free scrip: medication could not possibly diminish the impact of your talent—and neither could a well-placed hammer to my cranium.

Special Forces mention of the Nordstrom's cosmetics counter girl generator of a suspected seventy-nine page novelette featuring a fashion-forward band of anorexic community college private eyes who may or may not be saucy wenches but who definitely rock facials and great exfoliation techniques—that was the honest-to-God narrative premise—to whom he drafted the following: *I was tempted to publish your book on the titillating grounds that you composed possibly the best worst sentence in the glorious history of the English language: "The eating of these girls are unhealthy."*

Here's the thing, and you'll probably not understand this yet, but hear me hear me: "Sibella, I truly *was* tempted."

✳✳✳

THEN THERE WERE THE books he selected for publication. Careful what you wish for, conspiring author. It was the medium-rare writer who did not ultimately yowl that Myron was (drum roll, please) *controlling.*

Oooh, ah, no, please, not that, not that, I'm cut, I bleed.

Shut the fuck up, all you male and female pussies, if I may quote I know who. They tweeted and blogged about him without signs of let up or advanced literacy. They contended he had tectonic-plate-size character flaws, but that would imply he was in possession of one of those pesky things, a character. Yes, he drank too much. They contended he was as lazy as a three-toed book pubslothcist. Because you see, he paid no attention to particulars. For what they called crucial details (*Please send an advance copy to my wife who left me saying I would never amount to shit*), he called petty annoyances (*You truly think this meager book of yours proves otherwise, hotshot?*). Yes, he mercilessly flattered the commendably striving (independent book store owners, God love 'em) and the criminally self-indulgent (reviewers and advertisers) because he saw no way around exploiting them. Yes, he was untrustworthy, disloyal, dishonest. Yes, his mockery reduced to tears his vendors and his sales staff. He should have been thrown into prison, though sometimes he thought solitary confinement would amount to being a relief. At the very least, he should have probably dry-cleaned his ragu-stained blazer and recycled decades ago his George Plimpton-on-meth hairpiece of a coiffure that for a while he used to sport for ceremonial occasions. If he had any children, they would have disowned him. If he still had a wife he would have betrayed her by sleeping with her best friend—sort of like how his ex kind of did cheat on him. As for friends—

"I have friends I haven't even used yet, Sibella."

Touché, all you yeast-infected malcontents, Myron saluted you. Send him your wretched manuscripts. If you were fortunate, he would make you flush enough to hate him all the way to the bank.

✳✳✳

HERE'S A SWEET LITTLE fantasy in which he indulged. And no, it was not his everyday kind of fantasy (the one that involved some implausible tag-teaming of Monica Bellucci, Penelope Cruz, and Beyoncé). That was a big sweet Praying Mantisy.

(You want to complain about *my* TMI? How about Myron's?)

In this daydream of his, a striving but dismissible writer, desperately handkerchiefing for an ounce of acclaim or recognition, in mortal frustration goes to a fortune-teller, who allows him to ask one question.

"Oh, Madame Voyant, will I ever be famous?"

She peers into her crystal ball, rubs her eyes, and grins. "Yes, indeed, you will one day be world-famous."

He is ecstatic. "I knew it. I knew all the lonely hours of labor and the two-packs-a-day chest cough would be worth it."

"What the heck," the seer announces, "two for one sale today. You may ask me one more question."

"When?"

He had idiotically used up his second question, but she was feeling sympathetic. "You may ask your second question *now.*"

"Thanks, Madam. I mean, when will I be famous?"

"Oh, let me look... Ah, I see... You will be universally recognized to have always been a genius, the greatest writer of the century, on the day you die."

"Yes!" cries the exultant, unclear-on-the-concept, soon-to-be ex-author. For in his jubilation, he giddily darts out of the fortune-teller's house and into the street, where he is splattered by the crosstown bus and his name instantly becomes legend.

***

A CLARIFICATION AS TO the "small" in his previously articulated description of his *small* independent press. In comparison to the industry Brobdingnagians on the Mystic Isle of Manhattan, Hard Rain was indisputably Lilliputian. (Read a damn book someday, why don't you, Kelly?) He may not have had an impressive New York City address in the Flatiron or on Fifth Avenue. No, we were located in a nondescript twelve-story office building downtown.

To judge solely on the basis of the antiseptic scents and free-floating anxiety in the air, all the periodontists of San Francisco were holed up here with their jaws-pried-open captives. There were also various accountants, caterers, shrinks, and a crow's murder of "consultants." I never get what consulting means, or "life-coaching," which I probably could use, you are doubtless thinking. These consultants had chest-puffing, vague names that all sounded like The Blue Man Group, so I figured they were mostly trafficking in high-tech weaponry or guiding private school head searches for Packer, Brearly, Trinity, Dalton, and my alma mater, Spence.

In any case, Hard Rain operated out of six adjoining closet-sized offices and one conference room, everything lit up by fluorescent bulbs, and we had one lumbering table that could serve as an abattoir's butcher board, which is not a bad metaphor because that's where Myron chopped it up during editorial meetings and told us what we were deciding. So, yes, we were small and unimposing indeed. Dynamite and MDMA come in small packages, too. But here's the thing. You wouldn't believe how much money his privately held company made, and that's all right because it's none of your fucking business and he was never going to tell you.

But he did tell me.

"You're fucking kidding." That was me, gobsmacked, having heard the numbers.

What did Myron do with what my dad called, inscrutably to me, the "bread"?

Let's put it this way about Mr. Big Stuff: one New Year's he sent the entire overdecompensating staff (more upside to having a shrink dad: psycho jargon) to Las Vegas, all expenses paid, including first-class airfare and a couple of thousand in walking around money. Ask me, they should promptly resume atomic bomb testing on the Las Vegas Strip, but that's another subject. Year before, it was New Year's in Maui, same thing. And, no, he didn't accompany his crew. He relished the solitude and the quiet. Something tells me all of them enjoyed not being in his environs for a few blissful days. And this year's lumps of coal? Excuse me? Try criminally costly Bottega Veneta briefcases, where he stashed Missoni scarves. Complicated zigs-when-he-oughta-zag fellow, Mister Myron Beam.

In sum: "I was born to be a publisher."

I am not sure what his talent entailed, but whatever it was maddened and mystified his competitors. He unerringly selected books he believed the testicle-deficient big houses were too timid to risk publishing, enamored as they were of their own silly self-fulfilling metrics and scared-bunny forecasts. Some critics say the mainstream rich publishing houses underestimate the reading public, but they're wrong. To quote Myron, they don't underestimate them enough. In any case, King Myron generated royalty statements and issued checks in timely fashion (thereby never jeopardizing licensing rights), strangling the sub-rights into submission. That's something his greedy writers *should* care about: their own personal bottom-line.

But, no, inedibly enough, that's not the case. Believe it or not, what they ultimately craved was Myron Beam's devotion, what they ultimately desired was Myron Beam's admiration, what they ultimately needed was Myron Beam's abiding personal interest in their lives and their alleged creative processes. Are all writers nuts? You betcha, as Sarah Fucking Palin might say, a nut job who wanted to be president and who "wrote" a fucking bestselling book but never read one. Maybe the big houses did accidentally underestimate the public.

✳✳✳

IN FACT, ONE PUBLICATION of his stood at or near the top of the national charts for more than a hundred gynecologized weeks. Of course, this was back in the good old memoir salad days of yore (psychopathic parents, wall-to-wall pharmaceuticals, misty conversions, naked and heroic Tantric Yoga teachers, Celebrations of Nature and Fly Fishing, promiscuous motorcycle repairs, empathic stray dog or friendly wolf emergence, and so on). Godlike Oprah practically levitated with delight during the author's appearance on her show.

"God, I miss when Oprah ruled the world," he said more than once.

Thus it came to pass that Myron became the envy of the publishing world. Every now and then the brass of one of the conglomerated big boy houses in New York flew out and took him to places like The French Laundry in Napa Valley for dinner (try to get a rezzie, but think next decade, and after mortgaging your house to pay the freight) and made an offer with lots of zeroes to buy him out. They said things like, *You have captured lighting in a bottle.* Which was true. One cannot not argue with the obvious unless you work for the New York Knicks. Thus he would drink their first-growth Bordeaux and consume their tall, sustainable, locally sourced food, but he always took a pass on a proposed deal. What would he have done with himself if he weren't the publisher of his company? He was not in it for the money. Yes, don't be ridiculous, he craved all the money he made, but that's not the point.

"What's your *secret?*"

"Fuck if I have a clue, *Sibella?*"

If he had been a gracious gent, if he had had a single magnanimous bone in the temple of his beleaguered, undepilated (except for the top of his head) body, he might have thrown some credit onto his gifted authors and his crackerjack staff, including one junior editor.

I overheard one day an exchange between him and the social media guru, who was named—what else?—Caprice.

"You handle the social media stuff, right?" For a micromanager, he lost track of an astounding number of details (like other job titles).

She nodded, but then she wouldn't recognize a cop's trick question if she were shackled for running a three-card monte game in Times Square.

"What is it exactly that you do?"

Her bottle-blonde pageboy cut was a little too darling, if you know what I mean, but between us girls I wished I could wear my unmanageable hair that way. My dusky, wavy mop top combined with my chipmunk cheeks and elongated face severely restricted options in the salon and in my dating life. I sacrificially burned out a few intrepid flat irons before I gave up and experimented with a buzz cut. Now I warily watch my hair grow Chia-plant-like.

Yet to her or her life coach's credit, Caprice was not as dismayed as anybody else might have been by Myron's query, and he wasn't being hostile, and it wasn't truly a trick question—he wanted to know what was the nature of the work she did. But watch this. She actually fucking told him. She talked for five straight minutes, a thousand tweets' worth of nonsense, without taking a single breath. At the conclusion of her peroration, he thanked her sincerely.

When Caprice left her desk with iPhone in hand to do presumably some of that essential social media work or to go to the bathroom—or both, being a multitasker—he approached my crates, where I sat with eyes and mouth wide open, as if I had witnessed a wreck, which I sort of did.

"You heard *Caprice?* I didn't understand a thing she *said?*"

"Neither did *I?*"

"Just *checking?*"

Anyway—and that's a feeble transition I would cut the fuck out of any ms I was editing—in the staff's spare time when they were not playing games online or stealing music, they also pored over manuscripts that come in over the transom, a term whose etymology I pretended to understand. Must be a Britishism. When in doubt, it's British; when it's not, French. I have been known to have a tough time around the tea-sipping hundred-buck-bangers-and-mash UK gulag. You get stockaded at the London Book Fair sometime and you'll back me up.

"When a dog journeys," Murmechka might say, "he has no pockets and comes back with stories he wishes he could tell." Most of her proverbs involved the animal world—predominantly a certain Mr. Coyote—but I was philosophically resistant to her casual attitude in regard to non-homo sapien protagonist cultural appropriation if not exploitation as well as her default lunch order from the downstairs deli: tongue sandwiches, whole wheat, no mayo or mustard. Never mind the tongue, and never mind that it wasn't Katz's downstairs, but how could somebody eat a self-disrespecting sandwich minus mayo and mustard?

✳✳✳

IF YOU REALLY WANT to hear about it, Kelly, the first thing you'll probably want to know is all that David Copperfield kind of crap, which I think qualifies as a double-barrelled collusion. Spoiled alert: you're not going to be rewarded on that score. His childhood was, to him and to anybody not trying in vain to publish their latest verse epic in iambic pent-up-ameter, a nonevent. According to him, he did make an effort to remember primal moments, figuring he must have had a childhood, as who doesn't have one? That was what prompted him to see for a while a classically trained psychoanalyst, goatee and couch and white noise machine and all. Therapy proved a bust. The shrink periodically nodded off during Myron's Buster Keatonish silences. The psychodynamic moral of Myron's story might be this: his real life began the day he conceived of Hard Rain Publishing.

The second thing you'll probably want to know is, where did he get the big dough? (Duh, that's where my dad's "bread" comes in!) He wasn't a member of the Columbia Cartel and didn't reprise the clever visionary the world came to know as Signor Ponzi, but there could be some discussion on that sensitive subject later on, we shall see. Otherwise, drat, he didn't enlighten me on that matter, or unlock his ledgers for me. But wherever it was he found the capital, by whatever the means he came by it, he threw everything into the company he created out of whole cloth in a down, down, down market.

"The rest is *history?*" I guess.

Speaking of money—and if you are ever in doubt as to the functional import of Myron's remarks—whenever his publisher lips moved he was speaking about money. People harbor many misconceptions about the book business and about Myron, but one thing everybody knows is this: publishing ain't cheap. When he first started his company, he said he figured he could count on a nice little yearly loss for tax purposes as well as unbridled access to gratuitous tail. Unsavory, but true, let us all with a long face concur.

Well, how did that work out?

I will tell you what he told me. As for tail, honestly, not so much.

"I am, I think the word is *celibate?*"

"What? You're a Jewish Catholic *monk?*"

Not quite, and he explained, in graphic detail I may have to share with you, he was, well, "important." As his copyeditor I would strike out that typo and replace it with *impotent*. Moving on quickly now.

And as for those anticipated losses, no such luck. He said he made a profit every year without fail. It is a truth universally acknowledged, that a single man in possession of a good fortune must be in want of a publishing company.

Raise your hands. Who, besides Kelly, didn't see that collusion coming?

He told me a stupid joke.

"Hey, how do you make a small fortune in the book publishing *business*?" goes the wiseacre.

"Start with a bigger *fortune*?" Holy mackerels in a barrel.

Yeah, yeah, yeah. His rivals wished they could marginalize him. But they couldn't, because he *totally* killed in the book market. Editorial advisory: he *totally* rejected a book with extreme prejudice, he didn't care if it was cobbled together by the ghost of William Fucking Faulkner, if he caught one single *totally*. I myself did read *one* Southern Aggravationarian page, over and over, yearning for the peace that passeth understanding that was not to be and knowing why man will not only endure he will prevail. Con seder this re: Myron Beam's predispositions: unlike the Yokfuckingcounty author, Twain and Nabokov and Joyce and Proust never won a Nobel Prize. The bomb-maker's selection committee got Proust right, I will say that.

Through the fence, between the curling flower spaces, I could see them editing.

To finish off the point earlier adumbrated (*ooh la lah*, fancy dancy word, get me the copy desk!) *vis-à-vis* tail pursuit on his celibate, or whatever, part, or whatever:

First of all, don't use flaccid French turns of phrase anywhere in Myron's zipper code, or use the word "flaccid" at all around him, and before you trot one out, find out how to pronounce *flaccid*, as in not flas-sid, but flak-sid. If you are a grad student, you now have all you need to win a bar bet. But maybe think about hanging out next time in a real bar.

Whenever I hear Zou Bizzou Bizzou French, I want to go guillotine on the beret-bearing, Gauloise-puffing, The Metro Is Much Cleaner Than the Subway boy or girl. But Calypso O'Kelly's rogue *déclassé* in her notorious email that fucked him up earned a Myrulligan. The first ominous sign, if you ask me, of his lapsing judgment.

And B, as for flaccid, I might as well let you in on something else he intimated since you're going to find out much more compromising information about Yours Hardly, or not hardly at all.

His limp ageing ilk was the target demographic of a certain *genre* (I know it's French, merde) of the prissily denominated "erectile dysfunction" gang, but when he saw those TV commercials (featuring manly men galloping on steeds, stoking California beach sunset campfires, cocking firearms and I don't know what else while touting come-hitherish pharmafuckingcological advances), he yawned. His evolutionarily curious prostate existed nostalgically in his rearview (poor choice in images, I rant, but let's move on), and he was proudly, defiantly, ecstatically, exuberantly unable to answer any call to duty.

Did his plumbing's delimitation depress him? You might think so, but wait, there is more. The side effects of a lifetime sentence of detumescence without possibility of parole were mixed. One unfortunate proctological byproduct was a byproduct he experienced hardship producing: his—and I am sorry I must mention this, too—urination. Oh, the sluggish struggle before the public or private *pissoir*. (Who's going to edit this book anyway? I'm praying it's species-nonjudgmental Murmechka.) That was when his entire day and night seemed consumed by the gallant attempt to void his bladder, an activity occasionally interrupted by meetings, dreams, not taking phone calls, and nutritional intake at Carmine's or Avenue. But the *other* other byproduct—now that he had slide ruled out the old ruling passion—was that he had more time and energy to compose and not send out rejection notes. And not only that.

Because, you see, finally the gift of celibacy and/or impotence demuscled up my Jewish Catholic monk publisher to withstand the sallies (and the sashas and the cassandras) of feminine wile and The Strunk and White Elements of Guile, which redounded ultimately to his advantage, most especially the financial. Herr Doktor Freud, he a Hall of Shamer from the dead ball era, effectively struck out every at bat during his entire shameless career, but Buddhist priests and plein air painters and Myron the publisher would put in a good word for the sublime powers of sublimation. With that diagnosis, my work here is almost done.

Now, Sibella, may we finally leave this subject, umm, behind?

As occasionally happened during my college games, the crowd...
goes...wild!

You can never count on a junior editor for a fancy prose style.

"The cow chewing on its cud in the green meadows of
timelessness cannot paint a picture of itself," as Murmechka might
say. And often did.

How moo, how fucking moo.

"Sibella, want to hear another *joke*?"

"Not *really*?"

"Who did the blonde star of the movie based on a book fuck
on the casting *couch*?

"The publisher, and it's whom, and are you out of your
fucking mind? You can't make that non-joke anymore, buster.
You living in a vacuum cleaner, *Myron*?"

"We should go to Frankfurt next year. Good beer, *man*?"

Let us turn the page, mental reader.

But before we do, let me insert a qualification to everything
Myron said about writers and their books. Sometimes, very rarely,
comes along a writer with a gift he or she can barely control and
a book issues forth that changes lives of book lovers forever. That
was when Myron's brilliance shone forth. He knew that he had
discovered a writer who writes because there is no existential
alternative to writing and we will all bow down in awe before the
performance because it seems like anything but a performance.
It feels like genius, and we don't know how we got along without it.
Call Myron sentimental if you must, or call Myron an outrageously
lucky publisher, that's coolio. Because a great book is nothing less
than a miracle. Don't believe in miracles? Myron and/or I would
have felt semi-sorry and/or -sad for you. I suppose you never heard
of Hard Rain Publishing. And you have never known a publisher
like Myron Beam. Don't trash yourself. Nobody else has either.

This takes us all the way back to the debacle about to take
place, overwrought by the improbable Calypso O'Kelly.

A STREETCAR NAMED SIBELLA

ERE WE GO. LIGHTS, camera, faction.
H   Visualize if you will the misery en scène that morning.
We were still in the day after Myron's marathon reading the night
before and Myron had dragged me into his office and we had been
talking in his office for hours. I say we had been talking but I was
mostly listening. I was taking gnotes, struggling to track, acquiring
TMI about Myron and the house I never would have suspected
before, and I wasn't altogether sure I was liking it, and I continued
to prefer not to. At the same time, I could feel the staff tension
building outside his door. What was some junior editor doing
meeting so long with the publisher? What tricks was the tall,
scheming girl up to?

Finally, somebody cracked. I guess YGB couldn't take it anymore.

"Myron," said YGB upon entering Myron's office, and he
spoke with genuine emotion and urgency as he audaciously
touched Myron's shoulder. "You all right?" Myron deplored
physical contact, especially on the part of the editor in chief, and
you could see him about to rise up and poke YGB on the bridge of
his perfect, delectable nose, which would have been very upsetting
for a number of reasons.

Two wit:

You see, Young Goodman Brown truly was a handsome and
rakishly sincere Rhodesashish boy, and Dear Bleeder, I couldn't
help it: I liked him. You might say my affection rose to the level of
what used to be called in school a crush. That tender regard might

explain why I would catch myself smiling idiotically whenever my Teddy Boy was near. Watch out, though. Here comes Folsom Prison disclosure: he reminded me of Junior. That might be way TM of TMI even for the unlikes of me. Yet the truth is that YGB flirted with me all the time, and despite being a slow if tall learner, I deduced that my altitude didn't sicken or intimidate him. Of course, I thought Junior wasn't fazed by my towering over him, but then again, his current Greenback Squeezette isn't elevated enough to gain admittance to the big kid Matterhorn ride at Disneyland.

"Is Myron stroking out?" called out a senior editor once she saw his office door was open. That senior editor was the one named Kelly, and she feigned concern for Myron the way she also feigned intellectual competency.

That was Myron's cue. He told me he and I would take a break for now, continue our conversation later. I realized what he did not state: he had some reflecting to do about Calypso's book.

As I walked across the office, my head was pounding from listening to that Myronathon and from smiling at YGB. I could sense Kelly staring at me from across the way, on the other side of Murmechka. She was sporting a buttercup polka-dot yellow retro sweater set, which was clinging like Saran Wrap upon B-Cups of Lemon Jell-O. Her bra size probably matched her grade point average—as honestly, fair enough, did mine. The real reason she was pretending concern for Myron is that she probably had big plans today that involved the publisher (pointlessly pitching a loser of a book he would ultimately reject, if her track record and her outfit were any indication). These designs might fall through if, say, he were intubated in some ICU.

She would have been a good woman, I say, if there had been somebody there to shoot her every minute of her life.

She and I were a study in contrast. I was the non-Kelly. Myron called me a living breathing Mixed Metaphor, and said that I had him at *fuck*. Street urchin Spence debutante face-metal Ivy League potty-mouthed Upper East Side sonnet-writing Valley fist-fighting nonZen Girl Starting at Center Number 44. If I may quote my curriculum fucking vitae.

Little wonder that the meager wonder named Kelly hated me. Take a number along with most of the other senior editors, except for YGB and Murmechka. She had cause. This junior editor could take her off the dribble and posterize her senior editor ass anytime I wanted, and I could edit the final fuck out of a manuscript before she finished perusing a first draft. And she knew it.

Soon as I took my place at my milk crates, the moment I became a stationary target, she took aim and fired off her volleys, *boom boom boom*. "This morning when you saw Myron you said *what fuck the fuck*, which makes no sense and which means that every other word out of your mouth is literally fuck."

Chomp chomp, chew chew.

To which I could reply: "You are Kelliterally a literalist and also a devoted word *counter?*"

"Why is every other word out of your filthy Valley Girl mouth *fuck?*"

Admittedly, a not unreasonable question. Don't you hate it when unreasonable human beings do the unexpected?

"Fuck if fucking I fucking *know?*" said I, and meant it.

"You know, when you're sitting down, it looks like you're standing up," she added, an ad Sibellum remark if I ever heard one.

Chomp chomp, chew chew.

"I can't help it if you're a fucking dwarf, Kelly. But I take that back, because there's nothing wrong with *dwarfs?*"

"You're a height-ist and you're seven feet tall."

Chomp chomp, chew chew.

"I told you a million times to stop *exaggerating?*"

Yes, middle school and a publishing house do have a lot in common, and I'd been intolerating that sort of put-down all my life.

"Why you gussied up like a fucking *lollipop?*" I said.

"Why you costumed like a publisher?"

"I was going for assistant *professor?*"

"More like Myron suck-up."

"Don't you have a Norton Anthology you can sit on to give you greater stature around here since you can't read *it?*"

"Dumb jock."

"English *minor?*"

She's never found peace since she left his arms, and never will again till she's as he is now! Sibellude the Obscure gets the last collusive word.

***

Kelly's pointillist In Seine sweater told a man like Myron two things. One, perhaps he had been hasty if not rash when he opted for his sex-life-destruction derby. Yowza, more creepy and lots more to come, FYI, but what's a harmless man without a DOA dream? And day ux, Kelly had shown up at work planning to pitch him a book that had come in on that damned transom, which apparatus unfailingly seemed to hum along, barely keeping up with the literary production taking place in this great land of ours where everybody and his or her incestuous or adulterous or Scientologistic partner has a literary agent and a whirling dervish of a word processor.

Kelly and my catfight now temporarily over, why don't you take a break and go Goloogle up how many hundreds of thousands of books are published each year.

I'll wait.

You're back already?

Amazing, ain't it? Now imagine how many more are written that aren't published or self-published by anybody. I recommend a cold cloth to your forehead. These are the haunting, daunting numbers primarily responsible for packing writing conferences along with writers' medicine cabinets and wet bars.

The armature of Kelly's sweater notwishstanding, he appeared to be in no mood to be pitched by anybody, and despite being anything but a whip smart editor, she sensed this and would beddy bide her time. For a change, and unquestionably in order to irritate me, she took it upon herself to answer the fucking office phone. And next I heard her speaking to Myron across the way.

"Phone call, Myron, says it's urgent," she called out. She turned her attention to Murmechka: "You do something with your hair? I like it."

Publisher's Advisory: The next time the publisher gets a call that is not urgent will be the first. But here comes the suspenseful part. Would Myron, on this august occasion, take a phone call in real time?

Kelly kept talking conspiratorially to Murmechka: "This pushy biach on the phone says Myron will want to talk with her? Calypso *O'Kelly?* Jesus Christ, what a name. Sounds like a loose chick somebody met on a bad spring break trip to Aruba. Calypso Oh Plagiarizing My Name—she sounds like a good pal for the giraffe girl. Hey, giraffe girl," she directed her remark to me, "you need a friend?"

I did, and that was a subject for another time. Besides, Kelly and my dustup was producing immediate dividends in adjusting her attitude if not her buttercupitude. Do you see this, too? I was having a salutary fucking effect on her, and I was proud. As for Kelly and Murmechka, Her Lollipopness was always trying to forge alliances against me, but I had my doubts her strategy was working, since Murmechka safely hovered—considering her stature, a fantastical image—above the office politics fray, preoccupied as she was all day long on her personal projects, at least a few of which had to involve Hard Rain, no? Or was Mr. Coyote continually filling up her ear with words of wisdom emanating from Mr. Rabbit?

"Myron," Kelly tried again, "she says to tell you it's Calypso O'Kelly."

Though the calls to the publisher were predestined to be cast into the purgatory of his voice mailbox, Myron wanted us to inform him promptly when he received a call so he could promptly not take it.

"I'll take the call," Myron said weakly. And incredibly.

"What fuck the fuck?" I said again loud enough for the whole office to hear. He was taking a fucking call? Did he have a brain tumor?

Cue the Kellygian: "Again with the *what fuck the fuck*, again?"

And he waved me back into his office. Being a keen observer of human and giraffe nature, Kelly fumed toward Murmechka, and he closed the door, and turned on the unspeakablephone so I could overhear.

In his excitement, he fumbled for the receiver, which he dropped and scrambled to retrieve from underneath the desk. He bent over and reached down and when he rose up he banged his skinhead on the knife edge of the desk and yelped like a kitty cat.

"You?" he surfaced, mewing.

"You killing yourself?" said his caller.

"Not yet, thanks for asking."

"You seem to be in an agreeable mood this morning for a man who didn't sleep a wink. Which is how I prefer my men."

My breath was taken away. I could have used some handy cannulae. She had a voice like the wind in the trees, first autumn day, but don't trust me—in all the excitement, *my* head was pulsing like with the techno beat maintained by Eurotrash bands in clubs roped off to keep out the likes of me.

"You're tuned in to my sleep patterns?" Being at a loss for words was a relatively new experience for him, like helping a blind lady cross the street I hope may one day be for me.

"How could you conceivably stop reading a book like mine?"

"Wait, *you're* Calypso O'Kelly? I thought *he*…"

"Plus, your office lights were on all night."

"You were watching my windows?"

"This is not material to our ongoing relationship, Myron. I will see you at Avenue for lunch at one o'clock. Don't keep me waiting, time is of the essence. You didn't have lunch or dinner yesterday. You must be famished."

She hung up. He probably was famished, and not only for food.

You know what got to me? Not the ambiguity of the authorship or the identity of the caller. Not the fact that she knew he had been up all night or that Avenue was his hangout. Not that she instructed him to meet her. Not that she knew he had skipped lunch and dinner yesterday. It was that she said she and Myron already had a relationship. She was correct, not that I understood why at the time.

"What are you doing for lunch?" he asked me.

"I'm looking forward to my nice organic apple—"

"Good, I'm not taking this meeting alone."

"Shouldn't I stay here and read her book?"

"That's exactly what you shouldn't do. I need you with me. Don't tell anybody."

Don't tell anybody he needed me with him?

Who would fucking believe something as outrageous as that?

THE PURLOINED SIBELLA

MYRON WAS A CARD-CARRYING habitué of habitat of inhumanity and something of a luminary at Avenue, to which we had hastily repaired. The host advised him that somebody was waiting at his table. She didn't say "somebody" was waiting. She actually said, "Some vamp's expecting you." Vamp? Had we time-warped without warning? I concluded otherwise, because the host didn't invoke gams or heaters or gats, but she did point a nostalgically nicotine-stained, divining-rod of an index finger in what I presumed was a direction familiar to him but not me. It was my maiden lunch with Myron because my personal jeans mutual disarmament pact that I may have mentioned precluded such prior socialization. Then the host obliquely expressed a concern we all had cultivated today at the house: "Myron, you look like you need a drink."

Across the way said vamp was indeed lodged in Myron's booth. She appeared to be studying wide-eyed the bill of fare as if the text were sacrilegiously lifted from the Kabbalah or as if she had never before examined an esoteric printed publication known as a menu. I approached alongside my bedragglian boss. The guidebooks advise that projecting self-assuredness and power and standing tall are the keys to survival when happening upon a threatening creature in the wilderness or in an overpriced restaurant.

"May I?" he said to her.

"Of course, Myron. Glad you could slip away from Hard Rain."

I sat down flanking him, unable to take my eyes off her and her red dress and her shiny black tresses pulled back devilishly tight against her skull. She was woo woo put together, like out of a French magazine. Not a *Paris Review* type of magazine, wiseass, and she might as well have been wearing sunglasses, because I could not focus on her eyes. I was guessing she was old—thirty-four, thirty-five—but don't trust me, as along with my powers of perception I had been vacuumed into the vamp muthaship's suckational field.

As for Myron, he had never spent a sleepless night in his office reading, and his unsteadiness showed.

"What do you recommend, Myron?"

"What shall I call you? Calypso?"

She must have misheard the question and she held up the menu for theatrical effect. "I'm leaning toward Chicken Diavolo."

"That's an unusual name."

"Delightful, Myron." She hardly appeared to be enamored. "Tell me, who's this statuesque, exquisite gazelle keeping you company? You are both cutely clad in your identical academic chic white shirt and black tie."

If she were aiming for the jungular, I conceded gazelle was a notable improvement upon giraffe. Myron shot a glance in my direction. The astonishment in his eyes indicated the likelihood that that was the first instant he detected our unbespoken clothing synchronicity.

"Myron, is this your new lover?" And yes, she pronounced the word "luvah."

I looked around, to ascertain if this insane creature was referring to me, and I was taken aback when Myron chortled and chortled, which was nowhere in the time zone of polite, and I thought, what am I, chopped fucking *livah*? But then again that *was* a crazy idea and who uses the word "lover" anymore, and let's all agree I was obviously no wurst-ish candidate for downbeat pâté or AARP-eligible amours.

I introduced myself anyway, fuck her.

"Sibella is an intern," he said expansively, following up.

"Junior fucking editor," I said.

"Oh right, she was recently promoted to junior editor. And don't worry. She has Tourette's."

"So don't make any fast moves," I said, "though I don't fucking have fucking Tourette's."

She addressed me: "Sibella is such a lovely name, one that, sadly, is hardly heard any more in this world overpopulated by the Madisons and Rachels, the Jennifers and Sophias."

"Sibella does sort of rhyme with luvah, never thought of that before."

"Tell me, *are* you?"

What fuck the fuck? I didn't have to say it for her to get the message.

If you will.

"*Are* you a sibyl, Sibella?"

"Well, my last prime-time prophecy was that the Mets and the Knicks would win championships before my Alzheimer's kicks in, so I must qualify for the indefinite future as a fucking failure in the oracle department. Same time, I'm kinda savvy with bird entrails, if you have any in your fantastic handbag that need interpretation." It was a knockout bag on her chair, gotta say. And I myself wouldn't have deposited the messy entrails of anything inside it. "Is it a freakin' Birkin knockoff?" *Like you?* I didn't add.

"Such a lovely girl," she said. "You two make quite a pair, Myron and his Sibella. She makes you happy, I can see that, Myron."

Some people possess that rarest of commodities called charisma, from the Greek, suggesting the ability to perform miracles. In our secular age, we look askance at the whole divine intervention phenomenon, and charisma has devolved to mean something more restrictive and modest, along the lines of charm. I happen to possess the inverse of charisma, or charm. But that didn't mean I couldn't decipher that this woman had charisma to burn. She probably had more than adequate juice to turn me into a toad if the combined efforts of the book business and of Junior had not already rendered moot that feat. In any case, she seemed to be enveloped by a mysterious penumbra, and I know this because I would have been incapable of picking her out of a *Law & Order* line-up of red dresses. I was looking at her but not able to see her. She dizzy-dazzled, as if a million golden asterisks of collusion burst across the solar system.

Myron's cell phone rang. He saw that it was Young Goodman Brown, and he didn't pick up. He decided he was going to fire his Hawthorne-ignorant ass that afternoon, as he told me later. He'd warned him never to disturb his lunch at Avenue unless the building was on fire, only Myron didn't grasp then that, as it happened, it sort of was.

Myron resumed. "Gee, the suspense is kind of killing me, what do I call you?"

"All in good time, Myron, all in good time."

"One thing you could clarify. If you are not Calypso O'Kelly, are you his agent? And the whole question of Calypso's sexuality in the manuscript is a little ambiguous, to me anyway."

"I find men are turned on by ambiguous sexuality, don't you agree, Sibella? But Calypso doesn't subscribe to the whole antediluvian agenting business. Calypso is committed to guerilla writing, marketing, representing. For Calypso and for Hard Rain, there are market force fields impossible to be penetrated by agents, or for that matter able to be understood by mere mortals." Was she referring to another person named Calypso or was she speaking of herself in the third person, the way superstar jocks when post-game interviewed have been known to irritate the piss out of me by doing?

"Well, what mere mortal isn't fond of gorillas?" said Myron. "I've been called one myself. Tell me. What kind of forces are at play?"

She sighed. "The kind of forces that change the world, the kind of forces that will cause my book to fly off the shelves." And that's when I shivered. The temperature in the room dropped ten degrees. Charismafuckitall. "You must sit back and occasionally wonder why you and your company have been so fortunate."

"I never sit back."

I could corroborate that bizarre fact, not that I was asked.

We ordered. Chicken Diavolo for her. Dungeness Crab Louie for Reformed Myron and an oxymoronish jumbo shrimp cocktail for me. Bottom-feeders of the world, unite! We waited for the food's arrival and chatted, at which mind-numbing activity she proved incongruously adept, sort of like the condemned on death row serving high tea.

Nice weather. We need a lot more rain. But we're having a lovely drought. What's wrong with the Giants' pitching this year? She gets to California whenever she needs to but prefers the capitals of Europe. What will possibly come of the ill-conceived Euro? The Greeks, well, the Greeks, but the Germans, mein Gott, the Germans. Americans are perceptive and have sound reason to be disappointed about their current politics. Republicans are gutless obfuscators, Democrats, weak-kneed flip-floppers. Don't get her started on Trump. Americans and their ridiculously phallic gun-fixation. Equities vs. bonds. Italy vs. France. (You must know where I stood conversationally on that one.) Berlusconi bunga bunga mama mia. World Cup. Myron and she, the mind-numbing usual, Myron and she. If we didn't talk business soon I was going to hara kiri myself with a butter knife.

Thank God she got down to the subject and to her suddenly served-up Chicken Diavolo.

"You read the terms of the proposition."

"That I did, that I did," he said. "It wasn't as compelling as the manuscript, which was, I have to admit, intoxicating. Did you write it?"

"This pollo is perfectly prepared."

"And that's a lot of money you're seeking for what may or may not be a first-time author. Is Calypso O'Kelly a pen name?"

"You have an unsavory reputation for skimping on advances."

"It's a pretty primitive aspect of the book business."

"Money is the essence of primitive."

"Not to me. I feel sophisticated when I am in the neighborhood of my money."

"Is our lunch over prematurely and so unproductively, Myron? That would be very tragic."

"Listen, money's one part of any book deal. Novice authors always make that mistake. It's every bit as important, or more important, how a book is represented to the public—not to mention all the other contract terms."

"Do we need to order more cocktails to get through this silly portion of the fake negotiation, Myron?"

Cocktails? We had a winner, ladies and gentlemen. Another Bloody Mary for Birkin Baby Grrll, another Martini for him, a Diet Coke for me. One day I have to stop drinking that concoction. It might be a contributing factor to my uptalk. It might be stunting my growth and thereby inhibiting me from joining the Knicks, who need a lot of help on the boards these days because you can't win without rebounding, and you know what you require in order to rebound? A lot of want-to and strong anterior cruciate ligaments, both of which I have in spades.

"Have you accomplished everything in life you desired, Myron? You and your publishing house have been on a magical run for years. Has this brought you peace and joy? But surely not the way your young lover, Sibella, has? Fact remains, you have the whole book business on its heels."

"We call that an overstatement, where I come from."

"Your success can't be a matter of your judgment and intelligence."

He practically choked on a crab leg. "The things that come out of your mouth. Have you ever done business with anybody ever, whoever you are?"

"Don't mean to offend your sense of propriety. I thought you were more of a bare-knuckles bruiser, which is the reason you are the first and with any luck on your part the sole publisher to see the book presale. Ready to pony up for an exclusive? You wouldn't want this to be the first time you passed up a golden opportunity, would you?"

He liked her aggressive approach to business, which he could work with. And considering who Myron used to be, her aggressive approach to décolletage, with which he probably couldn't work with anymore. It was at this point I detected the faintest of petite erotic moles on her upper lip.

"You talk about luck a lot."

"I have kept my eye trained on your company for a long time, Myron. You probably don't realize this, but we might have almost met once, before you ventured into the book business. You must wonder why you have achieved so much in such a brief time. I may have a clue as to why. Care to know what that is?"

"My good looks? My infallible editorial shrewdness?" He palpated his hairless pink scalp, forebodingly.

"You are aging fairly well, but I don't think that's it. And your acquisitions? Let's say they are eclectic, to put it politely. Life is strange, Myron, but your success may stem from one fateful night in Venice. Do you remember the gypsy?"

"Gypsies are everywhere in Venice, like cockroaches, no offense to the Roma people." He didn't like this turn, or that she seemed to know things about him she shouldn't.

"Yes, but there was one particular beggar of a gypsy you came across on an evening walk in the rain, a gypsy to whom one fateful night in that moody, mysterious, labyrinthine city you gave one Euro out of the kindness of your heart. Venice is a place that yearns to be walked in any sort of weather. It was raining a hard rain, you might say. And she was such a sad sight, sitting under an awning on the street, a tin cup in her hand that was randomly pinging from wind-driven raindrops. That was remarkably generous of you, to give her a Euro, and something tells me that she appreciated it."

"Well, I have had my weak moments." Myron was looking progressively more and more disturbed.

"And yet, in such a moment of largesse, which took place in Piazza San Marco, when you bent over to put the money in her cup, she surreptitiously managed to pickpocket your wallet."

Myron looked stunned, as if an invisible viper had sunk its teeth into him, which resembled the effect occasionally produced in him by Murmechka and sometimes Caprice, only now the quadrants of his face appeared to have been rearranged by one of those expressionist painters whose work gave me a migraine at the MOMA.

"But then a miracle. When you got back to the hotel that evening, the concierge said your wallet was waiting at the front desk. He didn't bother to state the obvious, which was that in the long, bloody history of Peggy Guggenheim and the state of Venice, no pilfered wallet has ever been returned to its rightful owner. Amazingly, until then, you didn't apprehend it was missing."

"Who are you?"

"I am the one who considerately sent you the *Adventures of Calypso O'Kelly* and I am your lunch companion and the Chicken Diavolo is delicious, though we don't know the identity of the person—or was it the gypsy herself?—who left the wallet at your hotel situated on the lagoon, where you shared a suite with your lovely bride on the top floor."

"Really, who the hell are you?"

"You ask many irrelevant questions, Myron. Does he do this with you, too, Sibella? Men can be so irrelevant at the most inopportune times, don't you find, and most of the time in bed immediately after climax, for instance?"

Damn, she accurately intuited the ancient reality of Junior and me, but nonetheless, it was time for In the White Trunks Weighing Who Knows What Junior Editor Sibella to come out swinging: "Enough of this whack shit craziness, whoever the fuck you are."

"Ah, Myron, how sweet, Sibella is your protector," she said, pronouncing it *protectah*. "And not only was your wallet intact, there were more Euros than before. Five thousand more. That was no ordinary gypsy, is my theory—that would be anyone's theory. Legend has it that some gypsies possess supernatural powers. And she could have been one such. And she was touched by you, she gave you a gift that has not stopped giving. For take into account this one overwhelmingly salient fact: You have never wanted for money ever since that amazing night, ten years ago—you won't believe this, today is *precisely* ten years. You invested a single Euro that night, and you enjoyed a five-thousand-fold return. Since then, every investment, every business decision you have spun into pure gold."

"My financial run of good luck was nothing but the result of living in the age of irrational exuberance and the dot-com boom."

"Apple, Xerox..." she intoned.

"Jeez, remember Xerox? Glad I got out before the..."

"Amazon, oodles of Googles, pharmaceuticals, every build-it-and-they-will-come crackpot IPO move you made was brilliant."

Now things got stranger still. For at this moment, it was as if a cloud lifted about her and I could see her at last. What was happening?

And where was it happening? In me or in her? It wasn't that the pale erotic mole on her lip darkened and sprouted wiry follicles of hair. It wasn't that her fingernails metamorphed into raptor talons, or her hair transformed into a tangled nest, or her once fetching breasts turned into dugs drooping down to the table. It wasn't that her eyes gleamed like hobo campfires. All that would have been something. And yet, and yet, I saw into her. I had previously endured similarly disturbing, revelatory experiences in college, but they all involved psilocybin and being tossed into the back seat of the campus police car and the administration of a shot of thorazine at the infirmary. She cackled with what sounded to my unreliable ear like demonic delight. Had I stumbled into another job the way I had stumbled into Hard Rain? The job of a sibyl?

Dare I say.

Downward to darkness, on extended wings.

I was projecting like mad, and I needed a new job fast.

But then the witch winked knowingly at me, and only then did she speedily, olé aginously, revert to her original, vague, and fashionable Hermes form—or revert in my own mind, and what difference would that make anyway?

"It's such a pleasure to see you again, Myron. It's been a long time."

What fuck the fuck did she mean by *again*? She had never met my boss before, or so I inferred a minute ago.

She smiled. Consider yourself lucky you didn't witness that. Some smiles have the uncanny capacity to warm the whole room. Hers deposited stalactites on the ceiling. "I should have told you before. I was fresh out of Brown then, so ten years earlier I was twenty-one or so, and I had a much older Venetian lover, about the same age difference that exists between you and your Sibella. He was some prince or marquis or count, but since he was married, he arranged for a spectacular suite, and we could enjoy each other's company free of prying eyes. As it happened, we were a few doors down from you. I hope we didn't disturb your slumbers, he was very boisterous in bed. Any candidates to be my lovers are required to be." Of course, *luvahs*.

"You don't say."

"And here comes another coincidence, a rather dramatic one. You see, I came to know your former spouse, and she told me all about the theft and the wallet's magical reappearance. Ships in the Venetian night, shall we say?" She then added that once back in America they got to know each other much better from the Nob Hill club and routinely shared such intimate confidences after Pilates classes when they scuttled to a bar to soothe their aching muscles.

It clicked for Myron. His ex talked freely about his finances and liked to spend freely his money, and he was fine with the second part but not the first. And long before she became his spousal-supported ex, she was on the slow stroll down Don't Give a Flying Fuck Boulevard that led to the outskirts of Beamtown.

"It was *you*? You broke us up? You were the one with the Italian boy prince she was fucking? And your Italian princeling didn't object?" Myron was laughing. Mr. Full of Surprises Himself today.

"You find this amusing? I was hoping you would, it's all ancient history, isn't it? In any event, my lover and I were bored with each other by the time I returned to the States, and at Brown—well, being bi used to be a graduation requirement."

"I don't know whether to kill or kiss you." He might have used the word he probably meant instead of "kiss," but that other word brought up too many associations with his personal futility.

"You're not the first man, and by that I mean lover, to have said as much to me. But losing her seems like such a small trade-off, Myron, wouldn't you agree? I did care for her, if that is any consolation, certainly I liked her far more than you did, and she seems much, much happier without you, doesn't she? As you are happier without her, and much happier with your lovely Sibella. Your wife was never truly interested in men, that was instantly clear to me—as it should have been to you."

"Tell me why I should do business with you." I think he was asking in the spirit of a thought experiment. You know. Like what if Mary Ann Evans traded places with David Foster Wallace? (Gnote to Kelly: Not to be cruel, but Evans is George Eliot.) I didn't detect a note of hostility in his voice. (Agnother gnote to Kelly: The author of Middlefuckingmarch.)

"Please, Myron, these are questions that beg to be separated. Such a crass expression you insist upon using, and unlike your divine Sibella you don't have Tourette's, but if so, the truth is the truth. Let's let bygones be bygones, shall we? But the point of my little tale is this. Business is business, as Americans claim to believe. This incredible string of coincidences brings us to our little *tête-à-tête* today. I have been speaking of that fateful night in Venice when you decided you would do something radically new with your life, and when the wallet's recovery put you on the road to enjoying unexpected, unparalleled success to come."

"Then I wish the gypsy'd kept my wallet." Myron was pretending to be blasé? He was dancing too fast, which is what taking X will do, as I recall, but who could blame his X-less self?

"Of course, you don't wish anything of the kind. In fact, that was the very night you made your decision. You had been casting about to initiate a revolutionary change in your life. And that night you, *voilà*, decided you would make your splashy entry into the predictably unpredictable book business, or so your wife informed me, and as we all know, you have never looked back. You have tasted success the way no small publisher ever has before. Why, honestly, you've never been the same man. And what a lucky man you are, and what an extraordinary gypsy she must have been to be generous to you. That night changed your life forever. And tell me if I am wrong, but the name of your company, Hard Rain Publishing, didn't it come to you in a thunderbolt that very night you decided to go into the business—that blustery, tempestuous, stormy night in Venice when you chose the blustery, tempestuous, stormy publishing business? Isn't it strange about life, Myron, how our whole being changes on a dime, or in your case on a Euro? You wouldn't want to tempt fate and disappoint a gypsy who channeled her forces for your great and lasting benefit? Who knows what disappointments would greet you?"

"My wife had a big fucking mouth."

"She possessed many exquisite attributes, but…"

And then as she was getting to the part where she was going to enlighten him further about the mysterious Venetian night…

"Myron," I heard a voice behind us say and I leaped up in my chair gazellishly, there was that much tension in the air. Unfortunately, it was an instance of Young Goodman Brownus Interruptus. "We have a critical situation." Some boys have bad timing, as I should know, and if this book or my abdomen had an appendix, I could list all the examples known to me. And these gents have bad timing in whatever sphere of life where timing is everything, by which I mean in every sphere of life.

"The critical situation before you is that I am going to terminate you, something I should have done the first time you wore those pink socks."

"What's wrong with my pink socks? Sibella, tell Myron what you said when you saw—"

"Get the fuck outta here," Myron cut him off. For the record, let me stipulate that they were adorable socks and I felt bad for how Myron was humiliating him.

Then he leaned down, and into Myron's ear he funneled under his breath the rumor that was circulating throughout the intricate series of tubes that was purportedly the Heart of Darkness Internet: Mistah Figgy Fontana, he dead.

Fuck, if that news were true, that was as somber as Myron's suspected cardiomyopathy. As serious as any situation in Wolf Blitzer's Situation Room could possibly be. Figgy Fontana was a horse for the company, a thoroughbred truly, a reliable money-maker for years, and once again Myron's lead author this season with his new novel, *Swimming Buck Naked in the Hurricane*. Advance orders for what we were touting an irresistible beach read were through the roof, and Myron had preemptively ordered a second printing. But a "beach read"? Please track down the craven idiot who coined the sappy term and draw and quarter him or her. Who reads at the beach? The sunscreen, the wind, the fleas, the seaweed, the crab carcasses, the shards of oyster shells. Don't you hate it when the sand gets between the pages?

Myron had printed a barge load of hardcover *Hurricanes* in China, and Figgy was scheduled to start in a few weeks his national book tour on Myron's dime, starting with national television and radio interviews. (Nationalistically filluminate about conducting business with the repressive People's Republic of China if you must, but then you try running a publishing company with scrawny Lindsay Lohanish margins before you utter another self-satisfied plaint.) He took out full-page print ads in the national periodicals, not because he believed they paid off but because authors pucker up for that kind of publicity. Normally, he wouldn't bother to throw away money like that, but grand symbolic gestures were sometimes ultimately cost-effective when dealing with a delicate ego like Fontana's. Delicate, did I say? The man was a hothouse flower—if, that is, he hadn't been cut down by the Grim Reaper's scythe. But in any case that's not the proper botanical reference point. Think cactus.

Rest in peace, Figman, you soused-at-daybreak, unscrupulous pseudo-genius—if, again, the rumors ended up to be true.

It was clear that our lunch meeting was going to be abortive. Myron told YGB to go back to the office in case he was needed there. Because one place he was most definitely unwanted was here.

"He is gorgeous," said the Diavolo-devotee and Venetian sexplorer, tracking the editor in chief's retreating form. "Somebody could eat up that pretty boy with or especially without his pink socks. I swear he looks familiar, too."

I picked up my butter knife and wondered what artful damage I could inflict by means of it. "You slept with him in college?" Everything is permitted.

"Who can keep track?"

"Look," Myron told his baffling non-companion, "I have an urgent problem I need to deal with back at the office." Not that I myself appreciated what difference it would make by sinking his butt down into his ridiculously overpriced Aeron chair (chairs he also gave all his senior staff last Christmas).

"*The* Figgy Fontana?" She spoke with a whisper and she looked distraught. Was she momentarily concerned there was more than one Figgy Fontana? "I should have known," she said mysteriously, emotionally. Then she rallied her resources, clearing her throat and keeping her eye on the prize: "Meanwhile, you would not wish me to shop the book around, would you? You would be making an unwise decision, if you ask me."

"No, I'll buy it at your number."

Whose woods these are I think I know / His publishing house was soon to be pillaged though.

Without your gracious permission, I think I should take the opportunity to summarize my complex, nuanced, junior-editor feelings at this juncture, which I dared not express out loud, with regard to a publisher who never gave an author an advance (with the exception of Figgy Fontana, so please let's keep a candle burning) a penny over one or two thousand: six hundred thousand plus plus fucking smackers?

Myron wasn't in the mood to haggle. Not saying that under other circumstances (anything other than the possible demise of Fontana, and the ridiculously improbable gypsy story, and his ex's preposterous affair) haggling isn't always very big fun for a publisher.

She did not blink or blanch or do anything else beginning with a b, and she certainly did not blubber her gratitude. That's the sort of style he otherwise enjoyed. It was not much of a style, but it was his.

"Let me know when the contract is ready," she said matter-of-factly, "and Calypso will come into your office for the signing."

Six hundred thousand plus plus. Tell you what, gentle book buyer, to Myron in his current state of mentation—using the bossy word very pompously—that was a *steal*. Which made it clear to me how far gone my boss was. But to him this book at least enjoyed the added advantage of zero zombies and vampires, a minute percentage of whips and chains, and an altogether arresting shortage of wizards and British accents. Besides, if his lunch date and the gypsy were right, he couldn't help but succeed in any project he embraced. Every risk he took was, well, no risk whatsoever.

As she was speaking, she was confidently dining with brandished knife and fork in dueling hands, Euro style, and after she sent on its merry way down her alimentary canal a thoroughly masticated morsel of spicy poultry, she said: "All the money up front with the delivery of the manuscript, which has already been delivered, so due now." It takes genuine talent to eat and speak at the same time, something suspects being interrogated on *Law &* *Order* were gallingly good at. Because tell me, who eats a hot dog with kraut when being interrogated on a street corner as to the commission of a class A felony?

"One hundred K now, the rest upon publication." What the heck, a little rug-trading is Diavolo Chicken Soup for the Publisher's Soul.

"Half now, half upon publication."

"One hundred K now, the rest…"

She raised her palm. "Tell you what, Myron, you've been such a delightful lunch companion and you're clearly having a strange day, and you're a little bit in shock as a result of my revelations, let's say two hundred K now, and we split net receipts up to the number, and then once we pass that number, we get sixty per cent of the receipts and the first three hundred K in sub-rights."

"You're good, whoever you are."

"*Good*? Me? That's something *I* have never heard. And as a result of publishing my book, I imagine the gypsy's power will stay with you. I'm going to remain and polish off the chicken, if you don't mind," she said, as if she were uttering a veiled threat to the species if not the whole environment.

Myron helpfully pointed at the rogue chili pepper flake on her magnificent lower lip, which she gratefully attended to by means of her white napkin. Hey, they had a relationship, didn't they?

"Forgetting something, Myron?"

He wasn't forgetting anything. He put down all the cash in his pocket because there are at least two things you can bank on in the book biz: the sun will likely come up in the east tomorrow and lunch is on the publisher. Reluctantly, I admired how she did business. Very professional. Or at least very much like Myron.

"Condolences about our friend."

He looked confused.

"Figgy Fontana?" she said.

"Our friend? He is *my author*."

"Or unfortunately *was*."

"That's the thing about publishing a book and exploiting what are essentially licensing rights. An author's book not out of print exists continually in the present tense. The marvels of the back list are also not to be underappreciated—or carelessly over-reported."

"At least till rights revert on account of nonperformance. Poor Figgy Fontana, what a fantastic writer. I hope for everybody's sake the rumors aren't true."

"Hell with the paper contract," he said. "You can have one whenever you want, but in the meantime, you and I have a deal, with the splits going the way you spelled out."

"Deal. And Myron, the gypsy is never wrong. My book, *our* book, will make us millions. It is a foregone conclusion. The forces are at work," she said, "guiding you, guiding us."

They shook. She and I shook, too. It seemed the thing to do.

Let me tell you, a luvah and protectah such as I could not believe a cadaver's paw would be as key-cold to the touch as her hand.

You were not there for the beginning. You will not be there for the end. Your knowledge of what is going on can only be superficial and relative. That's an obscure collusion, Kelly, until you realize we had partaken of the nakedest of Naked Lunches.

Myron took off and I followed him out the door, but then I lied to him: "I forgot something, go on and I'll catch up."

I hustled back to the table. Before her a fresh Bloody Mary with a threatening stalk of celery that was so large it must have been biogenetically modified. And my mind was playing tricks again. She should have had those claws and talons and teeth and fire.

"I knew you would come back to me, Sibella."

"I see you."

"Of course you do. That's why he brought you along."

"No, I see you for the fucking thing you are."

"And what would that be, dear?"

"I have no idea, but I will find out. And all that Myron and Sibella luvah bullshit, what fuck the fuck is wrong with you?"

"Wanted to give the old man a little thrill, that's all, get his pulse racing. Are you frightened of me, Sibella? Don't be. In the meantime, remember what I am about to tell you. When all is said and done, you'll find, everything will work out to your lasting benefit."

"You're on notice. I'm a junior editor."

"And perhaps a sibyl on the side?"

"As a sibyl, I am an intern."

"See you in your dreams, Sibella."

Fuck if she would prove to be right about that one.

She removed the celery stalk from the glass and inserted it into her mouth. The snap executed by her brilliantine teeth popped my ear drums.

Defensive basket interference, score the bucket.

✳✳✳

GUSTAVE ASCHENBACH—OR VON ASCHENBACH, as he had been known officially since his fiftieth birthday—had set out alone from his house in Prince Regent Street, Munich, for an extended walk. (Lots of luck colluding, Kelly.)

In a few minutes I caught up with Myron, who was trudging along lost in thought, not an everyday sight. As he and I wended our way back to the office, I kept a sharp lookout for any more gypsies who might have additional plans to fuck up his head. Then again, on downtown San Francisco thoroughfares gypsies are as rare as Republicans and Dodger fans.

He was silent, but I couldn't resist talking. Yes, we were both upset about the Figgy development, but I was also thunderstruck he was throwing that much money at any book—and more than that, doing any business whatsoever with this...this, this, this... shifting namelessness in a red dress with a fancy purse to die for.

"Sibella, I couldn't stop myself. I can't believe she knew about the wallet and the gypsy and my wife, my fucking wife. I couldn't lose her book. Something came over me. I didn't want it—I *needed* it. I couldn't let any other house publish it."

I told him that he might have made a deal with the devil. A trite expression, but there it was. Devil, crone, witch, sorceress, voodoo princess. You pick the term.

He came to a full stop and we faced each other. "You felt that, too?"

There was no need to confirm his intuition.

"Something about her...it was like I could not say no to her."

When I looked into his eyes I saw that he meant it and that, gypsy or no, he was in for a dreadful spell, which meant I was too.

He said he had a question. "Figgy, Calypso, Venice, my ex. Without warning, in the last eighteen hours my world has completely turned upside down."

"That's not a question."

"To me it fucking is."

I didn't know what to say. "I look forward to reading her manuscript."

"But what if she was right about the gypsy? That all my success came from that supernatural source? I do have this problem: I have no doubt everything I publish is going to sell. And so far, so good. But that's not possible in the crazy book biz. A gypsy's spell did the trick for me or I am the luckiest publisher of all time? Which is it? Either way, I have been living a fairy tale. But which is it? Go on, tell me."

"Permission to speak freely, Commandante?"

"Permission granted, Intern."

I let that pass, he was having a rough day. "They could both be correct explanations."

"And maybe there's a third I'll never know. What difference does it make?"

He wanted an answer. For him, as I have said before and may well say again, there was no such thing as a rhetorical question.

We went out of the ruined place, and in all the broad expanse of tranquil light I saw no shadow of another parting from him.

THE RED BADGE OF SIBELLA

Back at Hard Rain's office, Myron's email inbox and voice mail were overflowing. The *Times*. The *Post*. *Publisher's Weekly*. *Library Journal*. *Booklist*. *Shelf Awareness*. NPR. Journalists seeking comment for an obit. All the influential blogs. But don't be intimidated by Myron's half-vast knowledge of the blogosphere, as he didn't know what anybody was talking about. As Caprice reminded him, with Twitter and Facebook using up most of the oxygen, a lot of blogs were on life support, thereby uttering three or four things in a row whose import neatly eluded Myron, and thereby also keeping intact her thus far unbroken record of incomprehensibility as far as he was concerned.

Myron was reeling. What I mean is, he was pouring himself shot after shot of Midleton's, his chosen Irish whiskey purchased at two hundred bucks a bottle. He kept a case of the world-class stuff under his desk. Everybody at Hard Rain presumed his downbeat mood was all about Fontana.

✳✳✳

While Myron and YGB huddled, I hastened to my crates to have a gander at the $600+K Gold-plated Kandy-Kolored Tangerine-Flake Unstreamedline *Adventures of Calypso O'Kelly*.

I was not forty pages in before I felt the upswell of nausea—the book didn't narrate such an upswell, the upswell was tickling my throat. I realized that Myron was going to throw six hundred thousand bucks into a litter box of a book. It was a criminally repetitive tale told by a blockhead of a narrator signifying nothing who found herself so very clever or clevah and who would give Nicky Narcissus a run for his money. Lover after lover. Luvah after luvah. Dinner after dinner. Dinnah after dinnah. Thrill killing after thrill killing. Ferrari after Ferrari. Silk sheets after silk sheets. Betrayal after betrayal. Villa after villa. Or viller after viller. Diamonds after diamonds. More betrayal after more betrayal. Incest after incest. Lafites after Lafites. Baccarat after baccarat. Yacht after yacht. Picasso after Picasso. Bon mots after—well, there were no bon mots that bonmottled me. Her singularest accomplishment? She gave decadence a bad name.

If this was considered writing, I didn't know what reading could be. And vice versa.

I ran cold water over my head for ten minutes in the women's room, and I concluded the manuscript was not, strictly speaking, worthless. That is, it wasn't *simply* a worthless book, or a bad book, or a failed book. It was a fucking Tour de France of an un-book. It was a non-book. Maybe not you, Kelly, but Murmechka herself could see that.

I'd wait for my opportunity to be alone with him to break the news. We could unwind this whole deal if I was half a sibyl, a sib or an yl.

The retiring fogs revealed an army stretched out on the hills, not resting.

Wolf, it's me, Sibella, here. The ICBMs have lit up the night sky, wherever we are. Wolf, what are we doing, why are we always at war, what do we know that is true, Wolf? Back to you, Wolf?

✳✳✳

As for Figgy Fontana, hey now, wasn't everybody jumping the gun? We had not received confirmation that the man's corpus was cold. When Myron called the reclusive author's home number, nobody picked up. Not a promising sign, though not a definitive one either, as Double F, in Myron's recollection, had never once picked up the fucking phone—which was one thing he and Myron once had in common. He would have called the author's office, but he said Figgy did not have a phone there. Reviewers and critics and scouts and event coordinators and bookstore owners and PR people were scrambling everywhere, Calling All Hemispheres, from California to Santiago, London to Milan, Paris to Frankfurt. And also Oh Canada and India and Australia, big buyers of Fig's books. Myron's social media girl, Caprice—just hold on a second. That's what she called herself, a *girl*, so don't get mad at Myron. Caprice noted that her world was blowing up. This, I take, would qualify as a significant development.

What to do about the Fontana tour—in case the worst turned out to be true? As for jumping the gun, I call your attention to Exhibitionist A: the editor in chief. A little too enthusiastically as well as precipitously, YGB ventured a gruesome suggestion: that he and the publisher and the junior editor keep to the schedule, publicly read from the book, and celebrate FF's lifetime achievements. Myron thought about it long and hard and gave the out-of-the-bandbox idea all the consideration it merited, let's say thirty seconds, and determined: No way, too cheesy. For one thing, Myron might have suspected what designs YGB had up his sleeve: privileged access to and face time with me, because YGB had to know Myron wasn't going with him on any tour, not even if it included a reading in the Playboy Mansion. In the meantime, the Fontana fears were boroughing like Staten Island down into Myron, right there in the chasm in his chest, where his heart once skipped an adolescent beat as he penned verse that did not do the job a teenager's poetry intended—unlike Junior's verse, which did the fucking trick to his unbemused *Muse*'s everlasting regret. After reciting his verse to some cheerleader or prom queen runner-up, did Myron manage to reach second base? He struck me as the kind of poor guy who got picked off on first.

I cringed to imagine the journalese treatment that Fontana was destined to receive if he were indeed past tense. Figgy Fontana, prodigious cult writer cut down at fifty-five in the prime of his career. Prolific and trendy author the micro-bespectacled younger demographic had wrapped their spindly tattooed arms around and sucked into their sootily T-shirted or braless beau zooms. Our own company website was overtaxed with consoling lamentational commentary and it seemed to have gone down temporarily. Caprice herself was going to blow up, I feared. God bless America, land that I love.

I must admit I did check Amazon, and I would ask everyone's forgiveness for my callousness and insensitivity if it weren't for the fact that that callousness slash insensitivity is my second calling. His books were bunched up in the top hundred in sales. What a boon for Myron's conscientious company and unconscionable me. The snooty critics had long ago lined up to worship Fontana as a natural-born, untutored genius, and the lackademics were probably already dusting off their book proposals for the elbow-patched university presses that would ultimately sell six copies of their tomes to the professors' immediate families and groupie grad students.

Figgy Fontana. I could see it, how the scholars would package and distort him. They would say the man was a Pynchon for the common folks. A Salinger for all the little people, who by definition resided beyond the Hudson. A Stephen King for the Rush Limbshockandaugh addicts. A Hemingway for the white collared. A Rowling for the post-adolescent. A Bolaño for the Nortoamericanos. A Morrison for people who won't read Morrison if their life depended on it. An F. Scott Fitzgerald for the non–polo pony set. A Roth for the uncircumcised.

Double F.: Talking about Figgy Fontana. Yes, he had a formula he could rightly claim as uniquely his own: spousal battery *cum* the earth moved post-coital gasping for breath; crystal meth *cum* "Can I get a witness?" revival meeting; hideaway country stills *cum* squeal like a pig; UFO sightings *cum* Serpico-like backwoods law enforcement corruption; Irvingesque endlessly italicized wrestling in the muddy river *cum* apparitions of the paranormal; alligator stew *cum* prepubescent pageant competition; rich whoring daddies in Cadillacs *cum* impoverished saintly mommas on the county dole; legless Iraq vets *cum* high school Biology teachers and their extortionist honors student friends with benefits; white-shirted

Mormon missionaries *cum* black-moustache foreclosure artist bankers; bounty hunters *cum* serial killers; marijuana farmers *cum* DEA agents and priests packing heat and crucifixes. All in all a heady brew, a strong concoction absolutely devoid of intentional humor. And I say as much admiringly.

Too many writers these days go for the easy joke, or the self-distancing and paradoxically self-referentializing gesture. Like me, for instance, you are thinking. That's about as far as they go, their raisin-debt. But you know, *Just Kidding* could serve for the subtitle or sell-line of any number of big books. But in FF's whole body of work there was not the slightest whiff of irony, nothing that smacked of "Come on, I'm merely writing a book after eating my dino kale and working out in the tony gym, don't take me seriously or I will cry." One thing I could say about the Figgy Fontana books was that he *always* meant it, every single chapter and hearse. If you didn't like it, his attitude seemed to be, fuck off and have a nice life. Readers did like it, and they signed up in droves, bored by the desexualized, politically correct, high-concept stylizations that clutter up the publishing marketplace. No wonder no New York publisher would initially take a chance on him. For which Myron gave thanks multimillions of times, and Fig should have, too.

***

SHE LIKED VICTORIAN NOVELS. They were the only kind of novel you could read while eating an apple.

I missed my apple that day, and eating it would have spared me the encounter with bat shit at Avenue. When I returned, it was missing from my crates' top, too. I was disheartened to see the core in the garbage can near Murmechka's realm of the ridiculous. In her defense, we didn't compost, however. Editors are always selling somebody out. Murm had boundless boundary issues.

I heard that. Yes, I *should* talk.

Breaking protocol here, with your permission, I would like to observe that Stella Gibbons's *Cold Comfort Farm* (colluded a few grafs above) is essentially without qualification my fave novel. Everybody should go read it as soon as possible, and if you leave for a while to do that, I'll bid you an Au Revoir Dogs (a great if brainless movie), and maybe things will work out with Fig and Calypso by the time of your return of the native. I saw something nasty in the woodshed. That is one of the finest non-non sequiturs ever decomposed. And my second-favorite novel is *Fifth Business* by Robertson Davies, the cranky Canuck with the ZZ Top slash Solzhenitsyn beard whose other novels were for me, way to go eh, more beside the point than a wine list at the White Castle, which I sometimes indefensibly feel about the Yukon Territories and denture-dependent ice hockey worshippers in general. But his *Deptford Trilogy*: go figure, sometimes a guy writes a book that takes off the top of your head and you don't see the scythe coming, like some sorry character in a Washington Irving story and nobody reads *him* anymore or James Fennimore Cooper ever since Mark Twain has his way with him, but I digress.

"Fontanists": that was a term cleverly coined by cagey Caprice, and I kind of liked the label, but it proved to have the all the traction of ball bearings on a greased pie pan. The people spoke, or texted, and *Fontaniacs* instead proved to have the sticking power of Velcro, and the name brand Fontaniac and Fontanamania stuck instead. Don't bring up this defeat with Caprice if you happen to belong to one of her seven book groups, none of which she ever invited me to join, which kind of hurt my feelings. Maybe she had heard of my reputation in my old book groups, all of which terminated me with extreme prejudice.

That afternoon Myron did what any publisher worth his salt and even Myron Beam would do under the circumstances. He instructed Young Goodman Brown to order massive reprints of all Fontanas and have them shipped stat at whatever cost. That decision would preclude printing in China (he couldn't afford six inert weeks being transported on a book boat cruise). Meanwhile, he settled into waiting for the big distributors to come begging with their Fontaniac hats in their hands. And what do you know? It didn't take long before they did exactly that.

SIBELLA REVISITED

USA Doh Day reported "reliable sources" to the effect that Fig had been suffering from some unnamed terminal cancer and committed suicide. There was supposedly a note left behind. This rumor naturally gave rise to speculation within Myron as to the implication of such a depressing deed. If you needed any more evidence to loathe the Hard Rain founder and publisher and president, let me peel this organically grown banana. As this rumor pertained to Fontana, Myron was pondering if suicide was a career-enhancing move or the opposite? Romantic, tragic gesture on the part of a tortured artist? That could be sold, of course. But was that good for business? Could be, definitely could be.

But suicide? More he reflected, Myron wasn't buying it. It was not long ago he had concluded negotiations with him on the new three-book deal. Myron would say that he hardly sounded self-destructive or despondent in his transactions with himself, but what did he know? Truth was, he had never met the man in the flesh. The banal author photo, taken by his son, which Myron couldn't talk him out of using on the jackets, was responsible for his visual assumption. All of which was fine by him. As long as the books kept appearing on time and in more than decent-enough shape, he didn't care. In fact, the freelance copyeditor said she regretted billing Myron because she added or corrected essentially nothing. Don't agonize for her, as she always managed to get over her pangs of guilt and shoot over the padded invoice anyway.

Most of Myron's exchanges with FF took place via email, he said, a medium that evidently challenged the author, if the AWOL spell check and the glaring deficiency of standard syntax in his messages were any indication. Which kind of surprised me, the chosen one who had been typing and reading all his emails, or so I had assumed—therefore I seemed to have been wrong about Myron's email tension deficit, too. But then there actually was, as Myron recalled, one strained and odd phone call.

Figgy liked to brag in interviews that he had no formal schooling to speak of, that he was self-miseducated, and Myron believed him, because writers—especially wildly successful (thanks to Myron) writers like him—come in all sizes and packages. Of course, Myron didn't get into the business in order to starfuckingly cultivate personal relationships with his authors. And thankfully, Figgy wasn't inclined that way. He didn't need Myron's personal validation to write. This is what Myron termed a match made in publishing heaven. In fact, when it came to business arrangements with the Fontana camp, he said he usually dealt with his son and occasionally his wife, who both served in the shifting and interchangeable roles of manager and agent and in-house worrywart. (That constituted yet another shocker for yours coolly: Myron used the phone for Figgy.) His son struck Myron as an embittered-by-existence sort whose acerbic sensibility he regarded to be queasy and quasi-congenial. He liked that Figgy was fundamentally a hermit, living in the California hill country hours away from San Francisco, far from an airport, not to mention a highway, with no neighbors within miles—as his son informed the publisher in an unguarded moment. That's why Myron was stunned when Figgy consented to do a book tour, which would have been a first for him. He had always considered that kind of thing to be bullshit. Whatever you could say about the author, he wasn't stupid.

This is what Fontana explained during one particular phone conversation with Myron, which I render with dubious confidence as to the infallibility of Myron's self-serving memory: "Peoples kin buy my books, I don't care if theys fuckin read thems, long as theys buy thems. Which is wheres you come in, Moron, if'n you does your job." As you can determine, his sort of drawl played unflattering havoc with Myron's first name. "And I don't need to trot my fat ass out in public so's peoples kin've the eye lusion they knows me or cares what the fuck I think about the prospects of world peas or the winner of the Stupid Bowl and who the fuck all I may or may not be."

When a man makes as much sense as that, who is a publisher to argue? All to say, what had changed his mind in the first place about the book tour and all the related nonsense? No idea. And while we're off the subject, here's another thing.

I understand a writer's persona and the real-life human being who created that persona don't necessarily neatly overlap. There's often a swaying rope drawbridge over a gorge between the two, much like on the campus of the college I attended and where I led my basketball team to loss after glorious loss, and the drop to the rushing waters below is a stone-cold killer. The sweet-tempered creator of sympathetic characters can be a dick and a sloppy drunk at the cocktail party, and the dominatrix in her bedroom can send her royalties to Catholic homes for runaways and orphans. Yes, writers are as complicated and unpredictable and as mixed-up as—well, some publishers and editors I have known. What makes writers different, it seems, is that opposed to the rest of us who simply have different sides to our impersonalities, their whole job is to live inside the heads of characters they have created. I can imagine that it could be tough for some writers, listening to all those jabbering voices, not always knowing which one is your own and which one is of your creation.

I had one other concern, trivial given the latest, but I was curious. When I thought about Figgy's speech patterns and the raggedness of his emails, I was compelled to wonder how such a writer produced manuscripts finished and polished such that a copyeditor barely lifted a pencil, and yes, I know, they don't use pencils anymore, buzz off. I feared that mystery seemed destined—along with his corpus delecti—for the grave.

BONFIRE OF THE SIBELLAS

I STUCK MY SMARTLY betoweled head inside Myron's office door. I smirked and rolled my eyes, noxious practices I once exploited with coaches and summer camp directors and math instructors and parents to anything but my lasting advantage. Little children, don't get started. It's a slipp'ry slope on a graph straight out of Trigonometry for Losers. You might end up one day a lowly but tall junior editor making confrontational remarks to your boss like this:

"Been reading, though that's not the word, the Calypso Catastrophe?" I said. "How many shots of Irish have you had?" I pointed to the evidence of glasses on his desk blotter in case he had forgotten.

"What are you wearing?"

Now he was noticing my appearance? Now? But he was referring to the towel I stashed in my gym bag and had wrapped around my head, which was sopping from the cold water that cooled my brain after being overheated by that foe book.

"Towel's a long story, Myron, which Calypso's isn't? Hers is the shortest nine-hundred-thirty-two-page thing ever written, because it ended on page one and a half?"

"Please don't tell me?"

"You know what? That manuscript?"

"It's garbage?" he said.

The Irish might be a judgment-enhancer after all.

"And I may be a sibyl wannabe, but I don't see any good coming from it so let's not publish this, please, Myron?"

"Too late?"

"Can we talk about *this*?"

"First take that towel *off*?"

And yes, our fucking uptalk had returned with attitude to burn, don't remind me.

Another unpleasant development bah-loomed on the horizon, however. This disagreeable development was fleshfully present in the foyer, dressed like somebody about to go on stage for her pole dance at the anything-but-gentlemen's club. I wish I had merely constructed another one of my betrayed-mark over-the-top metaphors. And I hold you discountable, Kelly, that I hesitate to use the word *literally* because this was the perfect occasion to give the thorny word a callback.

"You have a *visitor*?" The disgust with which I invoked the passive-aggressive "visitor" revealed, no doubt, my contempt for the thus-far-unnamed personage in question mark.

"A *visitor*?" whispered he, with trepidation. "Can you please take that ridiculous towel *off*?"

I could, and I did.

"Ashlay *Commingle*?" I should have whipped out my death *ray*? "More like *visatrix*?"

Had Myron forgotten they had an *appointment*? He was preoccupied, of course, by the turbulent goings on, but he didn't want to burn a bridge with Ashlay, and he could liberate a couple of minutes for an appointment with the likes of *her*? And yes, that's the distinctive spelling of his author's *name*? For reasons soon to be *obvious*? And articulating her whole name made it sound like a puzzling and filthy sentence, salacious subject and provocative *verb*? Ashlay *Commingle*? Okay, I'll *stop*?

Fine, all right, I mean it this time.

He put the bottle and the shot glasses into a file drawer for later disgustation. He wasn't completely hammered, so there was hope for him if not for Ashlay.

"Ashlay," he sugarly called out, "come on in, sweetheart."

Upon further review, maybe he was hammered.

On the other other hand, it never hurts to adopt a honeyed tone, whatever the circumstances, don't you agree? But if you do, you are beyond hopeless. I noticed all over again how Ashlay was terminally de Minnie Mouse diminutive (much like Junior's present meal ticket), which might account for my elevated bias against her. And to underscore this point or to assert for his benefit my higher-archical dominance in case Myron had forgotten, I made sure to position myself alongside his working girl lady caller as to primitively emphasize my standing, of which there was, in the first place, little doubt in my mind if not in yours.

Ashlay click-clickety-clacked into his manlyish cave and the two of them warmly and whiskily embraced. Normally, that sort of clinch would have been the highlight of his day, on subpar with his inevitable veal chop, and for the same reason. He wrapped his arms around her, his sternum against the tippy top of her crown. She was dressed in a rhinestone-studded, bone-white jumpsuit, zippered—I should say unzippered—to the nether region of her twenty-inch baby doll waist, but the effect seemed to extend all the way down to her six-inch black open-toed high heels, which barely got her up to five feet. Yes, or I mean no, no discernible undergarmenture in evidence, and Victoria herself had no secrets to hold back. Bronze chest, long golden locks, green adder eyes, something like Junior's micro-fantasy in the flesh.

Let me get something off my chest. Is it my fault that some of the women who bugged me were pervertically challenged? Sure, whenever somebody used the bleak expression "flying under the radar" I winced and took it personally. I couldn't fly under the radar even if I was doing the limbo. But am I mean-spirited and unkind to the undersized set, which included Junior's micro-trophy girl? I can see why you might be suspicious, but remember, Kelly also got my goat and she is not very short, and she Great Daned to call me a "heightist," a dumb-as-Kelly neologism (look it up, Kelly). Even so, did she have a legitimate point, which would amount to a first for her? I will have to think this through—as soon as I ever give a flying-under-the-radar fuck.

As you might be swift-boatly surmising, Ashlay used to be a porn star. Her movies remained in wild, pulse-racing circulation and I may have had my doubts about her, but there were a few problems with my reasoning with regard to her. Publishers jabber about promoting writers with a platform, an established presence that makes their books more marketable. Ashlay had a platform in spades, a fucking platform under strobes. Again, Kelly, thanks to you, another missed dopening for a "literally." At the same time, she was also a terrific writer, go figure, which you'll have to agree is tall of me to concede. Myron was confident the literary world was going to celebrate her when her first novel, *Slip, Slippery Girl*, came out. Besides the working-too-hard syntax, yet another damn *Girl* book title. Oh, well, at least she didn't live in Brooklyn. Even so, she was wickedly smart and as promiscuously entrepreneurial as Warren Fucking Buffet. She had had Xtensive Xperience in the Xciting and Xpanding universe (four X's in a row, personal best!) of X-rated entertainment (make that five!) before doing a one-eighty of sorts and procuring her doctorate in literary theory from Berkeley—though she would argue it was not really much of a do-ouevre for her. Berkeley was where I heard they didn't read books or teach literature any more, only texts and hothouse obscurity with a soupçon of self-importance. Sacrè bleu. Ashlay was her actual name, too. Her stage name was different, and in every sense classic, as you will discover if you don't know already.

Disrespectfully, a point of personal privilege, if you would. Thank you.

What the fuck was it with guys and their porn? Now it was cool? Now it was antisocially Xceptable? Now it was avant fucking en garde? Sure, some women claim to endorse porn, including some feminists, but I did not understand. Call me a prude if you want. Junior and you would have something in common. But for the broken record, I had nothing against a woman's free choice and sexual expression, though, as you have seen over and over, it obviously had plenty against me.

As it happened, Ashlay and her book had aroused my first argument with Myron when he acquired the intellectual property. We were promoting pornography, I contended. And pornography was demeaning to women, I don't care how many times the post-modern types trumpeted the supposed transgressive nature of porn and how it was a vehicoughle for women's empowerment, pleasure, subversion, and resistance.

Well, that's what I told Myron, and the first problem with my contention was that I was adamantinely opposed to censorship. But the greater difficulty for me was that, without being conscious at first of this, I was soon to be Chanel Ing my professorial maman. Never a good look for a growing or overgrown girl, and fuck, Mom usually made more sense than I ever wanted to hear. She lectured me on how feminism had had its first wave and its second wave and was now in its third wave. I was a big beneficiary, being a female Division 1 athlete, of the first and second waves. She may have been a feminist Doc Ball or Duke Kahanamaka shooting the pipeline, but she lost me at wave.

Myron countered that Ashlay's book was not porn, despite any fuckation narratively repenisented. Point, Myron. And it wasn't his place as a man to be judging the sexual choices women had made—except with respect to his ex-wife, where this principle did not apply. Again, fucking point, Myron. And true, it wasn't like Ashlay was a victim of the sex slave market—but if you dare to make that observation among certain rabbidinnical feminists, you could get your head handed to you the way Salome did in the Oscar Wilde play, because they would say by definition all porn actors were exploited. Don't tell any of them what I am about to say, please, but I found that argument to be an oversimpletonification. I know I'm fucking contradictating myself.

"Tell me, Myron. Have you seen her movies and did that influence your decision to take her book?" I'd bet Junior had seen them.

"Define *influence*?" We may have stumbled upon yet another one of Myron's uptalking stress points.

"I don't need to. You need to." But see? It wasn't my stress point.

"I'm celibate, I told you, *remember*?"

"Let's not do that again, I beg you."

"Come on, Sibella, you know Ashlay wrote a terrific *book*?"

"And?"

"And if you're committed to the dignity of women, why can't you give her work the respect it *demands*? The author is not her book, Sibella. Keep the two *separate*?"

"I will if she does." Time would tell. Man, it would tell a complicated story, and I had one question, which I kept to myself: How can we know the pole dancer from the pole dance?

✳✳✳

"You growing a beard?" Ashlay asked Myron.

The idea had never crossed her publisher's mind. He had never made it home to shave this morning is all.

"Sexy," she said. "I like it."

Maybe he *should* grow a beard, you could tell he was considering this *pogonic* choice. (Kelly, here comes my Oh I E D alert: refers to beard, Little Bird.) If he rubbed the top of his bald head, he was going to be a goner.

In the day's hubbub, he had forgotten what they were supposed to be meeting about, but she reminded him once she sat down and the seams on her straitjacket of a jumpsuit popped like tiny strips of bubble wrap. She was here to discuss marketing gimmicks for *Slippery*. Myron always had a soft spot for an author who was ambitious and didn't despise him yet. Then again, he always had a prominent soft spot for every woman, no need to remind you. None of her suggestions made a whole lot of sense to him. He *was* pretty optimistic they were going to finalize a movie deal in advance of publication. One idea she kept pushing was this: marketing alongside the hardback book a shiny monogrammed *Ashlay Commingle Special Scrunchie*. In her defense, back then was when desperate publishers were way gimmickacious. What was true then is still true today: only an idiot thinks an author knows the first thing about marketing.

"Scrunchie?" he gamely tried, authentically baffled.

"You know, scrunchie? A hair tie."

Sloppy seconds passed.

"Oh, Myron baby doll, you don't get it?"

Guilty as charged. No, wait. She didn't mean...

"Yes, now you're using your head, which is the whole point. A girl who reads my book is the kinda liberated fun-loving girl who might have lots of erotic opportunities to tie back her hair."

And yes, that referenced activity was the particular go-to move on the part of her grandiloquently mouthy protagonist. Boys and girls the world round would one day be pleased Myron was publishing her. Don't make me think about Junior again, please, and I was no fucking prude.

At this point I heard a shriek barely this side of human: Cry, the Unbeloved Country Kelly. Yes, Kelly, you B-cup busted your way into Collusionville, congratufuckinglations! You should answer the fucking phone more often.

SIBELLA FLEW OVER
THE CUCKOO'S NEST

THE NORMALLY DISCREET AND composed, except around me, senior editor was bounding uninvited and hyperventilated into Myron's office, and she was in such an emotional state that as a result an uptick had been stapled on her tongue at least temporarily, and her gum chewing took a sabbatical, too. And whatever possessed her today to start answering the phone?

"Myron, *phone*?"

"I'm in a meeting, can't you…?"

"Pick. Up. The. *Phone*?"

For some incredible reason he decided to obey. Myron's taking *two* calls in one day. What was he going to do next? Moonwalk? "Ashlay, you mind?" She didn't, she said, as she was in the moment tying back her hair in a way that probably inspired Myron to return to her book gimmick idea as soon as he got rid of this caller. It did have possibilities, I support hose. For her book, I mean, for her book—which was a real book, unlike others I could name. The voice he heard on the other end of the line proved to be a shocker—and I heard it, too, because he clicked on speaker. What? Had he just discovered today that he had a speaker phone? More revelations loomed for all of us lashed to the Beamish mast.

"Moron, Fontana here."

"Figgy, you're alive!"

"And mah dick's hard, too."

Cheap shot. Myron would let that pass. But that was Downtown Figgy Fontana.

"But thass not why I called ya, ta report the latest on mah plumbin'."

"There have been crazy rumors going around all day and I'm very happy—"

"I don't have time ta esplainidate. Moron, you en me, we's done. You git mah message othah day I gave yo phone grrl? I ain't gwyne on no book tour and I don't want ya'll to publish mah books no more."

"What are you talking about, Fig? What's happened?"

"None of you's bidness is what happed. But I'm thinking I might need a new publish, if I yever write a book agin, whichen I might not do anyways. I could say nothin persnal, but what the fuck, iss fuck all persnal, g'luck, Moron, not rilly."

Myron was thinking fast, but not fast enough, because he did casually mention the three-book deal for which Figgy had received his generous advance—although nowhere in the region of six hundred fucking thousand.

"Ain't hap'nin, Moron, we done. Mah fat sow's gotta bettah chance of makin bacon outta me then you en me got've doin enny mo bidness."

Myron could tell the phone was not the best medium for communication with a troubled author back from the dead and devoid of one ounce of gratitude, an author who had sold a ton of books a few times over.

"Let's not be hasty, Fig. Whatever the problem is, I can solve it. Let's talk, face to face, okay?"

"Gotta go, Moron. Been nice knowin ya'll, least when the checks arrive in the mailbox."

"About those checks, Fig—"

Click.

Double dribble, turnover, loss of possession.

Desperate times called for desperate measures—that's what they all say, and you know what, after all the desperate times that followed from that day forward, I began to believe whoever they are they could be right. When Myron proposed a sit-down, Fig did not rule it out. Myron made a decision. He was quickly scanning his options. It was time to pay the man a visit, talk this through like mature men, even if neither of them qualified.

He then made, in my opinion, a very impulsive miscalculation. Miss Calculation Herself, Ashlay, he thought would be useful company for his AAAA onto the Fontana Farm. If men are so predictable when it comes to women, how come I cannot predict them? I'll take my answer off the air and I'll check with the next genuine clairvoyant I come across. But, no, he was not thinking quickly like that. Her conversation along the journey would certainly be more diverting for him than YGB's—and he was already counting on taking him and me. The publisher's posse, riding to the rescue.

"How about let's take a little ride?" he inquired gently of his porn star darling, his entreaty instantly misconscrewed.

Ashlay knowingly winked.

"Not that kinda ride, darling. I'm impotent."

I intervened in vain: "This is not going to end well, to not coin a phrase."

"Guys *always* say that," she pouted.

"They do?"

"A ploy for sympathy. No guy wants to use a condom."

Myron was going to break out Ashlay's new book with all the Viagrified vengeance he could muster, but that was something he could not think about right now. He had some pressing Figgish business to take care of and Ashlay could lend a hand or another convenient body part. As far as he was concerned, it certainly wouldn't hurt to have someone like her alongside him in the Figgified midst. The good news? Figgy Fontana was not dead. The bad news? He was killing Myron.

"Ready to take a trip?" he said to Ashlay.

"You know me, Myron. I'm up for anything."

Are you beginning to see why I was all over the fucking place on the complicated Commingle Question?

✳✳✳

THAT MADE ONE OF US who were up for anything. Me? I was up for something in particular.

I did harbor this one microscopic hope. My Commingle-size hope was simple. Getting Myron out of town might work wonders. If he had the distasteful fiduciary duty to confront Fontana, something unexpected might trigger inside to get him out of his deal with Calypso O'Fucking Kelly once and for all. A change of scenery might magically dispel the trance Her Weirdness had gauzed over him. And it wouldn't be bad for me to get out of town either. Kelly could start answering full time the fucking phone.

I would be proved right about everything, you shall see, and then completely wrong, thereby continuing my lifelong pattern of being an unbankable sibyl.

Cannon to right of them,
Cannon to left of them,
Cannon in front of them
    Volleyed and thundered:
Stormed at with shot and shell,
Boldly they rode and well,
Into the jaws of death,
Into the mouth of hell
    Rode the six hundred grand.
Yes, they did.
Calypso! Gypsies! Ashlay Commingle! Figgy Fontana!
Poor fucking Myron.
Poor fucking me.

PART TWO

SIBELLA BUDD

COME DAWN AND PRE-COMMUTE gridlock, our cracked crew of Nervy SEALS assembled at the Worldwide Offices of Hard Rain Publishing. I was in mid-reason form. Without benefit of adequate caffeination, I double shot daggers in Ashlay's black-jumpsuited direction. And how many jumpsuits in how many colors did she possess? Did some movie of hers involve sky diving *bombs away!* onto some poor mook's erectile function?

My daggers were dulled to the point of producing absolutely zero effect on her, because Ashlay's self-esteem was off the charts and she was conned-genitally immune to my or anybody's censure. As for self-esteem, porn stars may come by this character trait naturally, and which may account for their supreme lack of self-consciousness before the unforgiveable, drooling, High Def cameras. She may not have noticed my presence at all. In any event, we had all defiled into Myron's car.

YGB was going to do the driving. He wanted to make up for the dumb book tour suggestion involving the publisher and me. Myron let him knock himself out, but he would store his lousy driving for later ammunition against the editor in chief.

With this excellent resolve for the future, Goodman Brown felt himself justified in making more haste on his present evil purpose. Or so I recall Hawthorne's and YGB's walk-on-the-wild-side tale. I would bide my time and pour lye on the lie of the manuscript of that O'Kelly witch and save some for Oh Kelly Editor if she came at me with a weapon or a Groupon coupon. For grating upon me was the high probability that super facial Kelly would ultimately love the O'Kelly manuscript. With any luck that gum chomper would never get her mitts on it and man nipulate Myron to her advantage.

According to the flight plan we filed with nobody at the TSA, we would arrive at the Fontana Ponderosa before noon, stay for a disrespectable span of hours and, with cooperating traffic, get back to the city at nightfall with Figgy's manuscripts and the last vestiges of Myron's self-respect in tow. Myron could cast the determination to go there in terms of demonstrating deference and concern, but of course he was merely protecting his investment. After all, Figgy had cashed the check for the advance, as Myron may have mentioned to me once or a hundred times before and which infuriated Myron to perseveratingly contemplate. (My dad taught me "perseverate," a juicy word for a shrink to use with his budding perseverating child, don't you think?) Book rights belonged to Myron, not Figgy, and Moron de Figgy intended to take possession pronto before any more madness or any *Tuesdays with Figgy* could be dreamed up by some rogue marketing intern, whom we did not have.

YGB ticked off his self-surfing road-trip check list.

"Lattes?" *Check.*

"Water?" *Check.*

"Organic apples?" *Check.* (Yes, YGB could be bothersome, but wasn't that sweet of him to remember my go-to article of produce?)

"*Anna Karenina*?" *Check.* (But there he goes again, typical guy. With this literary name-drop he was trying to score points with Ashlay. Myron mentioned to his new author that the editor in chief was a fool, but her raccoonologically Green Dayish mascara'd eyes indicated she didn't need to be informed.)

"Oreos?" *Check.*

"Triage Doritos?" *Check.*

"Drive the goddamn car," Myron said.

✳✳✳

I OBSERVED SOMETHING ABOUT YGB I had never expected before, although upon consideration I should have. He drove like a high school honors student who had completed Virtual Driver's Ed online. He was white-knuckling his way, ten and twenty miles below the speed limit, scrunched over the steering wheel like the quarterback over center in a slow-motion football game, continually earning the fist-shaking wrath and splenetic honking of many a fellow traveler, often a teenage girl in a red convertible Mustang or Minnie Cooperage who breezily flipped him off as she sped past.

Ashlay was alongside Myron in the back seat, and she was diligently absorbed in her reading of—yes, what else?—*Anna Karenina*.

"Oh Em Gee, this is better than *War and Peace*," she testified with some ardor, and I wondered if she herself had composed a Russian door-stopper she would have suggested putting an airline-size-bottle of vodka inside the covers.

Marketers. Are all of them frauds?

I was riding shotgun, and I took Ashlay's testimonial as my cue to insert earbuds and listen to my signature mix of funk and reggae and girl band music. Every now and then I kind of dorkily shimmied to the beat, which was to Myron's elderly, world-weary point of view, he would later confess, the six-six height of cute and the depths of his encroaching decrepitude. Manhattan prep school credentialed and later MFAd nearby, offspring of doctorates who resided on the Upper West Side, I myself had smugly never troubled to learn how to operate a motor vehicle. And about those creative writing degrees, I am afraid you wouldn't want to get Myron started. But if you had recklessly done that, he would want to be told what's the point of learning how to write like everybody else or your second- or third-tier writer slash professor whose manuscripts of experimental prose stylings would be rejected post-haste? In any case, I was, to him, miraculously untainted by my grad school indoctrination. I myself was not always convinced.

Before giving me my book assignment on the Wonders of Himself, Myron unjustifiably flattered me, saying I had cultivated an original editorial talent that might one day lead to my penning (old-school term or what?) my own book, and in the future attaining the position of senior editor. Sky's the limit, who knows? Oh, to be twenty-six again, he ruminated to me, though I was, as I said, twenty-five. But as he said, if he slipped by chance into a time machine that managed this neat trick, he would have wished that somebody please shoot him. Youth would be wasted all over again on the member of the member of this member of the geriatric set. He felt confident that if he had to do it all over again he would make the very same old mistakes.

It would have been easy to rationalize not taking me along for the ride to the Fontana homestead (important for somebody to mind the store, etc.), but Kelly and Caprice stayed put along with Murmechka, who would have some extra time to hone her paroemiographical skills. (God, I love the OED, and Kelly, the OED is this huge shelf-long book, a library you might say, where you can look up the meaning of words, but helpfully for you, the words appear in alphabetical order. Now you know your ABZ's, won't you come and sting with me?) Besides, he could defend my presence in the interest of presenting to the Fontana Family a united and significant and very tall front on behalf of the venerated author's loyal press—not to mention, I was trying out for publisher's non-amanuensis, which nobody else knew at the time. None of which contributed to the point of his bamboozling the ever-fetching, feckless, in my view, and once professionally fecking for all to see and then some, Ashlay to Commingle along as well.

There was a man in the land of Uz, whose name was Job, and that man was perfect and upright, and one that feared God, and eschewed evil. (*Eschewed* is going to give you a ton of trouble, Kelly, but let me help with *Job*, which is not pronounced as the second syllable of that specialty practiced professionally by Ashlay.)

YGB appeared downcast that my music appreciation inhibited him from regaling me with tales of his editorial and (by implication) sexual prowess (following a logic that might be born in the tempest of his handsome brain). Poor YGB: taking a job working for Myron, the boy must have had an insatiable appetite for disappointment. One night in the imminent future I would personally look into altering that pattern of dashed and dashing expectation. Consider yourself forewarned, forereader.

Myron used to say he never regretted hiring me as an intern, but he rued the inevitable day I would waltz into his office, ducking as not to hit my head on the lintel, wearing a carelessly studied hoodie and dark glasses, and advise him that I got an offer at some New York house. He would have no alternative but to match and rely on his personal charm to seduce me to stay onboard and not scurry back to the Upper West Side clutches of my folks and all of Danny Meyer's thousand-and-counting city-wide dining establishments.

The false Figgish rumors were retracted, so this was the time to get right in the man's stubbled mug. (As for stubble, Myron said his mug was itching like from marching fire ants, but he was going to cultivate a beard, because if not now, what was he waiting for?) After all, his was the Notorious B.I.G. little publishing house scrambling to hang onto its prized author. He would have liked to say that he was keeping reasonably restrained his high hopes, but if history was a predictor, those new books were going to follow the *dum da dum da dum DUM* conga line of his previous works (and the promising, forthcoming *Swimming Buck Naked in the Hurricane*) and dance right out the bookstore doors—or wherever it is fine books are sold these days. His spirits were soaring higher with each passing and depressing mile of California country roads, each passing biker gang member, and each passing RV whose dust we ate.

At some point, a pack of said sad bikers decided to have some fun at the ex Spence of YGB and the rest of us. Two rumbling, varooming hog Harleys negotiated point position in front of our car, slowing us down to about thirty, and two behind, and one to the side, nearest Ashlay Commingle's window. Those wacky Hells Angels, right? Funmeisters or what? Imagine what they must do for Secret Santas and Easter egg hunts. I have to say, their showfuckingboating was meant to intimidate. But they inspired Ashlay. She stood up in the back seat (remember: she was knee-high to a cocker spaniel), opened the window, unzipped, and flashed her impressive breasts for the denimed gentleman riding there, looking cocky as a country squire on a fox hunt, which this turned out to be. He looked pleased. Wait till he doesn't read her book.

"That was fun," said Ashlay, as the gang roared off into racketeering oblivion.

I didn't need to be a sibyl in the wings waiting to know what was not going through the minds of the two males in my car who would have sweet mammary memories.

✳✳✳

SO YES, INDEED, ASHLAY had a gift for disorienting the male species that rivaled her considerable prose skills. She wasn't alone in that regard when it came to disorienting Myron. Because what I wouldn't have expected was what he told me later he was thinking after that flashpoint in the car: once all the Figgish fresh streams of revenues were accounted for, he would hardly have to come deep out of pocket for the detestable, to me, ooo ver of Calypso O'Kelly, who would become, if he had his fragged way, his next Figgy Fontana.

As Myron said a thousand times, "I am a genius." You know, sometimes, I believe he believed that. And to tell the truth, so did I.

Somewhere along the journey, I turned to see that Ashlay's head fell softly as a cloud upon Myron's shoulder and she probably snored ever so demurely. Perhaps she was enraptured by Muscovite Ducky dreams. Myron himself was resolving to get a new car, equipped with something called navigation. He wasn't up on the latest car technology (or any other technology), so he was hoping the automobile business had advanced to the Jetson or Sergey Brin point of mass-producing, computer-guided, driverless vehicles. Anything to extricate the likes of YGB from the equation.

Around eleven, we arrived at the wished-for destination, the home base of the estimably not-dead-yet Mr. Figgy Fontana. There was his house number on the spooky mailbox, a mailbox that listed on the dirt road like a punch-drunk fighter. But the mailbox was in and of itself odd. We were so far off the beaten path that it was hard to imagine that the receptacle had ever been used as intended by the USPS or that anybody but a latter-day Lewis or a

Clark would deliver any Amazon boxes—or Myron's fat royalty checks. Our car rumbled over the beaten-down earth.

"You sure this is the place, Myron?" YGB reasonably inquired, considering the sight before our eyes. I am surmising he was asking as much because my earbuds were fixed, and so I assumed he was addressing me in a faint voice. I shouted, *"What!?"* And yes, I could exclaim and uptalk simultaneously, and with a little practice and adequate emotional desperation so can you.

"That's what the map said," Myron said.

Again, wild Keatsian surmise silent on a peak of Figgian.

"WHAT!?" I shouted once more.

Car stopped, YGB pointed with both hands in the direction of my ears. I petulantly removed the earbuds. It was a good song I was going to miss.

"Oh?" I said. "Oh my *God?"* I shuddered with awe.

For we had driven onto the set of an Alfred Hitchcock movie. There were three rusted-out, de-tired, and de-engined pickup trucks tenuously propped hood-up on cinder blocks. The trees—there were maybe five of them—looked to have been put out of their misery by a serial killer arborist. They were deader than dead. They were wilted and twisted like symbols of the Jack Londonian Collapse of Nature. Chained, unseen dogs that I imagined to be black and antelope-size barked vehemently from some dungeon. The house sagged off its evidently marshmallow-undergirded foundations and cried out for paint the way a dying man begs speechlessly for hydration in the Sahara. Parched ant-nest mounds of dirt served for landscaping. Window shutters drooped from their disconsolate hinges. On a bent flagpole proudly waved a tattered American flag that must have been used for target practice. All the scene was missing was a big epileptically flashing neon sign: V_C_NCY. Whatever Figgy had done with the money Myron said he had sent him, he had plainly not invested in property maintenance. I looked hard, but I didn't suss out a pink CONDEMNED tag or a banner declaring Abandon Hope All Ye Who Enter Here.

My eyes widened into histrionic search lights after I oonched my head in the direction of Myron. That is because the high sun bounced off my nose ring and glinted upon Ashlay's exposed, prodigious nipple, brown and shaped like a Milk Dud and seen by millions of movie-buffs and Internet-goers, but never before today by me, and now twice. I wished I was hallucinating, but I was not. My life had stood a loaded gun. No, really, it did. Watch what happened.

A double-barreled shotgun was pointed at Myron's bald pate, not to be confused, Kelly, with pâté, an objectionable food item because it is French. A weapon being pointed at him was, Myron would later testify, a unique experience, which in itself may come as a minor surprise as it pertains to somebody like him who has pissed off more than his fair share of disgruntled writers and madly invoicing tradespeople.

"Git off mah property," a woman declared. She was burly as an old brown bear and dressed in an unseasonably heavy wool house coat. "Git right now, or I will fill you all up with buckshot."

Slowly, very slowly, Myron lowered his window.

"I am Figgy's book publisher, he's expecting us." Not technically true, of course, but show me a publisher who doesn't on rare occasions strategically exaggerate morning, noon, and night.

His self-identification seemed to lift the gun moll's mood. Clearly she had not read the tweets about him and his company. "'Bout time," she said. She lowered the shotgun and smiled with her immense butter-colored teeth: "I was counting on you mighta brung my husband's money, Figgy Fontana's Publisher, which you owed."

What? That was a thought he did not voice. He was always fucking current with Figgy.

Ashlay roused herself awake. Noticing the shotgun, she gave signs that she was about to scream, but Myron swiftly covered her mouth, which for all anybody knows may have been the first time a man performed such an act upon her.

"Shut yer traps!" the big little Mrs. yelled, not at us but at the enthusiastically yapping unseen dogs. "Talkin' to Figgy Fontana's Publisher!" They must have been cowed because they obeyed.

Was it worth risking my life in order for Myron to claim his Fontanas? Sure, YGB's Myron would risk his in a heartbeat, but mine, his favorite supposed intern? Can you possibly be in the dark as to what chances he would take? Myron is a fucking publisher.

SIBELLA'S ASHES

IT WAS OVER A hundred degrees under the sagging shaded porch of the dilapidated house, and Mrs. Fontana handed each of us a free mason murky jar containing, she testified, lemonade. It looked more like a lab sample, cloudy and flecked. It didn't come with one of those little umbrellas like in Miami Beach or the Bahamas, just so you know. Citrus supposedly is victorious in its battle with scurvy, but despite not being technically a pirate and not having been recently vaccinated for tropical diseases, I was not curious enough to access the medicinal properties supposedly contained in the alleged refreshment beverage.

The four of us had been consigned to a rickety bench—presumably the stockade had a waiting list—and I positioned myself between Myron and YGB. My eyes darted toward the Mrs. shotgun, propped against an unreliable-looking rail, in case she got any ideas to stand her ground again. Ashlay situated herself to the side, yawning like a sleepy kitten after her long car ride, somehow not perspiring in the sauna-like air. Perhaps the klieg lights of her famous photo spreads had preconditioned her for such extremes.

As for Myron, he looked more of a mess than he did after spending the whole night reading Calypso. He would tell me that his head seemed to be swimming from the shock of the heat (or perhaps from the sight of the multiple-legged beetle that executed an expert water landing in his reputed potion), and he could not summon up the energy to remove his trusty blue blazer.

"You can see Figgy when he's done working," the wife stipulated. "He's back in his cabin." She pointed to some vague destination far, far on the distant moonscape, and the four of us peered dejectedly in that forlorn direction. I visualized the bones of the search party who had perished or resorted to cannibalism.

Fortunately or not, it wasn't long before my feverish fantasy life receded. That's because a menacing, shiny black SUV, tinted windows and oversized tires, rumbled onto the property, churning up a small cyclone of dust. At least it didn't turn out to be an advance Secret Service team scouting the surroundings in anticipation of a presidential powwow. Yet this arrival would cause a much, much more than momentary distraction, and it certainly would not prove fortunate in the slightest.

Out of the vehicle tumbled a dashing young man dressed in designer black duds, a man who looked to be a bit older than YGB. His sidekick was a woman, disgorged from the predatory vehicle and decked out in a fire engine red silk suit. They adopted a solemn gait as they reproached.

Believe it or not—and between you and me, to this day I don't—I happened to recognize the female visitor as they advanced upon the porch, which I hoped would remain standing after the weight of their footfall landed upon the unsteady boards. That red silk suit presence chilled me. Meanwhile, Myron's condition continued to decline, and he was appearing unsteady, his eyes glazed over. It was unclear how much he was taking in, if anything. I could tell without a doubt he had not quite registered these arrivals—because if he had, trust me, he would have reacted.

"Lord Almighty," announced Mrs. Figgy, but I was pretty sure that wasn't the young man's name. "Cable darlin'," she uttered with emotion and began to bawl. Cable was a name recognizable to me: it was the name of Figgy's one son, and somebody Myron had scuffled with in the past when he called up to "protect" his daddy's interests, which he alleged were being compromised by his publishing house, the house that had made his father what you or I or a sensible person would call what should have been a rich man. His mother threw her arms around his neck. "Your daddy missed you, Cable boy."

I looked over to Myron and worried. This time he did appear on the verge of stroking out.

"I know, Mama, I know, but Daddy and I been talking on the phone a lot," Cable said in a voice muffled as a result of his inserting his well-coiffed head into the mutinous bounty of her maternal bosom.

After a respectful pause, Cable's companion joined in the hug fest, and Mrs. Figgy obliged. That secondary hug didn't seem to warm her cockles or reflush her already flushed cheeks.

Her son's companion needed the bathroom, and without introducing herself she was directed inside the house. I'm no Emily Post Up, but that woman's social skills were sorely lacking. "We been driving all day, Mama," she said with, to me, an overdetermined intensity—and familiarity. Now, maybe the female visitor was indeed feeling nature's urgency, or maybe she wanted to get out of Myron's line of sight as efficiently as possible. She expertly avoided eye contact with me, and I have no doubt she recognized me, too. I am hard to miss anywhere, including in a crowd. Mama's parting word to the woman was, whatever she did, don't wander too far into the house, counsel which sounded enigmatic if not ominous.

Then silence settled over those of us left behind, like one of those serving plate domes they use in old-fashioned fancy French restaurants to keep hot those old-school dishes like brains—and have you ever tasted those innards, which for all I know the French might eat for breakfast? I hope not, because brains on a menu sounds repulsive, and mine were baking.

After a painful stretch of time, Myron opened his eyes and got a bright idea to break the ice. Ice would have been an anodyne in this brutal heat, and many years later I was to remember that distant afternoon when my publisher did not take me to discover ice. Nevertheless this is what rolled off Myron's parched tongue: "Weddings and funerals." I cringed over his crackled brain choice of hackneyed expression, as did all his captive auditors. Beyond that, his non sequiturian utterance indicated he was registering information at best obliquely and incompletely.

Half-hearted full disclosure: Like Myron, I am hypersensitive to hot weather. Living in San Francisco—and not in New York or Chicago or Florida or Texas—exempted me from such climatological depredations. What did Mark Twain perhaps never say? The coldest winter he ever spent was a summer in San Francisco? Well, Bay Area weather was ideal for me, and Junior and his herpes simplex were nowhere nearby, either. By the way, everybody knows Clemens was a great author, but not everybody knows he was, fleetingly, a famous publisher. (Key term for publishers to never forget when it comes to great success: *fleeting*.)

As for Myron's brilliantly witty "weddings and funerals," he would turn out to have been semi-prophetic. But he might as well have started breakdancing and spinning on the floor because the Fontana family along with my landing party all cocked heads in Myron's direction as if they all were correctly sizing him up for the fool he could have felt himself to be.

"If you say so," said Cable to Myron, before turning away from him and saying, "Mama, you're socializing today of all days?"

Myron, fixed to the bench and unable to move because he was para-non-compis Myronis, stuck his hand out and Cable seemingly regarded the white solar-deprived appendage as an affront, while Myron tried a once-upon-a-time conciliatory tack, now updated with the uptalk. *"Myron?* I'm your dad's *publisher?"* I wanted to weep. This is what I had questionably wrought in him, *this?*

"Jesus Christ," said the son, looking down at him in more ways than one, *"you're* the famous Myron?" He wasn't smiling, but at least he didn't mangle the name into Moron, the way big daddy Fig did. What did Doubting Thomas say when his buddies told him they had seen Jesus freshly risen from the dead, which Myron appeared to be? Until I put my hands into the wounds on his side, I will not believe. Cable was no such skeptic and most of Myron's wounds were psychological and unpalpatable. He pumped Myron's wilted-lettuce hand a couple of times for good measure. And at this point Myron sank down further on the bench and shut his eyes.

Cable was introduced to the rest of our scouting party, and he appeared visibly shaken when he shook Ashlay's hand, as any man with a pulse often has been.

"Caitlin should be back any second," he said to everybody, which sounded like nothing less than a warning shot across the bow wow wow. Yes, the dogs started up, and nobody else seemed to notice.

He did reserve one remark for me, which was not the first time I had been targeted with this genius observation:

"You're a tall girl."

"Come on, bro, don't blow my cover," I said sotto voce. "But actually, I'm not so tall compared to other Zulu warriors who can gut a man with a fucking glance or a spear, Caleb."

"Cable."

What kind of fucked-up name is Cable, anyway?

Myron tentatively revived. He didn't want me to go down that warpath again, he'd seen the bloody results, and he cut me off at the pass. "I am very sorry, Cable, that your dad seems distraught," he said. At least it wasn't a "weddings and funerals" type of remark. "He is a great and important writer—and, umm, man."

"Truthfully, Myron, I wasn't always sold that you held him in such high regard. I remember when my dad first told me about his 'big-time' publisher?" You realize that Cable did the dumb-as-dirt double-air quotation mark signs around "big-time," don't you? And thus was Myron snarkily punked tuated. "I'm sure we have a lot to talk about, Myron," said Cable, "when we get some time over the next couple days of your stay."

Myron roused himself, scrambling to respond to the terrifying invitation. If I didn't know any better, I would have sworn he had surreptitiously swallowed a few Oxy, he was so unsteady on his feet. "We wouldn't want to burden you." Or catch a dose of the Black Death. "Plus, we didn't pack."

"Mama has extra PJs and toothbrushes, not to worry." I would have no need for anybody's nightwear for reasons that will be made plain to you but were not yet then plain to me. Even so, the mind reeled over the prospect of undeloused clothing and the dental hygiene customs practiced locally. "And *what* burden? Hogwash," Cable said.

That was the liquid concoction we had been served by Mama Fontana?

Cable was multitasking, talking with Myron while he was at the same time belongingly ashessing Ashlay. He pointed up to the second floor of the house, somehow provocatively. "We got lots of spare bedrooms, and Mama would be hurt if all of you didn't spend a few nights—right, Mama? I'm glad you're all here for the services."

Services? That did sound like an omen straight out of one of the Hawthorny seven or so garbled gables or Cables, which collusion I feel confident would have been missed by YGB, who himself was visibly enchanted by the place where Ashlay's Tartlet Letter might have nestled. Myron would have to figure out how to slink out of the horrible prospect of a sleepover, but right then all I could sense was that he was appearing woozier and woozier by the second. On the other hand, it did occur to me that with a few extra hours to work his brand of magic he could gain better purchase on the three precious manuscripts.

"What services?" Myron said, this time out loud, voicing my own fearful puzzlement. Were we back to square one on the mortality front?

The Mrs. elucidated: "Fig's twin brother, he up en died t'other day, from the cancer bug." She did not appear overly ravaged by the loss.

The publisher breathed a sigh of relief and teethfully smiled. "I'm sorry to hear that," Myron said, and Mama Fontana registered the unintentional mixed message. I also deduced that that unhappy lethal development was perhaps what conceivably jumbled up the rash and unsubstantiated Figgish reports. "I didn't know Figgy had a twin brother," uttered somnambulistic Myron.

"Yeah, he was the smarty-pants one, Pork was." Which I had no choice but to conclude was the dead man's most regrettable name. Cable, Fig, Pork, what fuck the fuck was with these Fontanian names? Would some Gargantua or Pentagruel Fontana soon stomp out of the woodwork? And something told me I didn't want to hear the matriarch's name, but to look at her, a few wild spitballing guesses: Ax? Slab? Awl?

Mama continued in a way that explained why she wasn't in deep mourning: "Pork was thick as a post about everything 'ceptin book knowledge. Figgy and he fought their whole life long, but they was brothers e'en so. They kinda worked together on projects, like the cabin. They was like twins."

"They *were* twins?" Myron said, and I instantly wished he hadn't, because Mrs. Fontana looked at him as if he were an idiot, and remember this was someone who didn't look like her high school transcript was peppered with AP classes. And don't forget: Hot and Myron got along like McCarthy and Hellman. Capote and Vidal. Mailer and the female species.

"Said that, Figgy Fontana's publisher man."

This explained why Cable and his companion had arrived, for a funeral. But at least not for the authorial interment whose prospect had darkened the mood of our publishing house after lunch yesterday.

"Mah boy gradgerated the law school," his proud mother boasted. "Intellect of property, whatever that is."

"You don't say," said Myron. "Intellectual property, that's perfect. Congratulations, Counselor Cable." This professional accreditation hardly boded anything but ill, I feared. Here's when Cable's companion returned but remained unintroduced and on the fringe of the fascinating exchanges going on.

"Well, lots to talk about going forward," said the billable-hours boy, "lots and lots to talk about at the end of the day."

Going forward. People say that all the time. Also *at the end of the day.* I deplore these turns of phrase. I used them at every opportunity, particularly while going forward at the end of the day. One guess who said: "Crabs go forward by going backward over the golden sands and storms of time at the end of the day."

But ogler Cable wasn't addressing Myron or me, he was habeas corpusing Ashlay prima facie with his beady baby blues.

"Wesleyan?"

"Good guess. I was admitted, but selected Williams instead," she said.

"I had a feeling it was a W," he said nonsensically because nobody ever had such "a feeling it was a W" about anything in the span of recorded time. There are some people, in my de minimus experience of mainly de minimus lawyers, who have to not be wrong most especially when they are, so they say something that sounds like it means something or corrects a misperception

("I had a feeling it was a W"), when it doesn't and they can't. "The Ephs of Williams, my favorite mascot, right after the Hoyas of Georgetown, where I went to law school."

But the F-ing nickname of the Williams College athletic teams resonated disturbingly for me and possibly Myron. Time was wasting and, in a fast-breaking neurological development, Myron's head (he reported later) was starting once more its magic tea cup ride: he needed to get to Double Eph, persona non grateful.

"Wait, don't tell me!" said Cable to Ashlay Commingle. "I know who you are."

She appeared ambivalent. Happy to be noticed, despondent to be recognized. I was hoping she wasn't thinking about taking her business and breasts into her own hands and doing any more flashing, because we had had enough of that for one day, though in that regard I felt sure I stood in the distinct minority in this dystinguished and dysfunctional company. Doubtless, many people knew who Ashlay was, and her notoriety made her privy to the secret griefs not to mention briefs of wild, unknown men. Most of the confidences were unsought, and she realized by some unmistakable sign that an intimate revelation was quivering on the horizon. If you don't get that collusion or what intimate revelation was quivering, Kelly, you have to not pass Go and sign up for Ms. Redburn's remedial English class.

"Of course, you are the one and only Suzi Generous!" Cable declared. "I love your movies, seen them all seriatim, which are one of a kind, as are sui generis you." A pun is supposedly a low form of humor, and I should know, and no wonder low-minded Cable felt the compulsion to explicate. Another similarly low form of communication is open carry. If I were flashing heat holstered on my belt, I could test the comparables. As for Cable Fontana, ipso facto, lawyers couldn't graduate a fortiori without some rudimentary Latin, mea maxima culpa.

"I always regretted coming up with that Suzi Generous stage name, because then it stuck and I couldn't shake it. Call me Ashlay, I'm retired from the industry. I'm a novelist, or I will be when my book comes out."

"You're probably Myron's new shining star, good for you, good for him. I bet publishing and porn must have a lot in common."

"Far as I can tell, both involve a good deal of fluffing."

"But the money shot is the money shot pari passu, Suzi, I mean, Ashlay. You know, if you ever are in need of pro bono representation…" I was marveling over the spectacular artlessness of his come-on while fighting off my own sea-sickness, even as Cable was simultaneously relishing the prospect of Ashlay's overnight stay.

The bono of the pro bono offer seemed to earn her attention. "Well, funny you should say that, because you're an intellectual property guy, and I was thinking of patenting my own special scrunchie."

"Tell me more," said would-be counselor for the confused.

Alas, amplification and/or demonstration would have to be postponed.

"Visitors, guests, people, awl ah ya!" Cable's *mère* neighed. "I think the time's come," she said, and she prepared to lead everybody inside for the viewing of the Pork. She had anticipated some logistical concerns. "The mortician man M-bombed him, but he won't keep in the heat, so get your feets movin'."

Sad to say, Myron wasn't capable of accompanying us yet to sit down alongside Pork, and it wasn't because he ate kosher, which you already gleaned that he didn't, and it wasn't a matter of being offended by Cable's salacious and showoffy classical language exercise. He had a better reason, and one small problem loomed on his horizon, the place where his intimate revelation was quivering. In fact, Myron was, cheeky Kelly darling, *literally* fucking horizontal. For this was the moment he had fainted, knocked out in the second round by the undisputed heavyweight champion of the universe, the sun.

✳✳✳

WHEN MYRON GROGGILY CAME to, we were standing over him with gradations of concern on our faces. His head was bleeding slightly (from grazing the porch railing, which I was glad did not produce more grievous structural damage to his head or to the Fontana residence), and he appeared hollowed out like the innards of one of FF's rusted-out trucks. He was resting—more like fidgeting—on what was a filthy pillow case on Caitlin's fancy, overeducated lap, and he was being ministered by what I remembered to be her ice-cold hands. Her chilly fingers must have felt pretty good, I am compelled to concede.

Cable gave his endorsement of her professional competence. "Caitlin knows what she's doing." *When it comes to horizontal and sick men*, I completed to myself the teste monial.

When Myron uncertainly relocated his neurological bearings, he gazed up into his freelancing caregiver's dark eyes. Straining, he found his voice to murmuringly inquire: "Calypso?"

Yes, that's what I would have said, too, and Calypso is the name of the lovestruck nymph and cagey deceiver in *The Odyssey*, but that's another story. Homer had little to do with Caitlin, at least yet, but it was she who had been our heretofore nameless lunch companion at Avenue yesterday, and she was the conduit for the next big book Myron was going to publish—if he lived to sell the tale.

"What'd he say?" said YGB, who appeared genuinely concerned if not about Myron, about his next paycheck.

"Myron wants to hear Calypso music?" said Cable.

"Shhh," Caitlin hushed them and then addressed her charge. "Take it easy, Myron. You're dehydrated. Take a sip of lemonade." I could never forget that voice.

The reckless lemonade recommendation was all the proof I needed she could not be a traditional or alternative health care provider. I needed to expand my conception of the kind of healer she was. You may not know this, but there are certain diligent entrepreneurs who put up their virtual shingles and offer at exorbitant fees would-be authors editing and related assistance in the way of general manuscript makeovers. In the industry, they are called—step right up and collect your kewpie doll—book doctors.

As for that Tom-Ford-bedecked, Chicken Diavolo-consuming, email-bombing, Calypso O'Kelly gatekeeper, I could see Myron and I were going to have to deal with her. Caitlin slash Calypso may have been in her spare time a book doctor when not gallivanting (a Dad word) around Venice on the lookout for gypsies and wallets. You know how when the printer screws up and a blank page appears instead of page one hundred and twelve? The kind of thing that can happen, believe me. That's what it felt like to look at her: it was left up to me to fill in the blanks.

✳✳✳

CAITLIN—IF THAT WAS IN fact her name and not Calypso—and I remained outside with Myron while the others went inside for the "viewing" of Figgy's sibling.

"Pork's in the eatin' room," Mrs. Fontana had said leading the disinclined pack to the radically inclined Pork, "and he's awaitin'." That answered the prevailing question: not what was being served for dinner, but the identity of the man who was presumably lying tableside in state.

With the three of us on the porch, Caitlin, or whatever her name really was, pressed to Myron's clammy forehead a cold cloth of unknown origins but whose past purposes might have included engine-block clean-up for all I feared.

"Venice. San Francisco," Myron started and couldn't finish.

"Hang with me, Myron, the best is yet to come."

"Whoever the fuck you are." It was beginning to occur to me that if I myself did have a mild case of Tourette's, as Myron always asserted, it was for him possibly as catchy as my uptalk.

"You sure get around, Caitlin."

"You too, Myron. Thanks for lunch, which was marvelous, wish we could have talked some more. Got the contract ready?"

"You and Cable Fontana? Really?"

"You publish books and rub shoulders with writers and gypsies all the time. After Venice, haven't you gotten used to surprises yet?"

"I never unexpect the unexpected."

"Good, I can tell you're feeling your oats, which is good because you have to live long enough to publish my great book."

"Feeling a lot better than Pork Fontana, that's for sure, poor son of a bitch, cut down in the abattoir at the prime of his brother's career. Did you know him?"

I realize Myron wasn't making completely rational sense, but it was hotter than you would imagine and there were too many developments for him to keep track of in his condition. Twin siblings Pork and Fig: could be a kind of culinary breakthrough, I begrudgingly contemplated. Wonder what inspired their parents, and if their names were Cucumber and Nag, or Zucchini and Beef, or Plum and Catfish.

"Never met him," she swore. But according to her, it seems that Pork was the educated one, a legendary high school drama and English teacher who retired early a few years ago, purportedly to compose plays. This career turn possessed a sort of logic because he was always starring in some community theater production of *Surrey with the Fringe on Topahoma* or *South Pacification*. On the other hand, Figgy was homeschooled and formally uneducated. Pork was the good boy, the A student, the one following along the straight and narrow path. In his younger days, Fig was the shit-kicker, the booze hound, the one always on the prowl for trouble and women on the side, which he couldn't help but find. That's where he found his inspiration for those distinctive books, in his hard-scrabble life, not in literature.

"Where good books come from," said Myron, "is anybody's guess. It's always a miracle, that's one reason I'm in the business."

"That gypsy might have had some influence, too."

Come on now, you would have rolled your eyes along with me. She ahemmed and filled us in. Cable had explained for her benefit that anybody who knew Fig from the old days never could account for him writing as much as a grocery list, and that may have contributed to his decision to become essentially a hermit. The brothers spent a lot of time together up till the very end. They had a bond that Cable or Fig's wife never understood, but you will, in time. The brothers did fight a lot, true, but their conflicts seemed to keep them connected. And their odd names?

There was one conceivable explanation. Pork and Fig were the nicknames they gave themselves, I was forced to presume, while under the influence of psychotropic drugs that cognitively incapacitated them. I was correct they were nicknames. On the basis of their hospital birth certificates, Cable had informed Caitlin and so she informed us, long deceased James and Mary Fontana legally named the twin brothers Porphyry and Newton.

"Oh, no you don't," said Myron, surprisingly agile of mind. "Not Figgy Newton, no way. I may have lost consciousness for a minute, and I may have run into a tricky gypsy in Venice one time and almost you, but I am not buying this story."

Would that he would say the same thing about her *book*.

"Cable never said much about his dad or his uncle or the rest of the family when we got to know each other at Brown. I did later on get the picture that his dad had evolved into a dedicated writer. Not conventionally schooled and obviously unpolished, but then I read those amazing books of his and they made my head spin. The man wrote like a house on fire."

"When your house is on fire," I took my opening to Murmechkally mention, "that is not the time to stock the refrigerator. That's what a wise senior editor once told me."

Caitlin pretended not to hear, for which I could not really blame her, and went on: "And to hear Cable tell, nobody took a shot on his dad till he found you, and you went out on a limb and published him when nobody else would risk it. You're a 'big-time' publisher." Again with the air quotes? "A first class dickwad, too, says my fiancé, but a hell of a publisher, which is obviously why you called dibs on *Adventures of Calypso O'Kelly*."

"That's 'dickwad' to you," Myron corrected her, employing his own air quotes to dramatic effect.

At the same time, I could not contest the sum and substance of her assertions. My heart aches and a drowsy numbness pains my sense as though of hemlock I had drunk.

How many in our increasingly large circle, excluding Ashlay Commingle and wouldn't that be nice, attended a sepia-toned university? My college team lost every league game except against Brown, a point of humility that didn't need to be underscored at this tender button juncture. She had no view on my dumb, should-have-remained-internalized question, but she had one on another issue.

"Ashlay Commingle is a better porn name than Suzi Generous," she said, "which I object to unconditionally on the grounds of selfie-indulgence. But if she doesn't stop acting generously around Cable she will be commingling with the fishes."

Changing the subject, I mentioned to her that YGB was himself a distinguished Brownish alum.

"Remember I told you he did look a little bit familiar?"

To which I said, "And remember, Caitlinypso O'Gypsy, when I should have told you to keep your Venetian blind mitts off of him?"

Then Myron said, "But in the meantime I need to meet with Double F. Figgy's good, and I need his next three books, which I paid for, but between us and the slumped barn where the witches' coven is probably meeting, he's no Calypso O'Kelly. Wait, are *you* also no Calypso O'Kelly?"

Yet once more, O ye laurels, and once more ye myrtles brown, with ivy never sere, I come to pluck your berries harsh and crude and with forced fingers rude.

"Take it easy, Myron. You've been through a lot."

Something told me we were in for a fuckovalot more.

A CLOCKWORK SIBELLA

M YRON MUSTERED THE STRENGTH to get to his feet, with Caitlin and my grunting assistance, and we endeavored to enter the house improper through the extrasuperventilated screen door. As she told me the day before, I was his protectah—if not his luvah—and damn it, I should keep an eye out. As for the alleged screen portal, what could have been its functional purpose, considering its advanced state of disrepair? The mesh was shredded to the extent that it would Open Sesame for the winged depredations of blood-engorged mosquito swarms if not mated-for-life mourning doves.

Once inside, the temperature hovered I estimate at a comparatively refreshing ninety-nine degrees. You'd think Fig would have installed air conditioning. But no such luck. Myron turtled along, and the unscreened door had slammed behind us as Caitlin held his arm and guided him toward the muddled masses give me your tired and poor voices presumably emanating from Pork's next-to-final resting place. At least I hoped it was penultimate.

We ventured down the long hallway entrance tastefully appointed with a lynched sixty-watt bulb that swung from a codependent chain in the nonexistent cooling cross-breezes. The warped floorboards cartoonishly croaked. We passed an opened door and, giving over to his curiosity, Myron stopped to see what was inside the room. There was a bare wood desk and chair, and numerous boxes on the floor. It smelled dank as a cigar-humidor (a receptacle for my dad's only vice), and the smoke-stained

gossamer curtains drooped arthritically against the unopened
window. On the shelves were indeed a few books, but they were
all multiple copies of Figgy's publications. This must have been
where the Figgian magic once happened, because didn't Mrs. Fig
say that he worked in a cabin on the property? Nonetheless,
people are typicanooly and nosy too about the work habits and
surroundings of famous writers. They want to know what time of
the day they show up for business, they want to know if they write
longhand or on a computer, they want to know if they listen to
music while decomposing. I get that, I do. But you know what was
most peculiar about Figgy's office—if indeed it was or had been
in the past his office? Maybe Figgy had gone minimalist, or maybe
there was no Ikea within hailing distance to spruce up the joint.

"That's curious," I said to Caitlin. A writer with no books and
no computer, not a typewriter or pads or pens or pencils. Figgy
Fontana was legendarily eccentric, but who was this Spartan?

Caitlin was ready with the answer to my unasked question:
"Cable said his dad got rid of all the other books besides his own,
said they distracted him. And he was giving up his computer, too.
It was too noisy, and the porn that kept popping up all the time was
distracting him. He moved into the cabin he and his late brother
built by hand out back."

We passed along the corridor and soon came upon what the
unfailingly veracious real estate agents in my posh neighborhood
would have described as a "spacious and welcoming gourmet
dining room with classic, timeless touches that will bring back
memories of childhood," but which I, being an unreal estate agent,
would advertise as a place "where luxury and hygiene go to give
up the ghost." It was all-too-easy to imagine Mrs. Fontana serving
up healthy organic, locally rustled up fare such as BBQ roadkill.

In any case, there he was—evidently a man by the name of Pork
Fontana. But I would have thought it was Figgy if I hadn't been en-
couraged to think otherwise. Admittedly, I knew the eminent author
solely by that silly book straitjacket photo where he was rubbing his
chin like it was an Aladdin's lamp. Here Pork was stretched out on
the butcher block table. And talk about the flesh he was in. He was

enormous. He resembled a beached sea lion. A sea lion wearing a John Deere cap and a flannel shirt and suspendered jeans and work boots. His leathery sunbaked skin was beginning to postmortemly sag. He had the look of somebody who had fallen eternally asleep on the shore, and the M-Bomber should have thought to clean the dead man's fingernails. As he lay—watch out, Kelly, 'cause here comes a single-car collusion—dying, but mainly really dead.

I was looking at Pork, but I was thinking: Fig. I know writers come in all shapes and sizes, as well as all ages up to and including dead, but in advance I wouldn't have picked Figgy (or his twin) out of a lineup of bestselling authors. Literary types don't have to look like James Joyce or Joyce Carol Oates or a Joyce such as Joyce Kilmer, but it helps. I think I shall never see a poem lovely as Figgy. Let's hope that Jennifer Lawrence or Penelope Cruz writes a novel and one day is nominated for a National Book Award, because if they're irresponsible enough to put me on the jury I will do my best to make that happen. I lead an active fantasy life.

At this point my fantasy life and I were washed over by an odoriferous tsunami. A thunderstorm pelting me with offal. A C-4 detonation in the abattoir. The smell, the smell. The house itself reeked as if it itself had been M-bombed. *Hello, nausea, my old friend*, I sang in my bones like the sea.

✳✳✳

THEN IT HAPPENED. THIS was the moment Myron had been hoping for: Double F's grand entrance. It was disturbing but also fascinating to eyeball the identical twin of the deceased, dressed exactly as his brother and every bit as immense.

Myron must have summoned up all the strength in his beleaguered body and he ambled up to his wealthy and disturbed and unstable and unreliable author.

"Figgy, I'm Myron, your publisher, sorry for your loss."

"En I'm sorry fer yours, too, but we talked 'bout that on the telly oh phone." That unforgettable voice of his, half frog, half crow. A frow, a crog.

It was bad form for Myron to dive into that complicated business matter, but he would prove to have no corner on badness of bidness form. There was no risk of talking turkey, and besides, FF wasn't listening to or looking at his publisher. He was gawking at Ashlay, which, to be fair, sounds worse than it was.

"Suzi Generous? Dammit, as I liv'n breathe," he said King Leeringly to Myron's new author. "Know'd you anywheres, clothe or nekked."

It goes without saying, and that's a dumb expression because here I am saying it, he had zero interest in a colloquy with Myron.

"All happy families," said Caitlin, "something something."

The illustrious Russian author had once made a good point on that subject, which Caitlin couldn't collusively quote. But here was my point. I had not been wrong about lunch yesterday. She was no witch. This Caitlin was nothing but a grifter, albeit a talented and well-dressed one, but one whose game I had not yet figured out, and I wondered where she was hiding that Birkin.

What universe of insanity had we insinuated ourselves into? I couldn't wait to undiscover. But that's not true. I could. But Myron? Not quite. Because look what happed next: darkness filled his eyes and he dropped again, deadweight, to the floor.

∗∗∗

NOT SO FAST, MORTY the mortician man. Myron didn't permanently lose consciousness. His knees buckled! like that line in the great Hopkins poem, which Junior supposedly knew by heart, and which I doubted. YGB and Caitlin and Ashlay combined forces (*Mayday, Mayday!*) and carried him into the front room, and they deposited him on the mouse-castle of a couch. Myron had told me before that he needed to see his doc about his rocketing then plummeting blood pressure as soon as he got home, and that sounded to me like a fucking sensible idea. These unsafe skittery jags in BP, if that's what they were, might betoken a worrisome condition. Shoot me before I Google Search again.

On that couch was where he would stay for I couldn't say how long, but when his eyes opened, he told me later, it was dark outside and his whole body ached, head to toe, a random plunking on the xylophone of his skeletonic form. One thing he could detect with confidence was the resonance of advocate Cable's accusatorial voice as the author's son was speaking, Myron was dimly speculating, to Caitlin in the hall not too far away.

"Flu?" he said to her.

"Don't think so," she said.

"Being he's greedy and likes to roll in the mud, I'm diagnosing swine flu, doctor. Speaking of which, can we play doctor soon?"

Consulting my notes from Myron's account that he ultimately related to me, I understand the two of them laughed. Does anybody find remotely amusing this exchange relative to an elderly AARP-eligible man who is feeling like he is dying in a should-have-been-condemned house, one that might have served aesthetically as an inner-city shooting gallery, while another man is on his impromptu bier of a dining room table a few feet away? If you qualify, please send Hard Rain Publishing the first forty pages of your new work via the transom.

"I gotta get home," Myron managed to say. "Where are my people?"

My people? He said it, and examining the Myron arch archives I would say it was a first for such an expression on his part. He never thought of them, or I should say us, as people, much less his. My conclusion: he was in progressively shaky shape. I should have been by his side, but I was, comme on dit, surprisingly if seriously occupied upstairs, and you know what happens when a nation occupies another and they plant a flag, well, don't complain later that I didn't foreshadow.

"Myron," Caitlin said as she hustled toward Myron, barefoot and reportedly wearing nothing more than a checkered cotton nightshirt that was admittedly delightful to observe, whose buttons were not being called upon for decorous application. "You feeling any better? You had me almost worried. I thought about calling for help, though from up in these hills you'd have to be Medevacked."

"Did Sibella and Young Goodman Brown abandon me?"

"They went to bed hours ago," she told him. "Everybody's upstairs sleeping."

Or something.

Except with respect to Pork, who was more than asleep and downstairs. Alas, Poor Porkick, at that juncture I knew him not well.

"What time's it?" Myron couldn't raise his arm to look at his watch. He didn't think he had ever been that sick before. I knew I was right to suspect that pseudo-lemonade.

"Two a.m., Myron. Go back to sleep."

"Got anything for the pain in my head?"

She said it wasn't a good idea in his condition. What did she know? Myron wasn't a book upon which to perform her doctorly ministrations.

"Then get me a gun and let me end it." For the record, ungentle reader, you're not the first to call him or me a drama queen.

Myron couldn't tell where the author's progeny was, except for the fact that he was hidden deep in the shadows. As usual, Figgy's son piped up a mite too eagerly: "Gun? You want a gun? We got plenty of firearms in the house, Myron, but I doubt you have the strength to pull a trigger. Cait baby, beddy-bye-time."

"Sweet dreams, Myron," she said. "You're probably not as bad a guy as I thought you were. Of course, hardly anyone would be. We'll catch up by morning light. Big day's coming soon," she said with a thrill, leaning over him at a fetchable angle. "We got a funeral to get ready for."

"Whose?" he asked.

BANG THE SIBELLA SLOWLY

No cock volunteered for Myron's wake up call, and neither did the dogs do reveille. He felt a little better, it seemed, though there was no spring in his step. Maybe he should have stayed transfixated on the couch, but that wouldn't be normally advisable according to the directives of the Department of Infectious Diseases, considering the ruinous state of that piece of furniture upon which he had spent the night. He probably should have stayed as unconscious as he normally was in his San Francisco offices of Hard Rain Publishing and probably should have never taken his posse to Fontana Town in the first place. But if he had done that and I had never kept him company, I would have missed a most marvelous, unanticipated event.

Now comes the place where you are going to question me all over again with renewed skepticism as to the soundness of my judgment. But you will also appreciate that on this occasion I am going to restrain my impulse to offer TMI. You're welcome very much.

YGB asked me something at the right moment in bed last night (come on, man, use your fucking imagination) along the lines of, "We okay, Sibella?" You had to be there in order to catch how wonderful that might have sounded to me, but if you were, the double bed would have been too crowded for the unprincipals to circumnavigate. He and I were the apothefuckingosis of okay. And here's a sentence you never heard cross my lips before: I was very happy. (Enough, Sibella, I know you want to, but don't go there. You can resist everything except temptation.)

"Good," he said softly.

He was sweet and considerate and it felt right, the whole experience, to speak euphemystically, and don't allow that Spell Chechen Terrorist to autocolorectically sell me out. The closest we came to awkwardness had to do with—three guesses? No, not my length, which was kind of mattressly uncontroversial considering the horizontality. And you know, if anything, that factor inspired the opposite and ecstatic effect, truth be told. And not that I ruined the mood by babbling about books he had never heard of, much less read. Considering his relative book ignorance, that would have been shooting fish in a barrel, and besides, there wasn't a whole lot of pillow book talk, *ahem* and *ahim*.

Yes, the fucking tattoo.

"Says right here," he said, gently semaphoring a strategic and magical digit, "you are a *Muse*?"

"More like *amuse bouche*." Even by my low standards that is a tasteless pun if you mangle the bouche, and forget the mangle, too. At least I didn't quote the late great Marvin Gaye when he sang about textual healing. Miss that guy.

Ma mère et mon père, who could otherwise pass for brilliant, insisted I take French my whole time at Spence, classes I passed with meager distinction. I'll finally cop to my deficit, my usual defenses along with my clothes being utterly irrelevant in that boudoirish context.

But as for the French, man, here goes: not that they've been hanging on my every Anglophone word, but I now officially need to cut them a break. This century they have suffered heartbreaking tragedies at the hands of those uni-browed, virgin-shopping, de-Johnsoned terrorists. Very well then, let's start over. I have been unfair to those marching Marseillaise-crooners. Their cuisine may be criminally oversauced but it's damn good. I mean, nothing beats their croque monsieur and their French fries (but forget the mayo). And their vin? Got me there, too, though that's a question way above my editorial pay grade. The mossy-toothed existentialist philosopher Jean Paul Sartre killed God on the cover of *Time* magazine, but who subscribes to the existence of Jean Paul Sartre anymore? Nicely played, Deity. Their countryside is rapturous and their cathedrals and their museums and their movies and their clothes and everything else—all right, I give up. They win, fair and square. Sure, they make fun of tourists, but who can blame them? They're *tourists!* They are also very kind to tykes and to pooches. If only I could have mastered pronouncing the precious fucking "r" maybe I would have been more temperate off the top. If I were you, and obviously I'm not because you yourself are, I wouldn't bet on it. But then the French went and sealed the deal when they elected a president who is cool and smart and speaks better English than our potato head prez (all right, pretty low bar to hurdle) and somebody who married his high school teacher, which would warm the cockles of my heart if my cockles were not currently preoccupied. All to say, *Vive la France.* Seriously. While we're in a confessional mood, I also admit you have been correct all along: I am self-sufficient and high maintenance both. You yourself can order this combo platter if you exhibitionistically dedicate yourself.

"I'll bet there's a good story," said my editor in chieftain. "There usually is behind every tat."

"There must be, but I can't remember it, and if I did, telling it is the very last thing on my mind." And the very *first* thing on my mind I proceeded forthwith to consumatitiously demonstrate.

Afterward YGB said, and he could kill me with the honeyed sincerity of his voice, "Whatever the story may be, I hope you'll be my muse, Sibella."

Who was this boy to me, I yearned to know, and, God, I hoped my fantasy life hadn't manufactured the whole thing.

Let us draw the faded gingham curtain, venal reader, on this scene.

About the curtain in that bedroom, queasy reader? You wouldn't want to lay a finger on its long lost ginghamness without first snapping on latex gloves.

That's all from me, Junior Editor Sibella, reporting from her idea of the cobbled lanes of Paree. Now back to you in the studio, Wolf, and I gotta say you're looking mighty pale, do you ever get outside, see the sun? Qu'est-ce que c'est? Wolf?

✳✳✳

I AM SPEAKING ABOUT the morning after my night before when Myron lurched into the belly of the beast that was Fontana's ramshackle house, whereupon he came upon a sight previously unwitnessed: No, not Loch Nessie or a unicorn. It was rarer than that. It was YGB and colloquially me and not schoolmarmishly I standing alongside each other in the kitchen. He had never observed the two of us in such intimate-seeming proximity in the Hard Rain breakdown room or anywhere else on planet Earth.

YGB and I studied Myron—one word would be—*sheepishly*. And don't try to revise and inject *goatishly*, Murmechka. I have never been compared to any farmhouse animal (unless you are aware of any grungy grange filled with giraffe or gazelle herds), or spent a minute in any self-respecting agricultural enterprise, but I understand full well that sheep are supposedly meek and stupid. These were two adjectives that had never in the past been associated with Young Goodman Brown and Sibella of the Isle of Manhattan. Well, *stupid* was a viable candidate, but *meek*?

Because that is the moment the truth instantly cracked Myron like a beer bottle on the noggin during a college bar fight. He could tell that Meek and Stupid had slept together in one of those bedrooms advertised by FF's son on Expediency dot com. YGB's fantasy had, against all odds bodkins, come true. And so did mine. (If you only knew how hard it is not to embellish with narrative detail and selfies, but then again, you do.)

"You didn't," Myron said to us both in a hushed tone. "Tell me, please, you didn't."

"What?" YGB replied. Not his finest instance of oral repartee, I agree. And not at all like last night when he orally—

"You didn't," the boss repeated a third time in case we had missed it the first two.

Myron overplayed his hand, conveying contempt way over the border of *tut tut tut* with regard to the supposed desecration of professional decorum. Then again, Myron never played the hand he was dealt, which is what you are supposed to do in cards and in life. To my knowledge, in the end as you'll see, he *overplayed* every hand he was ever dealt. Maybe *that* explained, and not the gypsy, why he had all the success he had had, and also explained the dangers that loomed and the non-gypsies who targeted him.

Though this could not be fairly said ape pro Poe ravenous nevermore me, young people supposedly hook up all the time, as I read and have been known in the many moments of self-pity that I had called my life to envy. In strictly demographic terms, no big deal, right? Are you asking yourself if Myron was jealous? Was he possessive of his protégé, Sibella? If such thoughts cross your mind, you've been multitasking and not paying close enough attention, though who could blame you besides me? Perhaps it was none of his business what the senior and junior editor's relationship was, and don't think about inserting air quotes around *relationship*. That was our private business. But *none of your business* is the working definition of the business of a publisher like Myron.

"You couldn't." On the plus side, at least a slight variation on the prevailing Beam theme.

"What?" YGB said, suddenly having an awkward way with his tongue.

I added nothing because I was sensing anew the limits and therefore the instability of words, being a big fan of Gertrude Stein as well as being an excellent junior editor and the soon-to-be ex-colleague of probably my imminently ex–editor in chief.

Myron shook his head. Get sick enough and there's nothing you can do with the unraveling of the world.

"Sibella, are you crazy?"

There was a strong chance. But in a good way. As my precious Gertrude once O-Steined, the white hunter the white hunter is nearly crazy.

"You realize this is going to end badly for you, don't you?"

I said nothing.

"Of course you don't." I would locate his utterance somewhere at the midpoint of the sympathetic scale, somewhere far to the right of "Oh, you crazy kids!"

What could we say? If we knew what he knew, we might not have opted to do what we did, but I wouldn't wish Myron's romantic knowledge upon anybody, particularly me.

"Where's Caitlin and Cable, and, God, that sounds like a country music group."

"Saw them go into Figgy's former office a while ago," YGB said. Sleepy as he might have been this morning, considering you know what, he kept a watch on anybody who might affect his antisocial standing with his boss.

"What's that on the table?"

I espied the ominous blue cover that unmistakably betokened the mundane workings of the American judicial system that is the envy of democracies and the scourge of struggling publishing houses everywhere. Before this moment I had not noticed its presence.

"Oh, Myron," said YGB, "this was delivered when you were asleep, and I signed for you, like I always do in the office."

"You fucking did what?"

"Didn't want to wake you."

"You're a certifiable idiot." Harsh, even for Myron.

Yet YGB was visibly grasping the possibility that Myron had a case.

"Somebody's suing me, and I should have known. That constitutes improper service, but it was a matter of time before I was tagged anyway. Young Goodman Brown, you've learned nothing from me, but I hope you learned something from Sibella last night, which considering your obvious starting point, would be a long shot if you didn't. No offense, Sibella, you little minx."

"None fucking *taken*?" I said, not being brilliant and not being little and not being a minx and here came the fucking Uptalk Monster stomping through my mental bog more pissed off than ever.

Myron didn't bother to scrutinize the document. Who else knew he was here anyway, far from the madding crowd of his publishing offices and in the way more fucking madding crowd contained within this nuthouse?

✳✳✳

Bull by the horns: the cliché always worked for Myron. And the uncastrated bovine brute in the old china shop also had the virtue of being accurate with regard to him.

"Come with me," he said to his rosy-cheeked, still helplessly ebullient junior editor, and I obediently followed as he shuttled bull-hornishly down the hall. Yet with each bare footfall, I was beginning to note the slightest receding of my perfect feeling of satisfaction and delight. That deep down tingle began to get tangled up. Maybe there was a chance I had been a tiny bit unwise after all.

Myron pounded on the door of what was once supposedly Figgy's office. After a few moments, Caitlin appeared as she was buttoning up her denim shirt. She seemed to be having lots of trouble with all her buttons ever since she drove up with Cable— and what had come over the female race around me with their buttons and their breasts, not that I should talk on this of all mornings. Across the way the other half of The Caitlin Cable Band was pulling himself back together. Looked like Mama Fontana and Myron were the only surviving ones in this house not to have recently tripped the light fandango. I had briefly forgotten about Suzi, I mean Ashlay, but I didn't have time to follow my train of thought where it was going: off the tracks and into the gulley.

"Morning, Myron," said Cable to the window, zipping up, his back to the publisher. "Hope you're feeling better."

"You don't, and I seem to have been served." He waved the papers.

"A formality, Myron, nothing personal. I thought now's a good a time as any when we could talk man to man. I couldn't get you to promptly perform an audit of sales, but mainly the new contract looked hinky to me, and I figured I would protect my dad. If you think about it a minute, you'll understand."

"You believe I am ripping you off?"

"I wouldn't put it quite that way, Myron. As I say, I am merely looking out for my family, doing the diligence."

"Your family has been taken care of by me for a long time, for over a million bucks. Can you be that dumb and greedy?"

"You clearly have never read any of Figgy Fontana's books. If you had, you would know the Fontanas are motivated by the simplest of considerations: cash, cash on time, cash on the barrelhead."

"Your dad would be proud."

"I feel his presence all the time."

"Speaking of his presence, I'd like to pick up the three new books."

"That's not gonna happen till we deal with those pesky legal matters."

"You paid for a process server?"

"You're a guest in my dad's house, didn't want to offend you by serving you myself."

"About your dad, he did cash the check for the advance."

"Technically, yes, well, technically *I* did, as we were entitled to do by contract."

"About that purported hinky contract, you see, Cable, that's where the books come in, by contract."

"Contract law can be complicated, as any IP lawyer could attest."

"You're going to shop those books, aren't you?"

"Oh, I am sure you can avoid our taking such a drastic step, we've had such a fine working relationship for so long." Ready for this smooth move? Air-quotes around "relationship." What a dope.

In that cathouse atmosphere of litigious song and dance, I could say right then and there we may have been observing a clear-cut instance of wrongful behavior amounting to egregious tortious interference, which sounded less like law school to me and more like a dessert that backfired and produced unintended gastrointestinal consequences. And I would proffer my legal opinion indeed if, that is, it weren't for the fact that I don't know what I am talking about and that I ruefully regretted *Law & Order* never having screened a single episode hinging on this fascinating matter of jurisprudence.

"Calypso, sweetheart," Myron sarcastically addressed her, though I'm not sure why he shifted his attention to her. He was conceivably more of a romantic than I had counted on, a lesson I should have filed away for future use as my personal permission slip to run back home to Gotham City. "I hope you know what you're getting into with this idiot you got on the hook."

"Who's Calypso?" asked Cable. "Who's on the hook?"

"All happy families, something something," she said again, evidently thinking that it worked yesterday to semi-satisfying effect, why not try again?

On the other hand, she appeared disconsolate. Or she wanted us to think as much. They were nothing but a pair of Ivy League scammers, and my hunch was each was playing the other, as well as Myron and Venetian fat cats and who knows who else? I wouldn't say I was surprised, and I wouldn't say that they intimidated me, because facts are facts, and I apparently knew something they didn't know, that they needed Myron as much as—or more than—he needed them. Game on.

Cable asked Myron where he was going, their colloquy was just starting to get interesting. But this exchange had no chance of ever getting interesting in this or the next geological era and Myron had already made his move, out the door.

"Sibella, that's your name, right?"

"Yes, Caleb."

Cable was curious. He wanted to know if I'd be interested in hooking up with him and Caitlin for, you know, a three-way. Not very long ago I went through a phase during which every sentence I uttered ended with "bitches." Layup lines, *bitches*. Extra salsa, *bitches*. You get what I mean, *bitches*. It was diverting while it lasted, but it would have been wasted on these two bitches.

"You, me, and Calypso, the old striangulated slap and tickle me Elmo?" queried I.

"You lost me, but it sounds fun, no?"

"Fun? Honestly, it'd be more fun to paint Figgy Fontana's toenails. Why don't you proposition Suzi Generous? It's your golden shower opportunity. I hear she's usually up for anything."

"That's what I was counting on, too, but she turned us down before she went out for a run this morning. Suzi said she had zero interest in me, including on a slow day before a funeral, which is this afternoon, can you believe that?"

Though I was merely a tall Plan B, I thought I'd add, for the porpoises of his educational enlightenment, "Your history is a nightmare from which I am trying to awake."

"You're weird."

"I may be, but I am a junior editor at Hard Rain Publishing, your father's eminent publishing house, Caleb."

"It's Cable, I tell you, and I thought you were an intern."

"Fuck you."

"That's what I'm talking about."

"Bitches."

At that instant a most disturbing recognition flew into my mental windshield like a plump, collagened-up bug going a hundred miles an hour until The Big Sleep and then splat. All these post-Junior years, my body and I had witnessed less action than a federally protected Native American reservation mall church and casino combo operation at dawn. Then there was last night. And then, there was whatever this morning's invitation signified, and not that I would have ever taken it seriously in the time it would take me to get through a dozen Prousts. Perhaps Cable's crude pass shouldn't count, considering the off-the-charts high-slimage content, but as a good Spence alumna I could at least credit the request, repulsive as it may have been.

As I departed, Cable ventured a question for his girl. "Who's this Calypso they all keep talking about?"

Caitlin told him to shut up. I was for once wishing she indeed possessed those powers I once feared she possessed and would change him back into the lizard he was.

Myron was on his way out the front door, with me catching up in his wake, which I seem to do a lot and will do a lot more in the future, and I didn't need to be informed by him that we were headed off into the great unknown, or, since we had left one great unknown, a greater unknown. Or, same thing, we were off to enter the orbit of the Red Planet of the Great Fontana.

Dearly Beloved, we are gathered together.

Wolf? Wolf? Where are you when I need you?

THE SIBELLA JAR

MYRON AND MY EXPERT tracking skills were hardly to be tested that morning, which was good because they were sorely lacking for us tale of two cities slickers. It wasn't long before we entered a clearing when what to our wandering eyes should appear but a smart-looking idyllic redwood cabin neatly surrounded by a high, finished redwood fence, all Sick Family Fontanason. More different in appearance from the main house a building could not be. It was situated on a low-lying bluff, the kind of terrain where the cad and the lunatic the world knew as General George Armstrong Custer met his bloody and, by historians' consensus, well-deserved fate. After making such a connection, I did not fear an onslaught coming down from the barren hillsides. Instead we walked through the gate and onto the beautiful polished oyster-colored paving stones that led invitingly to the front door. We were about to confront Fontana about the lawsuit and determine what his role was in its initiation— as well as his future as a writer of books for the company called Hard Rain. Then and only then the raiding party could McMurtryianly ride in yip-yip-yipping and finish us all off once and for all.

The windows were closed and curtained but there were planter boxes outside laden with all manner of pretty, carefully tended wildflowers. The happy bees buzzed blissfully about. Hummingbirds darted and hovered, hovered and darted. The overhang on the porch was brightly adorned with proliferating purple and white wisteria. A poet's haunt. A determined Myron knocked on the author's door with authority of his own.

It was Ashlay who opened up the door. Did you require additional verification that this was one slippery girl? She was dressed in what looked to me to be her conception of workout clothes: skin-tight T-shirt, X-ratedly abbrev. mini running shorts, and pink tennis shoes, with a pink baseball cap emblazoned SSG for *Slip, Slippery Girl*, I guess, on top of her head. But no AC headband. In her grasp was her untrusty Tolstoy. At least she didn't run in yet another jumpsuit.

"Myron, you feeling better?" Ashlay seemed sincere, as why not?

What he was feeling was most likely what I was feeling: electroshocked. All we were missing was the attractive bit in our mouths to protect our teeth and tongue. We stepped inside the air-conditioned cabin and there behind a desk, on the other side of a 20 x 10 Persian rug, which had to be over a hundred years old and probably would have been offered for a hundred thousand bucks by some West Side Armani-decked-out turbaned rug seller, presided the raj, His Figness. He was in a white shirt with French cuffs and pearl links, and his oversized major literary agent type black-rimmed glasses inched down his professorial nose. His eminence grease hair was slicked back neatly. He had a book open in front of himself, which I was soon to find out was his own copy of Ashlay's favorite Russian novel, and off to his side was a computer monitor big as something in an air traffic control tower. The whole cabin gleamed and glowed. Ah hah, this was where he must have spent some of his enormous royalties.

"Figgy?" asked Myron. You would have double-checked, too.

"Who else would be in my office, Myron?" He chuckled. But perceptive on your part. You are correct, not *Moron*.

I cast my eyes around the place, his wall-to-wall bookcases packed floor to ceiling, the artfully recessed lighting. My quick scan revealed the twenty plus leather-bound volumes of the OED, complete sets of Shakespeare and Henry James and Austen and Mark Twain and Conrad and Trollope and Turgenev and Dostoevsky and Eliot and Proust (damn) and all the rest of the crazy canon guys and gals in impressive profusion. And a whole bank of contemporary poetry books, too.

No, Myron was not appearing woozy in the slightest, because his unreliable body had probably determined he had played the dizzy card once too often, but thanks for asking.

Ashlay spoke up: "Fig and I were discussing *Anna K*, which is his favorite book of all time. What a coincidence."

Coincidence, my sweet ash lay.

"Have a seat, Myron," said Fig, "and you too, Sibella," my first clue that he knew who I was. Myron and I both hunkered down into oversized red leather chairs, which matched the one Ashlay would use for her own ash. "Care for a cup of green tea? Suzi... I am not used to *Ashlay*. Suzi brewed some." He pointed toward the kitchen where stainless steel fridge and stove ruled the designer day, and on the countertop stood a post-mod tea cozy next to a cut glass vase embracing a splay of orange roses.

No coonskin caps, no wall-mounted rifles, no heads of elk, no fishing poles.

A regular writer's den. Check that. A writer's dream cabin.

I couldn't help but notice over the credenza behind him, against the back wall, an abundance of photos of great authors— Hemingway, James, O'Connor, the other O'Connor, Fitzgerald, Joyce, Eliot, Wharton, Plath, Nabokov (the one with the butterfly net), Dickens, Oscar Wilde, Isak Dinesen.

Oscar Wilde?

Oscar Fucking Wilde, you got a problem with that?

Kelly, do you know the etymology of the Italian word *credenza*? The root lies in the concept of belief, from the verb *to believe*. And that was the piece of furniture upon which, back in the day, the staff tasted food for a prince or a pope, sniffing out poison. What's not to love about the Italian language and culture and high risk dinner parties? And on that credenza of Fig's I noticed something very curious if not promising indeed. Three neatly stacked piles of pages, three-hundred typescript pages each I was reckoning. A Machiavellianish credenza would be the perfect place to deposit those manuscripted Figgies for tasting. What do you think I was thinking? I won't bother to ask what you thought was going through Myron's mind.

You would be wrong about one thing. Speaking for myself, I was not thinking. Too much was happening before me to think that far ahead.

"Fig and I were talking about love and death in Tolstoy," Ashlay said.

"Sure you were," I said.

"How one seems to follow the other," she added.

"In novels, love and death, like the night follows the day," said Fig. "But in life? Well, I hope not. Books are not life. Life is more interesting, that's what I have come to realize."

"Me, too," Ashlay said, with passion in her timbre.

Shivering his timbers, Myron I could tell almost wanted to agree, but couldn't, because as you know, he is, news flash, a book p------r.

"But betrayal, alas, is usually not far behind," she added.

"Sad but true," said Fig, "very sad but very true. And, Myron, where did you find this wonderful new writer, what a gem. Send me an advance review copy, would you? I'll surely want to blurb *Slip, Slippery Girl*."

Ashlay beamed and Myron Lastnamed as well.

So it went for an entertaining half hour or so, a veritable cliché for the bookish set. Chitchat chatting, don't you know, with an old lion of a writer recently back (in our minds at least) from the dead and with a fledgling peacock (technically, peahen) of a new writer whose professional past had been left behind for good as she sucked up a life of letters and the arts. *Ars longa* is a tried and true classical expression, though the *longa* of Ashlay's past had nothing to do with a life in letters. Both of them were indeed civetly sipping tea with the loyal and devoted and well-heeled publisher and his anti-heels junior editor who was probably glowing like a seventies luvah lamp from last night. I know I have commented that I don't care about the feelings of writers, because they are unknowable to anybody including possibly themselves, and that's fundamentally true, but something about today was making me reevaluate. For one thing, I was charmed by Fig, which I never would have suspected before. Based on what I told you, would you have suspected as much? Of course you wouldn't.

"Fig," Myron said, "what a fabulous office you have."

"My late, lamented brother Porphyry designed and constructed it. He had many hidden gifts. You like?"

"He had the perfect understated touch," Myron said. "It's so *you* inside these four walls."

"Well, I feel instantly productive when I come to work. But these days I cannot shake memories of my poor brother. I don't think I will ever be able to disassociate my office from my memories of him."

Ashlay and I murmured our condolences.

"Myron, I'm glad you and your staff and Ashlay found time to be here for the services. We should be getting close to the time."

That was our cue to get up and prepare for the obsequies. And about the lawsuit Myron had gone there to discuss? The subject never came up.

Wherefore art thou Porkeo?

✳✳✳

WE STEPPED OUTSIDE THE cool confines of the cabin to be sledge-hammered by the heat on the anvil of our heads. Wilting under the mind-bleaching sun, we hobbled along the beautiful paving stones that led to the outskirts of Figgy Fontana's writer's fortress. Writers need a stronghold of one sort or another. It might be a cave, it might be a studio apartment in San Francisco where they wear noise-canceling headphones, but they all yearn for isolation and privacy in order to tap their emotional and psychological resources. But the physical beauty of this author's workspace, well, that was impressive. And more than that. Fig's office was pristine and stunning and inspiring.

Once we got to the other side of the redwood fence, the instant Fig closed the gate behind us, however, he betrayed a signal that something grave was about to transpire. He was leaving behind that writer's artificial and secluded world of his. Ashlay's heart had been plainly filled up by the conversation, and something about her today was causing me possibly to reevaluate my views on her, and with renewed vigor she started running up the hill for her workout, for which she had been puta tively dressed. Her ponytail bounced beyond the harness of her suddenly appearing scrunchie, which *was* cute and functional and almost, I can't explain how, innocent.

When the three of us were alone, Fig pulled his white shirt out of the waist band on his beige chinos, rolled up his sleeves. He tugged the baseball cap down tight and low on his forehead, and he metamorphosed into the sort of man who had ravaged his three pickups and murdered those trees. And why was I wondering about those dogs we heard barking when we drove up? No clue. This next part is very hard to explain, and probably harder for you to believe, but this is the case. Since leaving the womb of his office, where he had been reborn before our very eyes, he had become his former self, somebody unfortunately more akin to the fellow Myron had come to know prior to our visitation.

"Moron, stay outta my cabin, ya hear me? And don't be bringin' any these baby giraffe girls."

Et tu, Figgus?

I concede I do walk with a lope, consistent with giraffes and cagers, which is the old-school name for basketball players because they used to play at the historical inception of the sport in a kind of cage. That was when bee ball was invented by Doctor James A. Naismith, who wanted boys to have something to do with themselves besides the obvious during the long, long Canuckian winters.

Myron and I were bewildered by this brutally abrupt transformation and Myron asked him to repeat what he said, because he couldn't trust his ears, and neither would you, not if you had been in attendance for our genteel conversation, the one where he and Ashlay and Myron and I, discussing in such a moderate manner books and what they meant and that I...

"Ya heard me. En ah nothah thing, ya ain't gettin' mah fuckin' books widout a fight, and ferget the damn dick-twirling book tour, Moron."

"Fig, what is going on?"

"Wass goin' on is dat we muss bury mah pig uva brother, witch is Pork. Witch is what he wuz, a pig what stoled my stories."

Beyond that, and inarguably, the man may have been making no fucking sense, but he was making more sense than I then knew.

SIBELLA OF THE D'URBEVILLES

THE CRADLE ROCKS ABOVE an abyss, and common sense tells us that our existence is but a brief crack of light between the two eternities of darkness.

Or in the case of Fontanaland, two eternities of perversity.

Everything was about to accelerate like a NASA launch countdown, and I am going to try to keep up because, Houston Street, which you ought to learn how to pronounce, Kelly, we were about to have a big problem.

The funeral procession was gathering into formation. The suspect funeral home guys had done their job, transporting the deceased's body onto a flatbed truck with a single strip of funereal black bunting. The coffin was cardboard and came from Costco, I'd bet, where you can probably buy a six-pack of coffins if you were a cost-conscious serial killer. This could have passed for high ceremony in this distant Martian colony. A dusty black van was idling, and I was hoping for it to be air-conditioned, having been spoiled by the cabin.

YGB, Ashlay, and I were in our places outside. Cable and his Mama and his Caitlin were there, too. The Hard Rain faction didn't have proper mourning clothes, unless you counted Ashlay's jumpsuit, which was black and as appropriate as could be expected under the circumstances, and did she carry a spare in her purse? And where did her running clothes come from? Then there were Caitlin and Cable: all in black. Mama in formal check flannel shirt. Sunglasses to the ready. Fig was at the graveside already, saying his private farewells, we were advised.

"Where's Myron?" Cable wanted to know. "Can't get started without the big-time publisher." Scorn in his voice dripped like acid. Smallist consolation: this time at least no air quotes.

Caitlin said Myron was flat on his back on the couch, having relapsed. "He's green to the gills."

"Myron's such a twit," decreed Cable dispositively, "such a tweakling."

We all piled into the van (giving thanks for the cranked-up AC that did not stand for Ashlay Commingle) and followed the truck in our humble cortege. In a few minutes we had arrived at the cemetery, where the briefest ceremony took place—a few valedictory remarks, and a lengthy bit of silence, nary a sniff to be sniffled.

The brother of the deceased got in the last word: "I'll miss ya, ya fucker."

And the body was lowered down and clods of symbolic dirt were shoveled by each of us with our most authentic fake solemnity.

✳✳✳

WHEN WE DROVE BACK to the homestead about an hour later, Mama Fontana said she had yummy refreshments. I know I spoke for everybody in my group when I say as far as I was concerned, dehydrated as I was, as it related to libations, not on your fucking life. I did snatch the last bag of Doritos and an apple from the car this morning, and that would tide me over. At the same time, I didn't know how Myron was feeling, but I had a pretty good hunch *where* he was feeling.

Our host and author pulled me aside and gave me a hard look. "You, baby giraffe girl, you'se comin' wit me."

"What about the, uh, refreshments and reception?"

"Fuck it."

Whew, saved by the fuck.

Something told me I could handle him if things went sideways. Then again, my overconfidence has been known to get the best of me. See: Junior. But if you do, remember what I told you: in a dormant and non-symptomatic state, his herpes virus may nonetheless pose a threat.

We headed off toward the inevitablest destination: that clearing where the cabin was.

"Ah will kill'm, tha sunovabitch, mebbe ya'll kin stop me."

All the more reason for me to go, to forestall prospects of mayhem. I might have dragged YGB along, if I were thinking more clearly, but perhaps I *was* thinking clearly, because I may not know much about the male species, but I do know that too much testosterone in one physical setting can prove combustible. Let the wild rumpus start.

✳✳✳

"MYRON," SAID THE AUTHOR to the publisher upon entering his cabin, "may I get you a cold beverage and how did you gain access, old chum?" As before, he had impeccably switched persona once inside the writer's Bourn of thrillers named Legacy, Ultimatum, Supremacy, and Identity, guilty pressure movies I wished I didn't like as much as I did, though I also wished I possessed that hero's knack for escapability.

As Gregor Samsa awoke one morning from uneasy dreams he found himself transformed in his bed into a gigantic insect. Gregor would prove to have nothing on the bestselling novelist. Someday I needed to check in with my dad for his transcontinental diagnosis.

"No thanks, I'm good, and the key was on the side of the nearest planter box, where people always put the extra one." Myron was adept at asking and answering compound questions as well as committing break-ins, being a publisher, and he was seated at Figgy's desk, three stacks of paper—those three manuscripts, I assumed—in place before him. He turned over a page, as if he had been interrupted mid-graf. The gently rustling sound the sheet of paper made was like that of quaking aspen leaves. Very pretty, to tell the truth.

"Reading something interesting, Myron?"

"Very interesting. One of my three books."

"And here I thought they were *my* three books."

"Well, I do have this signed contract that says I am legally entitled to them."

"You're going to kill yourself if all you worry about is business. Stress should not be taken lightly, haven't you heard? You must be heart-healthy when you approach your later stages in life. Look what stress did to my poor brother. Along with the cancer, true."

"You know, I had never heard about your brother's cancer."

"Well, it's a long story. And then it was flash fiction."

Whatever its length, it was evidently one that was not going to be told by him.

"Awful, awful about your brother. How long was he ailing?"

"Like I said, Myron. Long story."

"On second thought, how about a beer?"

When I came back from the kitchen run with three bottles of IPA (surprisingly good choice de Fontana!), I realized from their shifting side-to-side eyes we were, here we go, destined for a Thrilla in Fontanilla free-for-all or a strained conversation or both. I was glad there was a lot more beer in the fridge, because this might take a while, and everybody knows how critical beer can be during a tense negotiation. Since our last unannounced visit to the cabin, positions had been switched. Now Myron was seated where Fig used to preside, the best-selling author in one of the red chairs. I took my appointed place and, considering the downside of doing otherwise, I instructed myself to breathe.

"Can you tell me the back story of this manuscript here? *Cain Disabled*?"

"Catchy title, don't you think?"

"Not your best, not a humdinger like *Swimming Buck Naked in a Hurricane*, that's for sure. Sibella's pretty good with titles—" I was? Since when? "—and she and I will discuss when we get back to the home office. I'm not very far in, but the setup is fascinating and explosive, the pitched bloody battle between two twin brothers loving and hating each other. Is it a tad autobiographical?"

"Tell me what isn't autobiographical for any worthwhile writer? Each of his characters is an aspect of himself."

"I wouldn't have guessed you and your brother had such a violent relationship."

"He was a good prevaricator, is one reason why. The other reason why is you really don't know much about me and my brother, and why should you?"

"All storytellers are natural born liars, so my writers all tell me, when they're willing to talk to me, and by the way, thanks for talking to me."

"And I wish I could express gratitude for breaking into my office, but yes, and some people don't rightly know when they are lying, they think they are always telling the truth, like my brother, who never said two true things in a row. And like me he was a good actor, too. Porphyry was always getting the leads in the local playhouses, he could play act being me, you believe that?"

"But did you and he work together?"

He tilted his leonine head, signalizing puzzlement, but said nothing.

"Well, did he read and comment on your work?"

"Always advisable to get a second opinion, a reality check, a reading of the crapometer. And Pork knew about books. It's the only thing he did know anything about."

"As for that reality check, did the collaboration approach a type of editing?"

"You are attempting to be subtle, Myron. If you wish to be convincing, this is something you need to work at." Well, the author was perceptive. "You asking me did my late brother play a part in the writing of my books?"

God bless Myron, he didn't answer that question.

"'Cause, Moron, if'n you be axing me dat, I might heve to up'n whip yo sorry Jew ass." Crog, frow.

Then the author laughed. It sounded like choking. I've heard better laughs in *Texas Chainsaw* movies. His was unpleasant as the sound my washing machine makes before going clank and kaput with the clothes half washed and sopping with soapy water.

"Pretty good impression, no?"

"Dead on."

We were heading off into deep waters, and they were getting deeper by the second.

"You know, Myron, some people have stories happen to them and then there are other people who can actually tell the stories."

"I always believe stories happen to people who can tell them."

"That's slick publisher talk if ever I heard it."

Myron undoubtedly felt he was onto something. "What you are saying is the stories happened to Figgy and the person who could tell them was Porphyry. You guys are twins, so in some way, to put it very crudely and reductively, you are the same man."

Whoa, Figgy.

"Pork and Fig were not the same. Don't ever say that again."

"I'm trying to get to the truth here about *Newton*. That was his given name, right, *Porphyry*?"

What fuck the fuck?

"Don't say that. But I've been thinking. I've reconsidered, having gotten to know you and your staff. I will let you publish these three books after all. I told Cable he was getting too greedy, told him to let well enough alone, but he wouldn't listen, but he will from now on."

"I'm sorry about your brother, but that's a great development. Isn't it, Sibella?"

I was glad he wasn't waiting for me to make an affirmative non-denial.

"And you must be very distressed about your brother, whom you buried." Then Myron gathered himself up to deliver his coup de grab: "But my question after perusing this manuscript, and getting to know *you* today, is: *Who* was buried today?"

Hesitation long as the horizon across the Pacific. "My brother was buried, and you should show respect."

"Yes, your brother was buried, but is it Pork or is it Fig in the ground?"

"I'm going to have to ask you to leave."

"I'm not leaving without these books."

"I already said you could have them, didn't I?"

"Yes, you did." Myron paused. "Yes, you did, Pork."

What fuck the fuck, he said it again?

"My name's Porphyry."

Superfuck.

"And you, Porphyry, are the one who wrote the books?"

You know what I said to myself.

"What difference does it make who wrote the books? Fig was sick for a long time, very sick, advanced stage cancer and all, and he wasn't going to make it, and we made contingency plans in case the worst happened, which it did."

"And Fig's wife and son and his girlfriend, they are all in on it?"

"Nobody's committed a crime. The man died, it happens. He's my brother, and I loved him as much as I hated him, which was a lot."

"But you wanted the books to keep coming, as there was big money involved."

"What gave you the idea to come up here anyway?"

"The phone call yesterday, when somebody said he was Fig and he was done with Hard Rain."

"That might have been a mistake on my part. I was looking for leverage, since Fig was dead and I wanted you to cough up more cash."

"I already gave Fig the money, and we had an ironclad contract."

"Fig kept me in the dark, always took the credit, he thought I was exploiting him, and he never paid me half, which he should have done, only twenty-five percent, and only when he felt like it. After the first few books came out and sales were booming, I tried to get him to agree to changing authorship, *a novel by Fig and Porphyry Fontana*, but he wouldn't go along. He said he was the one who made the Fontana name famous and I would screw up the whole thing if I got my way. People were in love with Figgy Fontana, those books sold like hotcakes, which you know, because you got rich off him. Now do you understand why he was reluctant to go on a book tour? Because he couldn't be himself, because he wasn't the author of the books, his brother was."

"And you think you can keep the ball rolling, and nobody will notice?"

The wind set early in tonight, when glided in Porphyria; straight she shut the cold out and the storm and kneeled and made the cheerless grate blaze up and all the cottage warm. Kelly, let me help. Look up the poem "Pork's Luvah." You'll find it in that big fat Norton anthology you sit on. But I can't bear to see you suffer, so don't pull out your Browning Automatic: hint.

The mood turned perilous. "If you and giraffe girl both happen to die by accident, say a gun going off during a break-in attempt, so far away from the beaten path, nobody will know, that's true."

Myron said he hoped he wasn't being threatened. Porphyry said he wasn't doing that. He must have been channeling one of Fig's books, if, that is, they were books by the real Figgy Fontana.

"And nobody needs to know if you keep publishing Fig Fontana, remain on course, and the Fontana Brand will stay alive."

"What makes you think we can do that?"

This was when Porphyry became agitated. "Come on, Myron. Who the fuck do you think wrote the books? Me, that's who. I wrote the books. Figgy couldn't decline a verb or a drink." He paused, vexed. "Who was it who said that?"

"I call bullshit," I said. "You conjugate a verb and you decline a noun. Was it *Churchill*?"

"Could be," Fontana said.

"Dorothy Parker?" I tried again. Damn, I didn't know. Besides, I had other things on my mind, such as my mortality.

Myron went back to the subject. "But those were Figgy's stories."

"Which he couldn't tell, Myron! Didn't you a second ago say, stories only happen to people who can tell them? He and I used to fight all the time. His position amounted to: *You're a fat old English school teacher with good grammar and good manners, and nothing happens to you, it all happens to me.* But he was nothing without me, he wasn't Figgy Fontana without me."

"And you're going to have to stay in character for the rest of your career, playing at being Figgy Fontana? And when you come to your office, or his office, you can be yourself, whoever that is?"

"I can do anything I need to do to make money and survive. Learned that from Newton, the poor bastard. He never gave me any credit when he was alive, and now, he can't help it, I will get all the credit, thanks to you, Figgy Fontana's Publisher. And now I am leaving. Close up when you go."

"I'm taking the books, Pork."

The author got up to go, and as he reached for the door, he came to a halt. It's like the lights went out in the cabin, or like the equivalent of a riptide rushed through the room, and he transformed into somebody else, only for the life of me I would have sworn that he wasn't acting this time.

"Moron, you en giraffe girl," he croaked and screeched, "I's had enufa yore booshit."

He marched into the kitchen and returned with nothing I could see in his hands, but he seemed to have some imaginary object in his grasp, which he carried as if it were a rifle and which he positioned low on his hip. He took a deep breath and then he said his piece—or said his pieces—his eyes by turns fluttering, darting, snapping shut, then flaring:

"Fig, come on, man. What are you doing? Stop and think. I's dun wit fuckin' thinkin' thas what yore good for, Pork. These people are not worth killing. You'll spend the rest of your life in prison thinking about them and you will never be rid of them. Yas, yas, yas, they are like skunks in da hen house. Think anybody'd find their sorry asses we just bury them out here where nobody'd come in a hundred years and who would miss them nobody that's who. I don't think so, Fig, calm down, it will all be all right once you calm down. Think I'll have myself 'nother beer you don't mind you big fat pussy kissin' up to Moron. Myron is trying to do the right thing by you, Fig, come on, take a deep breath. Ya always wuz a faggot, Pork, always. Why'd I evah let you in why why. You needed my help, Fig, and you're my brother. Maybe I'll juz shoot you be good and done with both you and these bichez. Put the gun down, Fig, there's no call for violence. Like you fuckin' know 'bout vy lince things I could tell you it's all been vy lince all been nothing but shootin' up bichez from day one. It's fine, Fig, we can work together like before, nobody'll know any better, and Myron will publish our books and people will love you and it will be like it was before. Now's I's dead and burred ain't gonna be the same no more you fuckin' piece of shit. Come on, Fig, be nice, it doesn't have to be that way. Give me the gun. Fuck yer self I got the first amendment right to bear arms. Certainly, you have that right, but it's the Second Amendment and not here, not now, trust me, Fig, trust me. Like you wuz ever a good brotha to me fuck me fuck me you are nothin' to me. Don't get me upset, Fig, you know what happens when I get upset. Things happen neither of us like. Like ta see you uppen try you motha fucker you stoled my books you stoled my words you ain't nothin' without me. And you, Fig, you mother fucker, you are nothing without me. You hear me, Fig, nothing at all. Nowza, big brotha, let's git the fuck. Take the gun, Fig. Shit awe right."

He walked over to the desk, looked down on the manuscripts as if he were bidding them adieu, then turned on his heels, opened the door, and stomped out into the dusk without the manuscripts. Had we been in here that long, and what had we witnessed?

"Guy's out of his mind," said Myron.

I was trembling. "I feared he was going to fucking kill us."

"You realize he didn't actually have a gun?"

"But did he realize he didn't have a gun, that's the question."

"I think there's a big difference."

"Why am I scared?"

"Sibella, read my mind."

I did, and it wasn't hard to do. We ran back to the house and I summoned the others to the car, prontissimo.

I had watched the sickest, most twisted production of *Twelfth Night*, one without a happy ending, maybe one without any ending at all.

This is Dellyria, baby.

PART THREE

BREAKFAST AT SIBELLA'S

Y OU ARE NOT THE kind of person who would be in a place like this at this time of the morning.

Which is what I often felt behind my milk-crated desk.

Nonetheless, next day, we were all back in our not entirely unfamiliar places at the house. But nothing felt familiar. Myron and I were both traumatized, not that either of us would admit it. As usual, though, Kelly was smacking her gum and Murmechka was laboring over her whatever-they-were and a fierce-looking Caprice held cell phones in both hands as if she were a gunslinger and they were six-shooters and she was staring into her computer monitor as if it were the town's well the desperadoes had poisoned.

We kept everybody at Hard Rain on a need-to-not-know footing. Between us, though, before we made our hasty pudding departure from the Fontana Follies, Myron and I had agreed that YGB and Ashlay had no need to be told that something nasty had happened in the woodshed. At least until we figured out the implications and decided our next moves. As a consequence, there was hardly any car talk the whole way home. Everybody seemed relieved to have made a clean getaway.

Later that night in my apartment, considering what little use YGB and I had for pillow talk, we did not list the Figgian topic on our very crowded, intense, and on team agenda, so I buttoned my lips, if not in that way. I can guard the lane and protect the rim and repress with the best of them. He picked up on my disturbed state of mind and probed. You bet he did.

"Myron drove like a bat out of hell," he said, which was true, and it was weird to see Myron behind the wheel. "Something must have happened."

"Can we talk about this some other time?" Maybe when I understood and maybe when we weren't in bed.

"Do you want to talk about it?"

"Later." Much, much later.

"Whatever you want."

"It'll be all right, Myron's got this covered."

"I'm not talking about Myron. I'm talking about you, Sibella."

Interesting point. Tell me, what was the difference now between Myron's problems and mine? Besides, I was talked out. Afterward, I held my new boyfriend tight and we floated into a deep sleep as if it were a warm tropical sea.

No, really, it was exactly like that.

Shot beyond the arc is good, three points.

***

FOR THE RECORD, THE record a rational person or even I ought to be keeping, before we hopped in the car to go home, Myron and I tracked down Cable inside the house and away from Caitlin and his gun-moll momma, and we told him arrivederci. Myron also told him he better forget the lawsuit unless he wanted more trouble than he could handle. Like what sort of trouble? Like he would go public with the news that his father was dead and that Pork was alive and the true author of the books. How would he like that?

"That might hurt your sales, Myron. And to tell you the truth—"

"For a change." Too easy, I know, I know. Beneath Myron, yes.

Cue eye roll. "To tell you the truth, Myron, that might not be the worst thing in the world. But all right, I'll quash for now and we will let sleeping dogs lie. Keep sending the royalty checks."

It was Mrs. Fontana who was probably entitled to the Fontana moolah in a community property state, unless the deceased had made other fancy legal provisions with regard to those sleeping dogs—and along with you, I was forevermore wondering whatever happened to those invisible non-sleeping barking dogs at Fontana's. Myron didn't explicitly state that Pork wasn't getting a dime till it was all sorted out, because technically it was none of Cable or Pork's business.

"I'll show you the will when the time's right. I'm an IP lawyer, you think I would let this hippo slip through the cracks? Too bad Suzi Generous will be leaving us. She always lifted way up my, my spirit."

"One last thing. Sorry about your dad, Cable."

"Oh, yeah, right." I don't think he was in any of those famous stages of grief.

We had determined what was the grift in his and Caitlin's scheme all along. But at least Myron was mourning the loss of the man even if his creepy son was not.

"Take care of Uncle Pork. He needs psychological help."

"We all do, don't we?" The law of averages dictated the guy had to be right about one thing someday.

"And tell Calypso I will be in touch."

"Who is this goddamn Calypso?"

"I have no idea, but she's right under your nose."

I was pleased Caitlin was playing Cable. Those two deserved each other.

✱✱✱

MEANWHILE, OTHER MANUSCRIPTS WERE coming in over our legendary fucking transom, as per normal. Cozies and thrillers and sex memoirs and alternative history novels and those relentless books of verse. The poesy was dismissed forthwith, because we still didn't do poetry. This serial rebuff distressed me, as if I were rejecting at the pound a cute floppy-eared puppy or a rehabilitated pit bull that needed a good home. At the same time, *Hurricane* orders were nicely piling up. And Ashlay Commingle's *Slippery Girl* advance review copies were stacked all over the office and getting ready to be mailed out to every reviewer and bookstore owner along with all the X-rated purveyors in the country. In case you don't know how many so-called adult stores and websites exist in this freedom-loving land of ours, this was by a factor of five the largest ARC print run the house had ever produced. Predictably, German and French publishers had gobbled up rights to the novel already, and the rest of the Eurolemmings were gathering up right on schedule on the shores. We might be on pace for a monster year.

But you know what? Myron and I weren't feeling it.

It was all very well to say "Drink me," but the wise little Alice was not going to do *that* in a hurry.

Life that day in the house called Hard Rain Publishing: normal as normal could be. Normal, that is, if you characterized as normal what we had discovered yesterday: namely that Fig was dead and Pork was alive and that these three manuscripts probably had been written by both of them in some sort of bizarre collaboration, as had perhaps all of the other Figgies.

I had another question. Should we inform the police or somebody? Porphyry Fontana was not deceased, Newton Fontana was—maybe. It sounded to me that something like a crime may have been committed, but to my dismay it was yet another burning topic never covered in any of those million ripped-from-the-headlines episodes of *Law & Order*, my dependable go-to source on the subject of criminal justice. This story was not yet a good candidate for headlines to be ripped from, but I feared it wouldn't stay that way indefinitely.

Myron sequestered himself in his office, not answering his fucking phone as usual, waiting for the other shoe to drop, whoever's shoe that may have been. The three Fontanas were piled neatly on his desk, which he had cleared of every other distraction, but he was regarding these pages warily, as if they might rise up and bite.

✳✳✳

ON THE ROMANTIC FRONT, YGB decided we should keep our love affair private, no need for anybody in this small office to know yet. Myron knew, of course, but he was not the type to gossip, if he remembered—besides, he had more serious matters at hand. One day, YGB said, the time would be right for us to disclose. I concurred with his persuasive tongue in my mouth. I would have agreed to anything he asked, including wearing those pink socks of his to work if he wanted, and I was hoping one day he would want things like that from me.

He and I had conspiratorially timed our entrance into work that morning as not to arouse anybody's suspicions. We left my bedroom together this morning but staggered our arrivals into work and vowed not to acknowledge each other all day. This delayed gratification in itself would constitute a major turn-on for later delight.

Our stratagem brilliantly succeeded before it dreadfully failed.

Kelly was there first and I could tell she could tell something was up. First, she cornered YGB and they had a heated whispery exchange off in the distance. He told me in bed last night she had been pissed off with him about some trivial publishing issue, he could barely remember what it was, but it was nothing worth talking about and didn't we have better things to do, which we did.

Kelly glared at me from far across the office with enough heat in her eyes to roast me like a fucking s'more. When the moon hits your eye like a big pizza pie that s'more. Then again, everybody seems hardwired to sense when people are responding to their evolutionary dictates. We might reference pheromones, those mists of alleged airborne chemicals that signal the recent riot of sexuality, and that would have been a definite marker in my case and his. Murmechka, who may be the one human being who does not know the first thing about pheromones or human nature or Dean Martin or book publishing, for that matter, was holding forth.

"Good trip, Sibella?" she inquired, not quite accusatorily.

I told her it would probably bear fruit someday.

"Yes, the bear finds honey in the secret, hidden places and the wind is a guide to the falcon as the falcon is a guide to the wind."

This made me speculate that she did know more indeed than I gave her credit for. Or maybe she was feeling irritated after being left back during our field trip to the zoo that was Fontanaland.

Oh what can all thee, Knight at arms, alone and palely loitering? The sedge has withered from the Lake and no birds sing! I didn't know what to do with my enraptured self, and I should stop tracking YGB's every move, otherwise Kelly would scope me out, so I composed the email to Junior I had been putting off long enough.

✳ ✳ ✳

To: _____
From: sibella@hardrain.com
Subject: Your fiction

_____:

Apologies for the slow reply. I have been away on a business trip.
To an insane asylum.
Thanks for sending your manuscript. I have read the first hundred pages of *The Dream Calculus* with great interest.
In between sleeping with my editor in chief and ferrying Myron over the roiling shores of pending collective dementia and trying like hell to avoid the shoals of criminal prosecution. TMI, but let's face it, you had it coming.
This will be a brief email
Not that I'll ever tell you in so many words, but you broke my heart.
because
I can't believe you had the balls.
I would like to share your ms with my editor in chief
With whom I recently shared a fantastic multiply orgasmic experience.
and he may be better equipped
And no doubt about it, he is way better equipped in many crucial respects.
to respond to your book. He and I will certainly communicate with each other and get back to you asap with our decision.
Along about the time the Mets and Yankees play once more in the World Series or when hell freezes over, whichever comes first.
In the meantime, it's clear to me you have written a story that may possibly have broad appeal
Although not to this broad.

so give us a little bit of time to go through our internal processes. For now, I cannot help but be curious. In the publishing business, such curiosity produces what we call story questions.

You know, like what the fuck I ever saw in you in the first place and why I bothered to rewrite your now-illustrious poems.

I usually don't respond before reading the whole manuscript but I am making an exception in your case. Considering our past, I thought you deserved it.

Along with a Sonny-Corleone/James-Caan beatdown on the city street in our favorite movie The Godfather.

Your protagonist, Chas, has chiseled movie-star features and the body of an Adonis. Nice, but a stretch. He also has a "needy" girlfriend named "Susana" who played college "volleyball" and stands maybe six foot four. You might want to check the ms. Sometimes she is six two, sometimes six three. She attended "Packer Collegiate" (my old Spence rival) and grew up in New York (in a brownstone oddly reminiscent of my parents' home), and she pressures Chas to get a tattoo below his waist and above, umm, you know, that says *Muse*, to better guide her handiwork in case she gets lost in his eyes or his words or his whatever. That's about when I began to lose your train of thought. Then I go completely off the rails when I read that "Susana" has lots of face metal and ink and an apparently insatiable sexual appetite that borders on sex addiction for this Chas fellow— for reasons that are not easy to follow.

Or that anybody who isn't a sixteen-year-old boy would find credible.

One falls under the author's captivating spell, as it becomes all but certain that Chas harbors massive self-delusions of which he is barely conscious.

Strangely enough, much like the author himself.

In any case, Chas, as a result, finds himself needing what the narrator deftly, originally terms "personal space." At this point he oozes into the doll-like arms of a Munchkin-size heiress to the fortune of a Texas oil company. As I read your fiction

Which is one word for your complete and utter failure of imagination.

I was wondering if the average reader would feel as I do. Namely, that Chas is a doofus and a jerk, and that breaking up with his extraordinary and athletic and loyal and absolutely sympathetic girlfriend indicates that he had no clue about who "Susana" truly was or is. Betraying her would be the worst mistake he would ever make in his entire pathetic life. Only a dolt would do that. More on this later.

A lot more a lot later.

I wonder where your novel will finally go with the story of Chas and "Susana." Who knows? *The Dream Calculus* may end up being more the story of the estimable and big-hearted "Susana" than her disloyal, narcissistic beau. And someday "Susana" will find somebody more worthy of her.

Like an amorous and sensitive editor in chief, though in truth more worthy candidates for her abound on every single dating website in captivity, including probably the weird Christian and skateboard ones.

There is a remote chance Chas will become a more palatable character after he is chastened by inevitable, harsh experience that awaits any young man. Perhaps his heiress girlfriend gets bitten by a psychotic squirrel in Prospect Park and dies a very agonizing death from, let's say, rabies. Or she chokes to death at Eataly on a pizza crust because Chas was too busy writing poems to take CPR classes. Or their flashy new BMW explodes and she dies in a fireball somewhere in, I don't know, let's say Greenpoint, while he scampers to safety and, I don't know, big poetry prizes. But I'm spitballing what reading pleasures await me and the rest of your adoring public. All to say, you have aroused my attention!

And prompted me to anticipate the pleasure of kneecapping you.

Congratulations on all the good things that have come your way. And all that you richly deserve that will come your way in the future.

And, yes, I am loving California.

As I would love any place three thousand miles away from you.

Yours,

No fucking way.

Sibella

∗∗∗

I PRESSED SEND AND yelped. Not because my email server was the functional equivalent of a pin in a voodoo doll of me, but because Kelly was looming over me like a figure out of Wagner's Valkyries, only chewing gum. For how long she had been there I have no idea, so lost was I in concentration, which state of mind I would have vigorously recommended Kelly attempt to achieve someday.

"Does the editor in chief, *your* boss, know you are sleeping with *his* boss, the publisher? And that's why Myron took you and not me on the trip and why you and he spent the night in bed together there?"

Chomp chomp, chew chew.

What a delicious fucking development. See, if it is indeed possible to pick up on a young woman's ecstatic experience of a vigorous sex life, it may not be necessarily delectable who's her lucky partner in crime, which you supposedly shouldn't commit if you can't do the time, and I liked all my time with him and I wanted more more more, including more time. I should check on the latest brain research with my social scientist mom for confirmation of my scientific hypothesis.

"No, honest, he has no idea I am sleeping with Myron, Kelly."

"Would you like me to keep this scandalous intra-office news between us girls?"

Chomp chomp, chew chew.

"If you wouldn't mind."

Of course, she had tough choices to make. Would Kelly confront YGB, *her* editor in chief boss, with her take on the salacious truth, or would she go straight to Myron the publisher to lodge her concerns? I vicariously ventured into the arid wind-swept if not blown-dry wilderness of her thought process. If she went to YGB, her objective might be to piss him off enough to make him envious of me and therefore make *my* life difficult. Then what would he do? He might laugh in her face and tell her to mind her own business. On the other hand, if she went to Myron, she might try to get him to fire *me* on account of the publisher's compromising the pseudo-professional workplace environment. What would he do? He would laugh for a while and then might fire *her* for being unprofessional and reckless. Either intercourse she adopted would have been juicy fruit by me. I could tell she was working out her plan, which, if you knew anything about Kelly's strategic capacities, probably made her head hurt, and whatever her plan came to be, it was destined to be the wrong one. Then again, I could have been overfuckingthinking it. My money was on her kicking what she construed to be the whorenets' nest. That is, she might approach YGB and Myron both, gum blazing. As I came to conclude later about her plotting to subvert me, after other facts came to light, I understood why she might have never suspected YGB and me, poor thing.

"I could see why me keeping this to myself would work for you."

"Thanks, Kelly."

"Well, I have two words for you: dream on, bitch."

"That's *three* words, and you once used to be such a good fucking counter, too. You got an extra stick of gum?"

Chomp chomp, chew chew.

THE PRINCESS SIBELLISSIMA

Poor, sick, schizzy Porphyry Fontana, scum-bucket son of a bitch. If I may be so bold. To verify if a man could be simultaneously ill and despicable, let's check in with Junior—although I hasten to remind you there is no vaccine on the horizon for his herpes syndrome.

Myron figured out what he needed to do. I typed, as usual, the email he wanted to be sent to Pork in which he outlined the plan. Pork may have been mentally unstable or possibly deranged, but Pork had to inform the authorities of his identity, namely that he was not Fig Fontana, and that it was Fig Fontana himself who was six feet under. This plan assumed Pork actually realized that he wasn't Fig, of course, or that he was not Fig around the clock. Law enforcement could work out those legal and psychological niceties, that wasn't a lowly publisher's job. If Pork cooperated, perhaps Hard Rain would do the third printing, in which printing Myron would post an updated author's name on *Hurricane*.

Myron presented two alternatives to Pork, or maybe I should say Pork/Fig or Fig/Pork or Newton/Porphyry or Porphyry/Newton:

Fig Fontana
and Porphyry Fontana

Fig Fontana & Porphyry Fontana

One thing it was *not* going to be was *Fig Fontana*. Myron could make a case for change of authorship, and though he was conceivably opening himself up to possible financial exposure, he opted to take the high road—or a slightly more elevated road. The money he would otherwise make would feel dirty. Admittedly, the concept of *dirty money* as opposed to the other kind was a fresh one for Myron, along with his reluctance to acquire it. But now the new-fangled concept captivated him. Besides, big picture, if Pork hadn't been obliging, Myron wouldn't have in his possession those three new books stationed upon his otherwise cleared-off-by-me desk. Mostly, Myron felt he couldn't go on pretending nothing had happened, because something definitely had happened—although what it was, he wasn't sure. The original *Hurricane* contract with Mr. Fig Fontana was possibly legally enforceable by his estate, but it didn't seem morally enforceable. Needless to say, Myron was no intellectual property lawyer. Then again, if he had to be somebody like Cable to qualify for that distinction, he would take a pass.

"By God," exclaimed Sancho, "your grace has taken a great load off my mind and made everything as clear as can be!"

The other thing the authorship was not going to be was "Porphyry Fontana," or "Porphyry with Fig Fontana." Clearly logic was doing hand-to-hand battle with mystification and confusion. We would work through the complications of the next three books' authorship, as that big advance had already gone out. Maybe we would stay with the new formula, maybe the author would one day be Porphyry Fontana. We would cross that rope bridge over the gorge when we came to it.

Then the two men talked on the phone to confirm the understanding, as my publisher related to me.

"How are sales going, Myron?"

"Who am I speaking to? Pork or Fig?"

"Pork, Myron. Of course, it's Pork."

"Great, Pork. Sales are going gangbusters. All the early starred trade reviews were very enthusiastic, and keeping up with the orders is a full-time job around here."

Pork said he wished Fig was around to enjoy the success, and he almost sounded like he meant it.

"I decided, Myron. Let's go with the *and Porphyry.*"

That sounded reasonable, almost gracious on his part.

"You know, Pork, you might be in jail for a little while, if the police decide you and Cable engaged in any shenanigans. You can't go around burying the wrong guy and pretending you were ever dead."

Pork would take his chances. Cable was going to represent him.

"Well, then you might be in jail for a *long* while."

"Lissename, Moron, I's not takin' kindly to yas sayin' shit 'bout…"

Myron hung up as soon as Fig's Ghost made his appearance on the phone. He had nothing to say to Fig, who was both a dead man and evidently a personality that slitheringly insinuated itself into his brother's mind at the slightest provocation. In any case, Fig couldn't help Myron or Hard Rain. He was an inconvenience. And still dead.

This conversation was followed up by a certified letter, composed and typed by the junior editor. We both felt Myron was within his rights to make the change to *with Porphyry*, that it fell within the range of his publisher's discretion, and the house counsel grudgingly approved. Sure, Cable would come after Myron and Hard Rain, but that was the right thing to do. Simply because Pork didn't have a sure grasp on his identity or identities didn't mean Myron was off the hook. You make compromises in the book business. Compromise may be the essence of the book business. And you take chances. And you try to do the right thing whenever you can, which is not always possible, as I have learned full well.

Myron and I discussed another possible tact. What if we went with the story that our author suffered from a rare disorder, that he had multiple personalities, multiple identities? I got the idea and the terminology from my dad's monographs, and Myron listened attentively. It did have the advantage of seeming to be true, or mostly true, or at least mostly not false, and it did rely upon a sympathetic, nuanced reading of the whole subject of authorship and a sympathetic, nuanced understanding of the man or men who wrote the books. After all, Fig and Pork were one, or two, and together they produced their books. Of course, that move would have been dependent on Pork's willingness to divulge such sensitive information. But when Myron approached Pork with the idea, he wanted nothing to do with it. He was adamant that he didn't have any idea what Myron was talking about. He wasn't sick and he didn't want people to think so. As far as he was concerned, he wrote the books. And who that *he* was was not something up for debate.

Then Myron reached out to Cable and tried to enlist him in persuading Pork to accept this plan. Cable wasn't interested. "My uncle's a kook, but he's not crazy, and he'll never go for it. You, Myron? *You're* crazy. Keep the greenbacks coming."

✳✳✳

WE HAD NO CHOICE. We went public with the news that Fig was dead and held our collective breath. As a kid I used to sit in the back seat as my folks drove under the Carpal Tunnel and I held my breath as long as I could. I never did achieve my goal of holding my breath the entire length of the underwater passage but almost passed out once or twice. When I look back, that experience was a lot like what was about to happen.

It was the best of times, it was the worst of times, it was the age of wisdom, it was the age of foolishness, etc.

Talk about a hard rain. We needed an umbrella big as the Library of Sexual Congress. The Fontana news stunned the publishing world, which had been gunning for an opportunity to take down our upstart house and its egotistical publisher for years. First came the belated Figgy obits, which were painful to read, and were full of tough questions about Myron and our house, not to mention the whole Fontana family, which had pulled that ruse, and they wanted to know what we all knew and when did we know it, all those other grassy knoll and Watergate type questions. And then the critics scampered out of their rat holes with their sharpened incisors. The early *Hurricane* reviews had been indeed very positive. The new ones were anything fucking but.

"*Hard Rain's integrity has to be called into question. Fig Fontana is dead, but they published a book supposedly by him—a book that may not have been written by him. This was information known by*

*the house the whole time. Fontana's large and loyal following deserves
better treatment from...."*

*"Whoever wrote this has composed a fraudulent book. We don't mean
in a criminal sense, which may also be the case, but in a literary sense.
This talentless author, whoever he is, manages to offend every reader with
his thoroughgoing misogyny and misanthropy. His nonsensical vitriol
toward the LGBT community amounts to more than a technical failure,
it is relentlessly soul-sapping. Readers who get to the last page—and there
may be a few ruined souls out there who achieve that Herculean feat—
will accomplish it only while zipped up in their Hazmat suits...."*

*"Any reader expecting a novel by Fig Fontana will be disappointed
by this posthumous publication. This new book, which turns out to have
been possibly a collaboration between Fontana and his twin brother,
has none of the authenticity and pop of Fig Fontana's previous efforts.
Readers who are naturally mourning the death of an American original
will be dismayed by this desultory effort. They will see the seams of an
uneasy stitching together of an incoherent plot, and the desperate attempt
to meld two incongruent, clashing, clanging voices. One has to wonder
what role Hard Rain has played in the public deception that...."*

"Myron Beam's Hard Rain Publishing should be ashamed...."

"Embarrassment...."

"Disaster...."

"Travesty...."

We were reeling. *Swimming Buck Naked in a Hurricane* had
become overnight, instead of another hit, an unqualified bust,
the by far biggest dud in the history of the house. The returns
were filling up the warehouse and they were killing us, in a sense
more than the new, scathing reviews. The press had declared open
season on Hard Rain, a house they had always wished to take
down a peg or ten.

Porphyry (maybe?) called Myron in tears.

"What are they talking about? I was the one who wrote
the book, and all the previous books, there's no new author.
Nothing's changed."

Myron could not cheer him up because he knew from hearsay
and from other publishers if not from past personal experience

the vagaries of the book business and the unpredictability and unreliability of reviewing.

Besides, Myron had bigger problems popping up on the horizon. But he also had some loyalty to Pork, who was sort of one half of the author he had made famous. And I could see why he felt that way, although I had a more radical take. A collaboration between coauthors, which is what Fig and Pork seems to have been, is not a 50-50 proposition, it's a 100-100 proposition.

They want to get out of themselves and escape from the man. That is madness: instead of changing into angels, they change into beasts.

Myron asked Pork if he copped a plea when he admitted that the family made a greedy and stupid and illegal claim on Porphyry's life insurance.

"Not yet. I'm mulling. They offered me six months and two years' probation, but Cable thinks we can do better."

Maybe *he* could penologically do better in the end, but good news was not in abundance anymore for Hard Rain.

✳✳✳

AFTER MYRON ANALYZED THE implications of the drastic reception, he canceled publication of the next three Fontana books, and he thus formally notified the Fontanas. And he decided he would eat the advance. As a side note, Porphyry's writing career was over, at least at Hard Rain. Maybe he was a good writer and maybe those were good books and maybe they would be published by somebody else someday. It wasn't Myron's problem. Let God and *The New York Times*, if there is a difference between the two, sort it all out.

"Cable's probably going to sue me, but he was going to file suit anyway. Besides, he's been shopping those books already, so his case is going to look weak."

Could it get any worse? Yes. This is the saddest story I have ever heard.

"Sibella, I'm running low on cash, and I may have to take out a loan to make payroll. Keep this between us, all right? I don't want everybody to go into a panic, that's the last thing we need. But don't worry, you all will get paid." And then he added in this fraught context the scariest word in the book business: "Eventually."

"Tell me we can get out of the deal with Calypso." She had backed off on her insistence upon getting the written contract immediately, and said she was patiently waiting—but would not do so forever.

"We have an oral contract with her and I like to keep my word."

"What fuck the fuck, Myron."

Do you believe it had come to this most unlikely pass: that Hard Rain's future might be lying in the supple, seasoned hands of a Slippery Girl?

TENDER IS THE SIBELLA

ONE DARK AND STORMLESS night, shortly after Myron pulled the plug on the whole Fontana enterprise, I forced myself to read the entirety of Junior's book. It was my self-inflicted act of penitence. I am no guilt-ridden Roman Catholic, or any other sort of Roman Catholic, but contrition seemed to be consistent with the somber mood around the office and, besides, my slow passive play V's ah V J. R. had gone on long enough. Make a decision, Myron always said. And move on.

Easier said than done, lentil reader.

Birds build—but not I build. Time's eunuch, and not breed one work that wakes. Mine, O thou lord of life, send my roots rain.

Some couples are united by children, some by profession, some even by pets. Junior and I were united by poems, especially the poems of Gerard Manley Hopkins. Kelly, he was a Jesuit priest—Hopkins, not Junior—who insisted that all his poems be incinerated when he died. His executor disobeyed, thank, umm, God. But going back to Junior, he really loved Hopkins and I loved to hear him read aloud those spine-tingling poems, not that we were religious or anything, unless you think poetry is religious, and it might be. But now comes a tough part.

Here's what I discovered, fuck. Superfuck. Junior's book was not half as bad as I had counted on. At the same time, there was something strange about it, something transcendently or maybe eerily different I couldn't put my finger on. It seemed to be written by a Junior as viewed in a cracked mirror. In the moment

I couldn't explain how I came to this conclusion or what it meant. After all, Junior's most authentic self was in and of itself kind of a performance, so this could have been *exactly* his book.

Then again, maybe there was a much simpler, technical explanation. Maybe it was a matter of a poet who was striving to be a novelist, with predictably mixed psychological results. Horses of a different color, poets and novelists. It's a pretty rare poet, after all, who can do ordinary prose stuff, like convincingly getting a character into or out of a room or a scrape or a party or a marriage and not do it with plotless nonaplomb.

I struggled and struggled and stared and stared at the last page of the book until I fell asleep last night, but when I woke up in the morning I was relieved and saddened to find that I had come to a decision. One thing Myron always stressed: You're going to make mistakes, that's what the business is all about. Make sure you make the right mistakes. The great Yogi Berra first said that, and that philosopher ought to know. When I got into the office, I made the right mistake, I hoped, and I wrote Junior.

***

To: _____
From: sibella@hardrain.com
Subject: Your fiction

_____:

My editor in chief and I have had the chance to consider your new novel. It is quite a piece of work. The sentences are almost universally incredible. You write fiction like somebody who invented writing fiction, reminiscent of the way that Keats and Hopkins wrote their poems, as if they practically reinvented the language. I took abundant interest in reading it. You are a special kind of writer.

And a special kind of asshole. But I have to admit to myself, if not to you, that you can write. And why is there such a high percentage of fine writers who are jerks? It doesn't seem fair.

It is with great regret, therefore, that I write to inform you that Hard Rain Publishing is reluctantly going to take a pass. I am sure this treat will be picked up by some big house chosen by your crackerjack agent and you will enjoy yet another literary triumph as you march on inevitably to literary renown and more and bigger prizes. But the truth is, we are a small house and we can take on a limited number of projects, and yours, unfortunately, is not the sort of book our people have enjoyed much success marketing.

Technically, they have never before been charged with marketing a book by my spineless douche of an ex, who, fuck me sideways, can really write.

I wish our verdict were otherwise. But thanks for thinking of us, and of me. Let's definitely meet at Maialino around Christmas.

When the ducks depart Holden Caulfield's Central Park and where I buried my heart one winter day when you broke up with me in the vicinity of the carousel, staging by you, which I will forevermore object to on metaphorical if not metaphysical grounds. I mean seriously, Junior? Right out of Catcher in the Fucked-Up Rye?

Sincerely
and regretfully
yours,
Sibella

✳ ✳ ✳

As soon as my email blasted off into cyberspace, I realized where I had gone wrong in my email and in possibly my life. My bitterness clouded judgment. The rejection was more boiler-plate than it should have been, and when editors—or junior editors—take such cover, it shows that they haven't come to terms with their own feelings about a book. Perhaps it was better than they had the capacity to understand, and as a result they resort to stock language. Had Junior fooled me again? Or had he fooled himself? I was done with him, and after he got my email, he was going to be done with me forever. But then tell me why I felt miserable.

Then something else also dawned on me, as it had recently dawned on Myron. Even if we'd wanted to publish the thing, Hard Rain couldn't afford to now.

***

"Sibella, sit down, would you? I got an email from your ex's agent—I didn't forward you. She was apoplectic. She said her author was crestfallen and furious, but she assured me she was going to sell his fucking book and that I, Myron Beam, was an idiot to take a pass—"

"His book wasn't bad, and maybe better than that."

"Not high praise. And who cares about his agent? I trust your judgment, that's why I let you make the final call. I knew you wouldn't let your feelings about an author, one way or the other, get in the way of your decision-making."

He had never granted me such determinative sway ever before. Things were moving faster by the day with my job, and he seemed to consistently remember I was not an intern.

"I hope I didn't fuck this up."

"Look, I didn't call you in for that. Life goes on. Hard Rain goes on, for the time being. Don't worry, I can raise the money to keep us going. Wouldn't want to take any chances and disappoint that gypsy, would I? Sibella, another subject. A goofy one. Where did Kelly come up with the crackbrain idea that I'm sleeping with you—or anybody?"

"That girl is awkweird and she must be off her meds, that's where. Was she chewing gum? People who have a gum-chewing jones need to stay on their OCD drugs."

"She told me that you told her you were my mistress. Why would you do that?"

"I never said anything like that. For one thing, I would never use the word *mistress*. Too nineteenth century or Revolutionary Inroads."

"That's one of the problems with her accusation."

"I know. Off her meds."

"I think I kept Kelly around too long."

"Tell her you and I are not an item and she can stay at the company as long as she stops chewing gum."

"She chews gum?"

The things he missed, amazing, huh?

"It's like fucking crack to her."

"We can stop talking about Kelly. She is going to be immaterial."

That sounded ominous. True, I never wanted that masticater around, and call me sentimental, but I hoped she wasn't going to lose her job after being dumb enough to take me on. But he had a lot more on his mind today.

"Make sure this all gets in the book. You've got a lot to work with, after Fontana and everything. Speaking of which, how's it going, *our* book?"

Ah, *that* book, the Magnum Dopus. I knew how it was going. I knew where it was going, too. *Our* book was going nofuckingwhere. I had pretty much decided, as I had initially feared, I wasn't up to the task. I had too much or not enough insight to go on, and maybe it was both. Not that I didn't try, I did. I would pstare for hours and hours at the computer monitor and pspew out a pseudo-psentence and then erase it and the unforgiving pscreen would once more go blank blank blank. My psole companion, the cursor, would wink and wink and wink, like a timid pstuttery pstalker pslash flasher on the psubway. I didn't then, and pstill don't, believe in the existence of writer's block, which is nothing but a lame fucking excuse for not meeting a deadline, so that wasn't it. Was it psimply a case of Myron Block? Someday I had to tell him I was not going to write his book, or our book, but not today.

"Going great," I said.

"Ever want to show me a rough draft?"

"Sure, when the time's right." And when by some miracle somebody else composes a rough draft of *our* book.

"Does the protagonist get married in the end?"

"That *would* be some kind of twist."

There I was about to hit the metaphysical CTR-ALT-DEL. There was no way for me to anticipate that the next few minutes provided some real-life, all-too-believable turns. I have no idea if he planned it this way, but Myron was about to give me what I needed to get going on *our* book, and all I needed to get going with—using a word I don't use lightly—a vengeance.

✳✳✳

"WHY IN THE WORLD would somebody become a book publisher?"
said Myron.

This sounded like a perfectly good rhetorical question, and it
would have been had it been ventured by anybody other than Myron
Beam. But as I keep saying, Myron never asked a rhetorical question.
What kind of person never asks a rhetorical question, which is right
there a rhetorical question? I find that bizarre. *What is the meaning
of life? Who knows?* That sort of thing. And see? His big existential
question wasn't an example, however. Life itself may be nothing
but a series of rhetorical questions, but he wanted me to *answer* the
question, as if there were one and I was the possessor of the truth.

I did my best and I non-uptalked a while, raising all the
predictable points. Somebody becomes a publisher to make a
contribution to culture. To change lives. To help human beings
become better human beings, one of the most powerful and strange
aspects about stories. To bring out books that teach us how to read
ourselves. To usher something beautiful into the world. Blah blah
blah. Nothing stuck, and I couldn't blame him when he said:

"I don't think you have it yet, but you're getting closer."

"To make money?" I sent up my white flag.

"Well, that's not irrelevant, because if you can't turn a buck
today, you can't publish tomorrow. But there are a lot easier ways
to make money. Like opening a pizza parlor, because, unlike with
books, everybody loves pizza."

"You know, Myron, if I were a publisher, I would publish
books I love and take my chances in the marketplace."

"You make me weep, Sibella. I know I cannot figure out the
why of me, the why of Hard Rain, but I know Calypso's not the
key, and probably not Fig or Pork or any of the Fontanas. And if
you did what you said you would do, you'd be broke after your
first big book triumph, because success would go to your head,
and you'd take bigger and bigger chances and…"

I knew the litany of issues, I had been working for Myron long
enough to have memorized them.

"I would go broke, possibly, but I'd rather go broke than get
rich producing work I wasn't proud of."

Yes, I was still twenty-five, so there.

"Speaking of which, I have been giving a lot of thought to *Adventures of Calypso O'Kelly*. You are right. It's shit, it's unsalvageable. We can sell the book because Hard Rain can sell anything, but fuck it, I don't think I can stomach being around her."

"This makes me proud of you, Myron."

"God, to be twenty-six again."

"I am twenty-five."

"Since when?"

"Since three years after I was twenty-two, which is when you took me on as a junior editor, for which I thank you getting me out of New York and teaching me the business."

"You're twenty-five, you say."

"For a little while longer, till I am twenty-six."

"I don't think there are very many if any twenty-five-year-old editors in chief around."

"I suppose that's true."

"Well, you could be the first, because now that's what you are."

"What are you talking about? We have an editor in chief."

Well, we did once have an editor in chief, and I did once have a promising new boyfriend I had fallen for, too, but everything had changed, or so I was about to discover.

YGB had quit.

He called up Myron late last night at home and told him he had taken a job in New York. He thanked Myron for the opportunity and for all he had learned. And a minute later Myron got a call from Kelly. She also resigned, and she also took a job in New York at the same house as YGB.

When he noticed how I was taking this news (how the fuck do you imagine I was taking this news?), he said, "Seems like you and he haven't talked much lately."

Big jump on the part of the big cheese. "A little break, I thought we were taking, nothing serious, I assumed."

"I'm sorry, baby, I have to be the one to tell you one other thing. I don't have any question he and Kelly are, well, you know…"

It all fucking clicked. Kelly had been relatively docile the last few days, barely acknowledging me, and once or twice I caught her jaws in a rare state of immobility. And sensitive me had failed to detect her cloud-cover pheromones from probably her having spent the last two nights with YGB. Now I grasped what was behind her wild accusation. You could have thwacked me with the Collected Works of Anthony Fucking Trollope, all fifty or hundred volumes after hearing about that Kelly trollop, and they would have bounced harmlessly off benumbed me. It isn't often that I am speechless. Though it has been the case I have been boyfriendless for extended periods of forever, and that was about to be my condition all over again. I was a loser. I told Myron as much. He disputed the point, being that he was Myron and needed his new editor in chief not to be a loser.

After a few silent moments, I couldn't help it, I burst into tears. It was humiliating to snivel like that, but that is the TMI of the matter.

"Take a couple days off, get your heart and head together."

I looked over in the direction of YGB's office and saw that his desk was cleared. When did he do that and how did I miss the obvious? I miss the obvious a lot, you are saying to yourself, and you're right. I spend too much time thinking about myself, as if I were the center of the fucking universe. I will never put up a shingle that advertised I was a sibyl. But you have to admit, he was a fast worker, and you didn't see that coming any more than I did. I could learn from him. My exes were all good teachers, if not always in ways I would have preferred.

"And when you're ready you can take over his office."

It took a while before I could find my voice.

"It will be good to lose my milk crates home base, yet honestly, I kind of liked them." How come I never had a handkerchief? My mother always told me I should have one in my purse. Good idea, but I never carried a purse, so there was no safe haven there. I rubbed my eyes with my shirt sleeve.

"You can start whenever you want, editor in chief."

"How about this instant?" I was merely acting tough, but as I learned with hoops when playing against superior talent, sometimes acting tough can make you tough for real.

"You sure?"

"What fuck the fuck."

"Whatever you say, Sibella. Caitlin's coming in, she thinks to sign her contract."

"Perfect," I said and cried all over Myron's shirt some more. He didn't seem to mind half as much as I did. He was inured to all the weeping that happened around him.

We heard the office door open and close.

I wish either my father or my mother, or indeed both of them, as they were in duty both equally bound to it, had minded what they were about when they begat me...I am verily persuaded that I should have made a quite different figure in the world, from that, in which the reader is likely to see me.

✳✳✳

THE CAITLIN ALWAYS RINGS twice. But not this time. She just walked in and started swinging for the offenses.

"Where's my contract? I don't spy a check nearby. I've been patient for weeks and weeks. And your public image is smeared, and I hope you aren't trying to pull another fast one because your name is going to be dragged through the mud all over again."

"Oh, they're both right here, check and contract." Myron showed them both to her. "See?" But first, there was one thing Myron wanted to know.

"Only one thing?"

He didn't take the masterfulbaition.

"The wallet," he said. "This time tell me the truth about my wallet pilfered in Venice, it's not making sense to me."

"Yes, the famous wallet that launched a thousand licensing agreements. I don't know why I should give you any satisfaction. Then again, we're in business together now, what the hell. The plot's a little convoluted, but I'll tell you. It's nice to have one's work admired.

"You see, my fabulously rich Venetian lover and I were strolling in the rain that night—like you. We saw the whole incident unfold before our very eyes. We couldn't believe how stupid you were.

"'Did you see that?' 'What?' 'Gli Americani in Italia, lambs to the slaughter.' His English was impeccable. His principles, anything but. He reminds me of Cable. He almost reminds me of you, Myron, but those are subjects for another time and place. By the way, never put your wallet in your inside jacket pocket and, if you do, never lean down before a gypsy, Myron, never. It was my lover who witnessed her lifting your wallet. She was quite deft, and being a native he knew the scam better than I. For somebody like him, Venice was one gigantic, floating crime scene. Isn't that sweet? He also regarded Venice as one enormous living art installation. You should have seen his personal gallery, a mini Peggy Guggenheim. He had so much money, he barely knew what to do with it except for splurging on art and on younger lovers, like me, whom he flew around the world for his personal use. Anyway, after your pocket was picked, you wandered off, blithely ignorant and probably feeling good about yourself for having given the poor gypsy lady the Euro. We could tell you were going to be lost right away, heading off in precisely the wrong direction, which would not lead to the hotel. In that regard, you were blameless. Venice is nothing but a network of byways that go off everywhere but where you wish to go.

"We knew you and your wife were guests in the hotel. You never noticed us, of course. We approached the hag who had stolen your wallet and confronted her. He told her he would give her a hundred Euros if she gave us your wallet. He threatened her with getting thrown into jail. She counted the money you had inside the fold and said make it two hundred.

"Then he told me he had an idea. 'Let's play a little game with the American tourist. Let's give him a little shock therapy. It can be our little science experiment slash human art installation.' That was when he inserted five thousand Euros—God, he was phenomenally rich—into your wallet and we hurried back to the hotel before you could get there. He gave the concierge another hundred to swear him to secrecy."

"And you waited ten years to reach out to me with this manuscript and make your play?"

"Well, I did reach out to your wife not long after Venice. And she leaked to me, unwittingly, of course, information about you and your new business. Which proved my lover right. He created a monster with his living art installation."

Myron most certainly had not forgotten that part. "That's a long game to play, ten years."

"Ten years, they go by in a flash, don't they? Let's say it was all in the service of art. Ars longa, somebody once said."

I couldn't let her get away with that. "Fraud longa, too."

The slow play stuck in Myron's craw. "Ten years, really?"

"Well, I am a deliberate writer."

"Of nine hundred fucking pages," I said.

"Look, Myron, your wife wanted me to play you sooner, but she and I drifted apart, and I got involved in other, well, projects—and lovers. How's she doing? Never mind, I don't care. And then Cable and I reconnected a couple of years ago."

I could not resist: "On weasels dot com?"

"Sibella, grow up, why don't you? Listen. When Cable and I reunited, I took up the manuscript again. And then Figgy, his dad, and I got to talking about his 'big-time' publisher." Yes, the fucking air quotes. "Fig told me all about you, told me how easy it was for him to write books that you bought from him, and I got inspired, though I later found out he was lying through his teeth. He would have cheered me on, had he lived."

"Pack of wolves," I said.

"There was no supernatural force behind me? That Venetian night was an omen of nothing?"

"I wouldn't say that. Life is strange, and full of unreadable omens."

"And unreadable books," I said, "like yours."

"But the bottom line is," Myron said, "I have been nothing but lucky, no magic involved?"

"I don't know much about publishing, but I'd say anybody who thinks he's got books figured out is deluding himself. You don't need brains, you don't need business models."

"I knew I was a natural."

"All you have to be is lucky to make it in the business. That's why I'd call your success the most magical thing in the world, Myron."

"Thank you, Caitlin, that's what I needed."

And then he brought up to his eye level the contract and the check and held them there for an excruciating moment.

"No," she whispered, previsioning accurately.

He tore them both up. Satisfying music to my new editor in chief ears. So satisfying that I didn't in the moment connect this deed to the financial reality: Myron was tapped out, at least for now. He didn't have the money to pay her even if he had wanted.

She was shaken, and it took her a few seconds. "Should have listened. Cable predicted you would fuck me over."

"We gave your book the consideration it richly merited, but Hard Rain is not going to publish you, Caitlin. We're not the right house for this book, or for you, or for any member of your extended future family. One of the axioms in the industry is you don't publish books, you publish authors. And you? You're not right for us." He didn't bother to add that his vanishing liquidity was a contributing factor for his decision, and I didn't, either.

"I wonder how long it will take Cable to sue your ass for breaking an oral contract."

"I never agreed to any deal, did I, Sibella? Good luck in court, Caitlin." Unless she had taped our conversation before, that was the badda bing end of it. I have to admit that I am a little bit surprised how remarkably easy it proved to be to deny the truth, the truth that he had made that precise deal in the restaurant that day. I bookmarked this lying moment—to wipe off my mental hard drive later. The book biz is tricky. By which I mean the book biz is cutthroat and unconscionable, but in an honorable way.

"Sibella, are you enjoying yourself?"

"Living the dream, Caitlin, living the dream. Now *you* are a sibyl?"

"And let me predict another thing: you will regret you ever met me."

"I already regret it," I said.

Myron said to her, "Not that you planned to be, but you have been a big help."

"Don't mention it. And I mean it, don't mention it ever again to me. You have no idea what you have accomplished by betraying me."

"What fuck the fuck. Who betrayed whom again?" I said.

"I have to get to work. It would have been nice to pocket your six-hundred grand, but I'm a pragmatist. If by some chance you escape a lawsuit for breach of contract, there's always a next time and a new book."

The Writer's Pledge of Self-Allegiance: there's always a next time when it will all work out.

"Where you working, Caitlin?" Not that I cared.

"None of your damned business, sweetheart."

***

"Ever been to Venice, Sibella?"

I guessed Muscle Beach didn't count.

"It didn't work out well for me in Venice last time, but we should go on vacation, you and me, what do you say? We could use a break, while my credit cards still work."

I would have said that it sounded to me like it sounded to you: *What fuck the fuck?* He didn't intend the invitation to mean, you know, romance and so on, I can assure you, or I can pretty much almost assure you if I know anything about men but since I don't I had better hold my fire. Because I didn't care if Venice was floating on a torrid lagoon of romance, Myron the Doge's gondola wasn't able to float, as you know, and my armada was nada. For him, it had been a tough morning, a tough few weeks. That probably explained his proposal.

Finesse is not a commodity I stockpile. "I'll be sure to avoid gypsies and Euro trash if I do ever go."

"You know what today is, Sibella?"

Of course, I did. It was Friday and I was looking forward to spending the weekend feeling sorry for myself and eating Grape Nuts for breakfast and dinner.

"It's my birthday. Number sixty-two."

"Fuck, we need to celebrate."

He didn't think so, and it was at this point a funny look crossed his face and he said, "All of a sudden I'm not feeling so good."

"Was it something I said? Don't go passing out again. Last time that caused more trouble than we could deal with."

"I am going home to lie down."

I asked him to tell me precisely what he was feeling. He said he was light-headed, he said his chest felt like it was in a vise, he said his arm was pounding. His eyes looked glazed and then he couldn't say another word, but his mouth was moving.

I called 911.

***

IN SOMETHING LIKE TEN minutes the Fire Department showed up.

If I get an extra life, I am going to be a fire fighter.

You chew aspirin because it works faster. Seconds count when it comes to possible blockages to your heart. Amazing, how much knowledge you can acquire when your boss is lying flat on a gurney.

I was also thinking this was shaping up to be a strange birthday for Myron Beam. I was hoping and hoping it wouldn't be his last. I was impressed by the Fire Department. They were intensely engaged in all manner of activity, hooking up electrodes, taking his blood pressure. I was holding Myron's hand. I had never held his hand before.

It was delicate and soft. A little girl's hand, a writer's hand.

They asked him what hospital.

"The hospital in Venice."

"It is beautiful in Southern California."

"No, the Venice in Italy."

"Great, I've never been. But maybe we go somewhere we can drive our rig instead."

THE NAKED AND THE SIBELLA

BEHIND THE DRAWN ER curtain he was attended to by what appeared to be a score of supremely professional and ethereally kind men and women, a diversity of age and race and ethnicity, a snapshot of both California and New York, which qualified as my two homes. More EKG's, a chest X-ray, two more nitroglycerin tabs, blood draws. The oxygen refreshed. The monitors beeped and chuffed, buzzed and hummed.

"What day is it?"

"Who is the president?"

"What is your name?"

"Where do you live?"

"What is the year?"

"What is your name?"

"What is the year?"

***

EVENTUALLY, TIME DRIFTED AND slowed and suddenly we no longer appeared to be in crisis mode, at least as far as I could tell, but why should you trust me? Myron appeared to have stabilized, for now. The doctor, baby-faced enough to have once been a fellow student of mine, gently but firmly broke the news. (Sibelladvisory: I don't think he was an intern.) The doc said Myron's ticket had been punched for the night. He was going to be admitted, once he got out of the ER. *If* he ever got out of the ER, he intimated, semi-ominously. The first furious rounds of blood test results and EKGs were encouraging, but we had some ways to go. Myron balked at the prospect of a hospital stay. "It's my birthday." He lied and said he had dinner reservations. He didn't ever need a reservation at Carmine's. The attending made a cameo and glanced at Myron's hospital wristband identification to verify. "It *is* your birthday." He returned two minutes later bearing a chocolate cupcake with swirled blue icing, a tongue depressor doing duty as a candle. "Happy Birthday." Nice, no?

Go on, Sibella.

On birthdays, Myron told me, he usually tried to write a poem. Would he ever stop surprising me? His attempts invariably led to meaning-of-life dime store philosophy, he said, which is the death knell of poetry. He long ago resigned himself. Never would he compose his version of Dylan Thomas's great "Poem in October": "It was my thirtieth year to heaven..."

Okay, you got me. I've been temporarily laying off the collusions for a while, for obvious reasons.

In case it isn't too late to fill you in, I can suggest in what strange regard I must have held Myron when I say that I would never have imagined him to have a birthday. Yes, of course, he had to have been born and it must have taken place on a certain memorialized day. But it never crossed my mind that he was the kind of person who had a *birthday* or that anybody including him would ever note the occasion. Birthday cakes, songs, parties at the zoo when he turned ten, baseball bats and piñatas, trying-too-hard cards (*Happy Birthday, Mister President*...), skinny black tie presents.

The fact is that at Hard Rain we never acknowledged the day, and accountability for that oversight must be borne, at least partly, by Myron himself. No, I didn't conceive that he popped out of an egg, but I also never associated him with the conventional markers of life that make event planners and card companies wealthy. All to say, a little late to Myron's birthday party was I. Because here he was experiencing the possibility of the ultimate conventional marker of life: its termination. Feel free to wonder if I myself popped out of an egg and I can see why you might be inclined. FYI, my mother has the research results to argue to the contrary.

Thanks, Mom, and I owe you a call. And who taught you how
to text? I wish you were here with me right now.

Stop, Sibella, stop. If there are any moments you should stay in,
all you Deepak Chopra Kale-Munching Types out there meditating,
those moments would definitely include being in the ER alongside
your hospital-gowned boss with a PICC line in his arm.

Within a few hours the birthday boy's chest pressure had
alleviated. Calm settled over the scene, the wait for diagnostic
resolution commenced. Had there been in fact a cardiac event
and was Myron at risk? They didn't know yet. The two of us were
inside this darkened, curtained-off space and I felt the hours pass
slowly by, like floats on the never-ending Macy's Thanksgiving
Day Parade. He dozed off and woke up and then dozed off again,
and he surely wasn't up to a conversation. Having nothing else
to do, I struggled to resolve mentally all the problems with Hard
Rain and Fig and, honestly, YGB. I got nowhere, and Myron was
adrift. But he was, as I said, stable. Silenced and stabled. Being
nothing but a reluctant tourist to such a rarefied alien domain,
I wondered what the weather and the food were like and if they
all dressed like Murmechka.

A gauzy apparition-size wonderful nurse appeared. Petals on
a wet black bough. Things had now calmed down enough for a
collusion or two. I don't believe I hallucinated her and I wished
I understood the appeal of haiku. But you sit in an ER for a long
time and see what kind of inane connections you make. In four
hours, this nurse said they would draw more blood. They were on
the trail of an enzyme called troponin. It is a reliable indicator of a
cardiac event, and they needed a retest. She looked optimistic. You
might assume, as I did, that optimism is in short supply in an ER,
but you would be wrong, as I was. The nurse once had an Italian
boyfriend, she confided, apropos of absolutely nothing, but if you
hang around an ER long enough you might think everything is
apropos of everything else. She said every woman needed at least
one Italian bad boy boyfriend. I couldn't validate that contention,
though Caitlin certainly might, and yet the idea sounded oddly
attractive today. I cannot recreate the context, but she threw out

some idiomatic Italian expressions, including "Ti voglio bene," the charmingly indirect Italian way of saying "I love you."

Thanks, Google. Sometimes you rock.

You know how when somebody is starting to learn a foreign language, they can't help showing off and saying stuff like "the word for *pie* in Latvian is the same as the word for *flounder*," yuck yuck, and they sign off emails in chummy unspeakable Croat. Well, this nurse was full of language lessons herself, but it was more than okay here in the ER. In case you find this information handy, say if you're sleeping with somebody—why must I punish myself by bringing this up?—you say, "Ti amo," but "Ti voglio bene" you can say to a good friend or family member. She wasn't addressing me or Myron, but considering the day and the life Myron and I were having and the kind of people we were no longer sleeping with, it was consoling and encouraging to hear the love sentiment expressed by a human being in our midst.

Unless I had completely lost track, I was in the middle of the longest stretch of waking life—thirty-six hours—that I could recall when I hadn't been occupied by reading a manuscript or a book. Or Proust.

When Myron fell back to sleep, I couldn't help but attend to the disembodied voices bouncing off the ward's walls. The abject moaning, as of a suffering animal, from a far-off corner. The demented but eloquent articulations of an elderly woman one bed over. The rich baritone of docs examining one patient after another.

"Where did you get these bruises?"

"How many times did you fall?"

"Do you remember if you ate today?"

"Take a deep breath."

"Does this hurt?"

"How about this?"

Myron stirred and, as if he had awakened after a long journey on a plane, which could have been similar to his experience, he might have had a funny taste in his mouth. I know I did. He had a few things he wanted to say: "As lightning bolts go, this one I should have seen coming. Where else would I wish to be on my birthday if not here? It is good to be reminded, as if I needed to be, how brief life is, how tenuous the hold we have on our loved ones. The makings of a poem? No. At the same time, this dime store philosophy seems anything but."

I had never heard Myron weigh in like that or say something like "loved one." The title of a pretty good novel by my favorite misanthrope, Sir E. Waugh, now that I think about it. Which made for an unfortunate connection insofar as that novel was about the funeral trade.

Once again, let us return to our regularly scheduled pogrom.

Hours later, after the troponin search party returned, Myron's doctor informed him the test results had all gone his way. "It's probably a tiny risk to be discharged, but let's not take it. You need to see the cardiologist in the morning, do a treadmill test. Happy birthday."

A few minutes later, guess who walked in wearing her blue scrubs?

Wrong. Not Ashlay, who has already made too many surprise appearances. Here is a little giveaway clue. There was *Dr. O'Kelly* stitched on her chest in the area where she would have had her *Muse* tattooed had she once been as drunk and stupid as me or I.

"Myron, how are you feeling?" said Caitlin or Calypso or Dr. O'Kelly.

"You really are an ER doc?" he said.

Who saw that coming? (You're lying, Kelly. I can tell when you're lying—the giveaway is your jaws are moving.)

"My shift started and why would you ever doubt me?"

I myself had six-hundred thousand plus reasons he could doubt her.

"Looks like you had a fake heart attack, but they'll see for sure tomorrow. And if it was a fake heart attack, it doesn't mean that the next time it won't be a real heart attack."

I had a question for the grifter. "This is what you call your bedside manner, or is it bedside manners? Because you're short and short on both."

"Will you ever be able to stop yourself from saying whatever crosses your mind?"

"Let me think. No. Fuck you."

Myron's turn. "That was some act you cultivated, with your book, your depraved rich boyfriend, the Cable connection. You went to a lot of trouble to publish a book, which means you're like a million other people. But you and the whole Fontana rat pack, all pretty good actors. How much of what you told me contains a grain of truth?"

"A grain? Everything I said had a *grain* of truth. And it was fun while it lasted, wasn't it? I had you in the palm of my hand for a minute, you have to admit."

"Speaking of admissions, do I have to spend the night?"

"That wasn't my call. But I'll be back later, before you're sent upstairs. Rest easy, Myron, you son of a bitch. You should have bought my book. But you're probably right, it sucks a little. As do lots of your books. I'm working on a new one, and I'll send it your way when it's done. But I am sorry about one thing. It was a mean trick, what we played on you in Venice. See, Sibella? I have a smidge of a conscience. And I have sworn off decadent rich Italian boyfriends forever."

Should I have introduced her to the nice nurse with her bad Italian boyfriend issues that she didn't regret? Pass.

"And don't you worry, Sibella, I'll take good care of him. I always knew you two would end up lovers." *Luvahs*.

She brought up another topic. "Meant to ask you before in your office. The beard, Myron? Since when?" His facial hair was flourishing and the itching reduced to a nonfactor.

"Since the very day we had lunch and you and I made history, or almost did. You like it?"

She shrugged so as to indicate not so much.

"Thanks," he said. "I'll keep it."

I had one other thing to bring up with her: "Been mulling. The whole Pork/Fig extravaganza—and Pork's multiple identities. You're a doctor. I suppose. Was that real, or was that another piece of Fontana bullshit?"

It was the minute before that I formulated in my mind the question, and without planning, I was asking it. I do that. How do

I know what I think until I say it? It turned out that Caitlin had one more surprise up her lab coat sleeve.

"Define real."

"You know, like a heart attack real. That real."

She laughed that chilly laugh of hers. "Oh, Sibella, you are such a sweet tall child. But finally, bravo, you figured it out. Took you long enough. Congratulations. Isn't Porphyry a great actor? Multiple personalities. Dissociative identity disorder. Seriously? Please. What a brilliant play. He had you both going, didn't he? That was a beautiful plan Cable came up with, I have to tip my hat. And about Porphyry, never underestimate a desperate man who feels he has one last chance to make it—even if he has to hang on his famous dead brother's coattails. And never overestimate an arrogant man, like Myron, who's had it his way for far too long. He trusts his judgment too easily. Soon as you both felt pity for miserable, cunning Porphyry, we had you by the balls. Too bad you canceled publication of the three books. They were pretty good in my opinion and they would have sold if you knew how to be a publisher again, if you ever went back to the good old days. Free advice: don't make any future excursions into Fontana Town."

"Fuck, you guys are good," I said. "Though not in that way. Don't you have to be on your way to first do no harm? Give my sympathies to all your lucky patients."

Getting an MD degree and an ER job didn't necessarily mean she had any brains any more than being a human meant she had a heart. I was glad when she took off. I was always glad when she departed any room or space I cohabited with her. Maybe she had squandered all that was left of her charisma somewhere in Fontanaville, which like Las Vegas would siphon it off like a bucket of silver dollars before a slot machine.

"Of course," said Myron to me once she was gone, "she could be lying again."

"There's always a chance with her, you're right."

"Well, in any case, this was some kind of birthday," he said. "How about let's not do this again next year, shall we?"

I told him that was a deal I could live with.

"Me too. But I am glad you were here, and glad you'll be at Hard Rain. It would not be the same without you."

I heard him and his plain-spoken words in a new way. What do they say in Italian? Right. *Ti voglio bene.* I was also convinced that tonight I was not going to allow anybody to die. Hell of a plan, huh? Having never received a job description of the junior editor job I did, I never bothered to ask for a job description of the editor in chief. Anybody would assume that one key bullet point would have to be: Keep the publisher alive and fucking kicking.

Like the Leopard says, "While there's death, there's hope."

A PASSAGE TO SIBELLIA

WEEKS PASSED AND I finally signed up at the Y and crossed that off my bucket list. As for buckets, I had missed hoops. I love the smell of a locker room: the foot sprays, the talcum, the menthologized ointments, the damp towels, the bittersweetness of adhesive wraps around ankles and wrists. I love even more the echoes bouncing off the gym rafters. The screech that your sneaks make when you make your cut and the Sleepy Hollow sound of the dribbled basketball and the sweet rippling of the net when a shot from distance goes in, yessssssssssss, *swish*. I always felt at home at a gym and on the basketball court.

I was in pretty good shape in general, still had my wind, could run up and down the court, but it would take a while for me to get back into basketball shape. Nevertheless, it was easy for me to get into a coed five-on-five pickup game, that night after work being no exception, and there's a word you don't hear much anymore: coed. Can't say I miss it. I never knew the names of my improm two or four teammates at the Y, and they didn't know mine, and usually players don't introduce themselves. Considering how much back- and butt-slapping and high-fiving takes place during a game, anonymity always struck me an adorable affectation.

During warm-ups for the we-got-next game, I intuited that most of them had played some kind of organized ball, college or at least high school, and that would mean they were acquainted with the elements of balling: screens, pick and rolls, clear-outs, box-outs, pass and cut aways, the man/ball/man/ball defensive mind-set. We shot free throws for opening possession, and my team lost, so we were going to begin on defense, my specialty. First team to twenty-one wins, three-pointers count.

The eight guys ranged in age from thirty-ish to fifty-ish. There's always a duffer suffering from male-pattern baldness at the Y with a big black brace on his knee and a white headband and he manages to talk himself into a five-on-five, and this game was no exception. There were two females, by whom I mean me and a woman in her late twenties who was a lot shorter than I. Unless I was wrong, and these days there was a solid chance I was, she was a ringer, and she was a gunner, and she was going to give me trouble, because the girls were going to guard each other, and my game was more inside and hers outside. My plan took shape: she might be able to shoot better outside the key, but I could capitalize on my height and post her up and score from in close. Points under the basket are precious. They appear effortless to the uninitiated, but they are anything but.

Immediately before inbounding arrived the touchy moment of negotiation. Who goes skin, who goes shirts? Touchy, that is, in the context of female participation. I've seen it happen that females keep on their shirts if they find themselves on the skins team, and everybody compensates.

My "man," the other girl, took charge. She was not of that phony, gentlemanly school of thought. "We'll run skins," she called out, as she without hesitation whipped off her white T-shirt. I was glad she had not learned any lessons from Ashlay Commingle, because she revealed her white sports bra and stomach-crunched muscles, and her skins teammates complied and took off their shirts. Good, I thought, I wouldn't have to feel self-conscious about my ink concealed under the navy blue T-shirt and, fuck, I needed to do something about that someday.

Skins brought the ball up past half-court, and the designated ball handler, shortest guy on the court, as usual, executed a nasty crossover dribble and blew past his ankles-broken defender and took the ball right to the rack and scored. Okay, our opponent might be pretty good.

But we weren't bad ourselves. And we had a not-quite-secret weapon: the fifty-year-old. The fifty-year-old gym rats who frequent the Ys of the world are the only ones who get to have names on the pickup court, but their names are all the same: Old Man. Old Man is always on the court for one reason, and I don't mean to relive his glory days. He doesn't rebound, he doesn't defend, he doesn't pass. Bank on this: Old Man can fucking shoot the rock. Without hesitation, our Old Man demanded the ball, then he stepped beyond the three-point line and more quickly than I might have expected he got off what was essentially an old-school set shot. Nothing but net, *swish*.

Game fucking on, and bring it, Old Man and Shirts. My adrenaline freely flowed. It was exhilarating to be sweating and running and crashing against other players and nobody was being a pussy calling ticky-tack fouls and I was glad to be doing anything other than thinking about books so don't bring this subject up for a few minutes, we were balling. Playing hoops and publishing books may have things in common, but like I say, not now, give a girl a break.

Back and forth, in and out, side to side, went the contest, and it was close. The game provided the most purely physical enjoyment I had had in a long time—and there's another thing not to remind me of, the other kind of physical enjoyment I had not had for a while. The girl I was guarding had scored a few baskets on me, but I had more rebounds than she did, so she and I were basically even, canceling each other out. I respected her game. Shirts needed to spring open Old Man a few more times, and we would high-five each other after victory and take on the guys, all of them metrosexually unshaven, waiting we-got-next.

At a crucial instant, score tied 18–18, I set a pick and the opposing player stuck his hand out to ward me off. He grabbed my breast in the process. This happens, my boobs are not destined to appear in the *Sports Illustrated Swimsuit* issue, and it's fucking basketball, which is a high-contact sport. But maybe he wasn't used to playing against girls, because he blubbered a dim-witted apology. I lost all respect for him.

What fuck the fuck. It's basketball, it's not like you groped me, and I'll survive, and you watch your nuts, buddy. We played on. And taking advantage of his distraction, I pivoted into the lane and got a pass close to the basket, the perfect lead for me, two feet away from the hoop, which is where I made my living in college, and I went up, as I had done a hundred thousand times in my life, expecting to make an uncontested two.

My opponent had other ideas. She met me at the top of what I once liked to think of as my leap, which shocked me, and she blocked the shot. She didn't swat the ball out of bounds, she sort of tipped it, volleyball style, gently, and the ball came back down to the floor and then bounced back into my hands after I landed. Given a second chance with the ball, I went up again with renewed commitment.

She fucking blocked it again. Again, softly tipping it, and I grabbed the ball on the bounce and went up, this time pissed off.

Same result.

Three shots in a row from under the basket, three blocks. I don't think I had been blocked a total of three times during all of high school and college combined, and here it happened in one series at the Y.

I went up again. With the predictable consequence. Just so you know, the fourth time is also not a fucking charm. And she was toying with me, too, not swatting the ball out of bounds, but at the same time not taunting me. She was determined to block my shot again, and she knew that she could. Everybody had stopped playing and watched, and stood around, mesmerized by the girlo-a-girlo game-inside-the-game. Fact is, I had never witnessed serial rejection like that with the exception of my romantic life. My teammates must have realized the mood on the court had turned too strange to continue and we needed a break and somebody called time out and everybody went to their water bottles.

"Hate to break it, but you're not going to score the ball on me on the inside, girlfriend," she said to me, as if this were merely a statement of fact, and not an in-your-face insult.

"See, that's an expression that irritates the fuck out of me. *Score the ball?* The hair-gelled and the Michael-Jordan-bald announcers on TV say this all game long. What else would you use to score if not the basketball?"

She took this as an opportunity to look up and make an observation to the gym rafters. "Spence girls are nerds." But her apparent denunciation of me and my alma mater was uttered with a jokiness and with a sweetness that rivaled her jump shot. Trash talk is au courant in the pros and often in college, but at the Y? Frowned upon. Bad form. If you want to hear real smack, though, come to an editorial meeting. Brutal. But I'm trying not to think about the business for a minute.

Somebody please explain to me why I got up on my high horse and defended the good name of my K-12 alma mater where I had spent ten years getting through twelve grades until I received my diploma. Because the truth is Spence was a good school, and it was good for me, not that I knew as much when I attended. How many important experiences feel like that and are understood in retrospect and don't remind me.

"How would you know we're all nerds?" Or that I went to Spence in the first place? And another, bigger question to take up with somebody other than her: Do we ever graduate for real from high school? "Sibella's no fucking nerd."

Two problems with that last assertion of mine. One, I *was* a fucking nerd, and two, Sibella spoke of herself in the third person. This tit-a-tit was not going to end well.

"Packer Collegiate, that's how. I watched you play when you were an eighth-grader and I had graduated, and you were talented, but with predictable non-moves in the lane, which is still true. To this day, you never learned to use your left hand, or do a basic head fake, and you still have your white-girl Spence hops."

"We beat Packer like a drum."

"That's because, like I say, I graduated." She laughed.

You know what? I believed her.

"I like playing against you," she said. "You're a challenge."

She was being kind, but not patronizing. Packer punkette that she may have been, she was no punkette. And does everybody on the East Coast at some point end up in California for at least a while, as if the whole country is a box of puzzle pieces that you shake to the left to make everything inevitably slide westward?

The game finished soon after, and they won, and she and I hugged. A guy hug, more pat on the back than chest bump, and

I went downstairs and took a longer than necessary shower while I imagined she played the next game and the next one after that and her team ran all the other teams out of the gym. I wouldn't bet against her and you shouldn't, either.

She had said she recognized me. I had never seen her before in my life. At the same time, she reminded me of someone, or so I thought as I scoured the Sibella memory banks. And then it hit me. She reminded me not of someone but of something. She was no candidate for soul mate or even a date for coffee, don't get me wrong, but she reminded me what I used to have: friends. Where did they all go? Didn't I use to have them? Where oh where did I ever put them? I use to know where friendship happened. In my life.

I was having a bad night and I was feeling sorry for myself and for Myron and for Hard Rain, and I was standing under the shower head for too long and wasting water, which is not an environmentally responsible thing to do, but I couldn't budge. Sure, my job was eating up my days and nights and weekends. Moving to California didn't help in that department. But those factors didn't explain everything. My relationship with YGB I saw for what it had been, an empty fling, with a few pleasant high points, but essentially a nonevent. Of course, he never called me to break it off and say it was him not me, which I myself knew better than to ever believe. He didn't even bother to break up with me by text.

That hurt, I have to say. A guy who breaks up with you by telling his boss he quits—he was never going to be a keeper for anybody. And then the guy hooks up with a pretty gum-smacker.

In any case, I could use a friend. Not a virtual one, either. I was feeling sorrier for myself by the minute. All on account of some game? Man, if this kept up I was going to have to get a dog.

Whippets are beautiful dogs.

Stop, Sibella. You are going off the shallow end.

I mean it, whippets are very sweet, elegant, athletic. So we'd have nothing in common.

I would learn how to drive. Everybody in California knew how—or thought they did. Then again, their freeways are free-for-alls. Oh, and I would need to steal a car. And in San Francisco a place to park, which would cost more than the car itself. Objects in the rearview mirror, as all the cars inform you, are closer than they appear. Ain't that the truth? Life in the fast lane? Never happened, never gonna happen.

Life in the remainder bin for me, more like it.

If I were you, I'd skip to the next chapter, it's getting pretty maudlin.

As nobody ever once said with reference to me and my game: You cannot stop her, you can only hope to contain her.

Gratuitous advice from somebody who ought to know better: Don't play a pickup game when you are in a vulnerable mood and you didn't know you were in that mood, but whatever you do, don't get smoked by a Packer Collegiate girl.

Here I was twenty-six years old, being schooled at the Y during a casual pickup game that was not really casual, and schooled as much as I ever deserved to be. I may have discovered that I was washed up on the basketball court, and it didn't feel half as bad as I might have expected—which, paradoxically, made me feel worse, and I know that makes no sense. Here's something that might pass for making sense: It was time for Sibella to grow up. Fucking Caitlin could be right. There were more serious games left to play. If I hung up my sneaks I would miss the gym and the competition, but isn't life all about letting go? Life may be nothing but a series of losses.

I warned you to skip ahead.

Once when I was in college my dad came to a big game, and after we won he took me out to dinner, shrinkish dad and his Unshrinkable Sibella daughter savoring quality time. He asked if I had learned anything during the game. He was keen on questions like that. Despite his quirks, I love my pops. It had been a hard-fought game against a better team and we went into overtime, but we clawed out a victory, and I was spent and looking forward to getting some sleep that night for a change. I took his question seriously and then I told him I did feel satisfied. But I did not learn a single thing, I had to be honest. Saying as much, I sounded dumb, as if I should have learned a little bit, but he didn't think so.

"Isn't it funny," he said, "how we only learn when we lose?"

You can see coming what I had to say, but this time I meant it. "Say more, Dad."

THE INCREDIBLE LIGHTNESS
OF BEING SIBELLA

MONTHS LATER OCCURRED TWO major book developments I am professionally as well as unprofessionally obligated to report, one involving the Hard Rain publication of Ashlay Commingle's book and the other involving the un-Hard Rain publication of Junior's. The two books will in peculiar ways converge, as you'll see, on the sales charts as well as in my mind. Due to our house's supposedly temporary financial difficulties, Ashlay's book was excruciatingly delayed, such that it practically coincided with Junior's. His had been snapped up and rushed into print at a dizzying, land-speed-record-setting pace.

On other fronts, Myron had completed the cardiological testing, thanks for asking, including the echocardiogram. That is an advanced medical procedure that generates a fascinating and critical quantitative measuring stick called the ejection fraction (the percentage of blood leaving the heart after contraction). I confess I would have to take a hard look at any manuscript on the slush pile titled *The Ejection Fraction*, which sounds like it could be anything from a thriller to a AI love triangle to a book of poetry, which maybe we should just publish for once. Myron passed the tests with flying colors, but he had been summarily placed on notice: take better care of yourself. As a result, he was going on regular walks and watching his diet.

The Dream Calculus was released by YGB and Kelly's publishing house. Inevitable or what? A long while had passed since my Never

Going to Happen on My Watch in My House email and YGB's Xile on Lame Street, and the breakup didn't sting in the same way anymore, but if you believe that you should gin up a self-help book proposal and then immediately run it through the paper shredder and get a new life, which is some self-help advice I should instantly snag for myself.

Back to Junior. He always had this disconcerting effect on me. And you can tell I am stalling. This next part related to Junior's book upset me in about six different ways.

His book was YGB's much-publicized first acquisition, a six-figure deal with options for the next two novels and a commitment to publish his future books of poetry. One can imagine how much he relished taking a book Myron and I had passed on. His new house was going all-in on him. Kelly was assigned to be his editor, and those two worked closely together, the thought of which warmed my heart like a lava spill on the brothel-packed ancient town of Pompeii.

The critical response was unanimous and it was, fuck the fuck, adulatory. The work boomed and made a Krakatoa noise echoing across the whole book world. *Calculus* was greeted with a front-page rave in the *Book Review*. It shot up the bestseller charts. All the trades had given it starred reviews, and the bookstores had no trouble hand-selling the hand-fuck out of it. Life must have been sweet in Park Slope for him and his Smart Car-size wife. He was the newest darling of the literary set, and his picture appeared alongside her while attending the big book release champagne-and-caviar parties in New York, LA, and London. People were already speculating how the big prize nominations were all but inevitable. And a big box office movie star spectacularly optioned it, too.

Tyger! Tyger! burning bright in the forests of the night.

I was downcast, and I apologized again to Myron for taking a pass.

"You can't look back, Sibella. Every publishing house has regrets. Do you realize how many editors and publishers passed on classics? *Catcher in the Rye. One Hundred Years of Solitude. On the*

Road. *Lolita. The Name of the Rose.* And the list goes on and on and on. The important thing is we go on, and we do better next time."

"I fucked up."

"I can't tell you how many times I fucked up."

"You can't because you never fucking did fuck up like that."

"Give yourself a break, Sibella. If it's anybody's fault it was mine, giving you the final call on the book. I might have been sensitive to the fact that you and I were both reeling from the Fontana mess and the Calypso near-catastrophe, and neither of us were on our game."

"It was a better book than I acknowledged. You want me to step down as editor in chief, I'll do it. Somebody ought to fall on her sword around here."

"I didn't know you owned a sword, but as the employee manual stipulates, keep yours out of the office, Sibella. You hungry? I could use a little lunch at Avenue. I hear the kale burger is scrumptious."

I wasn't hungry, and the veggie burger enticed me not, but I also didn't feel like sitting at my desk pummeling myself. I was also unaware there was an employee manual, which I bet the editor in chief was supposed to be aware of.

"I'm going to get that fucking Chicken Diavolo," I said as we walked out, contemplating culinary revenge.

✳✳✳

THE NEXT PART OF this story shows that, while my judgment on Junior's book may have been foolish, in the end it turned out to have been the best ill-advised decision I had ever made. Yes, indeed, it was celebrated, and its charms and wonders I may have been too blinded by personal resentments to be able to depreciate. But powerful as Junior's book was, it wasn't *Junior's* book.

His college roommate went public with the proof. I recalled his roommie, Brewster. I always wondered how Junior and Brewster got along so well living together in the dorm, since they were temperamentally opposites. Brewster had, shall we say, a strangeness about him, and a very low affect. Asperger's, I would have guessed, or as they say these days *on the spectrum*, and when I discussed my observations with my dad, he had a hunch I was probably right. Naturally, Brewster's monomaniacally Ahabish, relentless commitment to his work was impressive. He always seemed to be on his computer, reading day and night, or writing day and night, and it seemed that he hardly ever slept. I know this because Junior and I would say goodnight and go to my room for euphemistic privacy (having a single, a benefit bestowed upon the captain of the basketball team). Brewster never made eye contact with me, and I question if he ever registered my name.

"He's an odd duck," Junior would say, "but he's harmless. Half the time he's working on something, the other half he is doing the whole thing all over again. And have you ever seen a boy's dorm room with no dust bunnies? Brewster has two vacuum cleaners." I had never been in another boy's dorm room and therefore I couldn't comment on any bunnies, but I took his point. "He is smart," summa cum loutish Junior said more than once. "He puts me to shame."

Full disclosure, which won't reflect well on me: Remember the time I took Ritalin before a game with disastrous consequences? Well, where did I get the kill pill? Junior stole a few from Brewster's stash. Junior denied taking any Ritalin himself, saying he preferred the black beauty Adderall, but looking back, I doubt that.

Sorry, Brewster. Please forgive me.

What I didn't know was that Brewster was obsessively keeping a meticulous diary, and that Junior one day when his roommate was out for a long stretch to attend classes he read it. At some point, too, he must have photocopied extensive sections. What possessed him to do that? I don't know, but Junior was one of those writers from early on who was perennially on the prowl for material and experience he could exploit for his own calculusating purposes. And if you assume that I assume I probably qualified as nothing but more material for him, you are probably my editor about to delete that whole whiny train of thought.

The Dream Calculus was essentially the product of Junior's plagiarism. The book contained over a hundred pages lifted virtually verbatim from Brewster's electrifying and beautiful and very distinctive prose. You never know who gets one, as Vonnegut wrote, referring to somebody's junior, however. Perhaps Junior presumed nobody, including Brewster, would ever notice or make the connection. What I didn't realize initially was that Calculus had been revised since I saw it—for which improvement I would have credited slash blamed Kelly. Once I had a chance to examine the published book, I could see that Junior's protagonist, Chas of the Adonis Bod, had radically metamorphosed into a fascinating autistic poet. Lawyers were prepared to release publicly the relevant pages from the thousands of pages meticulously composed by Brewster, when he shared that room with Junior. It would be obvious to any objective reader that Junior pilfered the young man's work, which of course he never tossed out, and passed it off as his own. Here's one place where Junior could have used a book doctor—and an ounce of integrity. The lawyers pleaded for relief in the form of an injunction against the continued publication and distribution of the book and also seven-figure punitive monetary damages for plagiarism as well as for the pain and suffering Brewster endured.

Junior's house kept its cool as long as it could. Then after the higher-ups read the supporting materials sent by opposing counsel, they acted. They recalled all the unsold copies, retracted the contract with Junior, and demanded repayment of his advance. It might have been easier for Junior if they had thrown him into prison gen pop.

✳✳✳

MOST OF THIS INFORMATION I picked up from the scandal-mongering book press, but some I picked up from Junior himself. Get ready for this.

"Nobody's talking to me anymore," he said to me over the phone. "Thanks for taking my call."

I closed my door for privacy, and also to disallow anybody from seeing tremulous me. I tried to sympathize with my ex. Yeah, I know, shut up, please.

"You were right to blow off the book, Sibella. I should have taken that as a sign. And then the new editors, especially Kelly—you used to work with her, you know how talented Kelly is—they got pumped up over the new voice, the groundbreaking material. It *was* groundbreaking. Brewster's groundbreaking material. You would have known better. You would have seen it wasn't me."

But who the fuck was the Real Junior anyway? And another thing: life had to be difficult at home, too.

"Chantal's going to leave me. I can feel it. She's disappointed, she put me up on a pedestal."

I knew that inclineration, once upon a time, because he needed a pedestal to be eye to eye with me, and I almost felt bad for his slide down that Park Slope.

"I'm doing it again. I'm lying to you right now. My wife already kicked me out, and I'm staying in some fleabag hotel in SoHo. She says she wants a separation for now, but I know she'll get a divorce or an annulment and shield her family money from me—to make sure I can't use her trust fund to pay off the claims."

I'm no attorney, but her legal strategy sounded dicey. I'm also not an ER doc, but I did seriously fear he was going to hurt himself.

"No, I'm not drinking too much. Just enough. They say vodka is kind of easy on the liver. I've fucked up my whole life. Where do I go from here? My agent dropped me, and nobody at Yale will return my calls, and after the news broke, everything I had sent out came back rejected overnight. And the *Sunday Times Magazine* is going to do an exposé. Won't that be fun? That's after they canceled the puff piece they were going to run about the hottest new young gun author, umm, which used to be me. And get this, this is beautiful. Guess who's got a new book contract? Brewster."

We talked a long time and I sensed he was building up to something, and I turned out to be right.

"It's pretty lonely here. My lawyers said I shouldn't call Brewster, but I did. I apologized to him for everything, stealing his book, stealing his damn Ritalin and Adderall, which never did me any good anyway. And he was cool, said he felt bad for me."

I couldn't hate him, now that he was hating on himself competently and legitimately. I never liked piling on, or running up the score in a basketball game.

"Sib, I did have an idea."

Here it was, his other Tod's Shoe about to drop.

"Like I say, it's pretty lonely in New York."

That is what he said about the crowded metropolis that was the greatest city in the world, which I myself missed more than I would ever admit. How much was he drinking today?

Mothers of America let your kids go to the movies!

"I was thinking I've never been to San Francisco, and getting out of town would be a good distraction."

Tell me, what girl doesn't love roses on Valentine's and diamond ear studs and, most of all, being embraced as a distraction?

Get a travel agent, buddy. Oh, right, they don't exist anymore.

"I could see you, Sibella."

You in the back row playing Angry Birds Candy Crush, tell me why I didn't hang up.

"If you were up for it, I dunno, I could you know, like, stay with you."

You over there texting your boyfriend, tell me why I didn't shoot myself.

To be clear, I didn't have the means to execute that plan or myself, and I didn't have the words for a minute.

"You're not saying no, Sib."

That was true.

"I'll hop on a plane and I'll stay with you for a little while, till, like, the tempest quells, for old times' sake? Whaddaya say, Sib?"

Forget the old times' sake, which was bad enough, did he really say *till, like, the tempest quells*? The *like* was bad enough, but the *tempest quells*? What did Sib ever sib in him? Since your answer to that question is to be located within the capacious confines of the null set (the single concept that made me smile during my entire dystinguished math career), you will have trouble with the next development.

You probably think I am a doormat, you probably think you would never entertain such a crazy idea as the one I was not being entertained by. You may well be right. I am the last person to argue, since you've come this far along with me. But you didn't know Junior the way I didn't know Junior. Being anointed somebody's *Muse* at a tender age entails some serious lifelong responsibilities. In Museland it's not always sweetness and light. You take the good with the bad. Or more often than poets care to remember, the bad with the really fucking awful. But most important to recognize, muses are by nature and temperament unpredictable if not fickle. The instant you take them for granted and attempt to sing your full-throated song, your mouth fills with cement.

"I'll think about it," I said.

I want to do with you what spring does to the cherry trees. I always wished somebody would one day go the full Neruda like that on me or at least not call me a distraction.

If you are staring bug-eyed at the page (never a good look, incidentally, so cut it out if you ever want a fulfilling social life, as if I should know), and lingering in incredulity over the Junior book scandal as well as my being sort-of-tentatively-open-to-the-idea-of-reconciliation-sex scandal, strap yourself up for the next part.

WIDE SIBELLA SEA

BREATHING DOWN THE NECK of Junior, as his star-crossed book was shooting up the charts before spectacularly crashing, was Ms. Ashlay Commingle, author of *Slip, Slippery Girl* (Hard Rain Publishing Inc., San Francisco, California).

"You know, Myron, if we had *Dream Calculus* in our pocket we'd have the *two* hottest books on the planet."

By the way, since you might be wondering whatever became of inserting into the book the hair-tie gimmick, Myron looked into it, but the cost was prohibitive, and he was having those cash problems, so sayonara, scrunchie. Not to worry, Ashlay would work around that disappointment, as she always managed to do.

When the ax fell on that neck of Junior's, Myron and I gloomily celebrated missing that bullet by promiscuously mixing our metaphors and our feelings, which is, under normal circumstances, never a good thing to do around an editor in chief, including one as green as I and not me though *me* could be syntactically defended as being the object of the preposition *as*, but in general I advise you not to push your luck, Kelly. Then again, normal circumstances hardly ever applied to Myron and his company, and I should say *our* company. In any case, that meant we had only *one* of the hottest books, but for a house like ours in the straits we were in, that was what we needed. In several months the cash would be flowing in, and before too long we might get back on our feet after surviving the fallout from the Fontana brouhaha. We needed to propitiate the book gods, pay our respects and beg for future forbearance. I would check with Murmechka as to suitable symbolic slaughtering candidates.

Isn't brouhaha about the dumbest word in the language? It also looks stupid, like February, which always looks misssppppelllled. I cannot swear I have read every single entry in the OED, but that will not hinder me from nominating the word for bad dog noun of all time. You won't be shocked to hear that its etymology goes back to the fifteenth century, when, as you know, Kelly, dinosaurs still walked the earth.

And though now you would never be in a position to edit my book, my dear old Kelly Girl, I feel nostalgically attached to you, and semi-codependent enough to keep you nearby in my imagination and on your perfectly painted toes. You know what they say: keep your friends close, your pedicured enemies closer.

✳✳✳

TRUTH IS, BIG REVEAL, Ashlay was okay. More than okay. I'd been wrong about her. You heard me. Please, suh, may I have 'nother slice of 'umble pie?

For there is no creature whose inward being is so strong that it is not greatly determined by what lies outside it. Jeez, George Eliot, she's a big-time baller.

Look, I had my issues with pornography and my opinions had not changed. But my mind changed about *her*. I could no longer see her as demeaning herself and allowing herself to be exploited. And every word in that last sentence makes my skin crawl. And, no, despite being tempted, I never did pay to view her cinematic ventures, which surely compromises if not undercuts everything I have said or will say on the sujet de Suzi Generous. Even so, she had made her choices and she benefited or suffered as she did. If I wanted to start critiquing lives, I needed to start with my own. Wait, that's what I have been doing for a couple of hundred pages. She and I had our differences, but nobody made a movie featuring me doing something I may have regretted later—at least I hope Junior didn't film us. I cannot say I ever heard Ashlay express a single regret about her X-rated career, while you have heard a thousand regrets about my life. Next stop, Lincoln Center.

I wasn't nominating her for beatifuckingation, don't get me wrong, since I don't have much clout in Vatican City anyway. And she and I wouldn't have gotten to know each other much better if she ascended by her lonesome into heaven. I was overseeing her publicity, and we traveled together on one leg of her book tour, the West Coast. Caprice did the other leg with her, the East Coast swing. Ashlay took my gently framed advice to tone down the porn costumery, which, between you and me, might have been a small risk, given the expectations she brought to every appearance— and those expectations were very explicit, like her once-upon-a-time career. But she decided she wanted to be taken seriously as a writer, and damn it, she succeeded. I have to clean up my own act at this late stage. Show some respect, Sibella.

I would show plenty of respect, as would the book world, who lapped up her tale (stop it, just stop it, I said). Starred reviews abounded in the trades, and the indie book stores welcomed her as a bright new luminary into their bosom with open arms and lots and lots of publishing One Love free publicity. Her Amazon page listed five hundred plus four- and five-star reader comments, and it was early in the book's life. Speaking of those Roman Catholics, the solitary sour note was sounded by their media moguls, who normally reserve their Jane Ire for abortion and evolution and gay marriage, but who took an abedding interest in *Slippery Girl*. They didn't appreciate that the clever and cleavaged and brilliant protagonist fell head over heels for a man of the cloth, who responded in predictable and spectacular ways—but erected not to leave the priesthood in the process. No, instead, protagogirlist herself returned to her childhood Catholic roots, and a refreshed love reblossomed, a love that finally turned, and I mean saved by the belle on the last page, Platonic. Passionate, but nonsexual. Curveball catches the corner, strike three. The Catholic reviewers missed the pitch by a mile. And once again the crowd went wild, because negative publicity, especially of a religious tint, engenders a backlash—a backlash when it comes to books in the form of a pop in unit sales. Her sales popped like Fourth of July fireworks.

As I said, I accompanied her on part of her national book tour, where I witnessed her signing a thousand books and submitting herself to the huggations of a thousand slobbering admirers. A large percentage of these acolytes wore her trademarked patent pending AC hair ties, which she had marketed with extraordinary results. And you guys out there, thanks for reading books like girls and thanks for showing your true colors for the readings, but what is with your ponytails and your AC hair tie? I think you need to take a hard look at your life. If I may continue. What a powerhouse was she. And she was a terrific reader, too. Theatrical and funny and self-deprecating, in all the right places. She was a revelation.

Over time, we got to know each other, especially during the post-appearance get-smashed-togethers in late-night restaurants and bars where she could unwind after her performances. From filing her information with the Library of Congress, I knew she was a lot older than I was, which you might not be able to tell because she was visually stunning and did not look her age. We discovered that we liked some of the same books and movies, and that our domestic backgrounds had similarities. Her mom was a homicide detective (my anthropologist mother was a kind of detective) and her dad was a shrink, like mine, and on cue we rolled our eyes in tandem when we fondly recalled daily therapy that took place over mac and cheezie. As most parents would have done, her folks had not approved of or understood her movie years, but unlike many others, they were open-minded enough to stay connected with her, and they never for a minute cut her off. Then when she went to grad school and then published her novel, they were over the moon with her. Neither of us had siblings. We talked of the pros and cons of being only children, acknowledging that we couldn't imagine having had a different life. I don't pretend to understand what motivated Ashlay throughout her life, but then again, for some reason I found that elephant-in-the-room interest on my part to be irrelephant. Instead, I began to cultivate genuine affection for her, and I think she felt the same way about me.

***

ASHLAY'S DRINK OF CHOICE was a Cosmopolitan, a pretty in pink drink that is too sweet for my tastes. It does look mouthwatering in its iced Martini glass presentation, I will say that. Me, I liked my beer, a hold-over commitment from college, unlike the other college commitments that did not hold over, though in my defense, I usually opted for the obscure, local, artisan beers that I discovered along the way.

One night after an especially strong reading to a huge gathering that tuckered her out, she consumed a lot of Cosmos, and I was keeping up with one beer after another. We were at a table in the bar of our hotel, some place in Portland or Seattle or Denver or Santa Fe, I can't remember. It possibly could have been Austin, which isn't on the West or any other coast, but if you were a resident of Austin you likely were confused to have landed in Texas in the first place, period. For certain it was one of those generic hotel bars, often empty as a schoolyard after a fire drill, same bored bartender wiping glasses, same track lighting, same music bubbling in the background, same salesmen guffawing over the same jokes to each other propped tenuously on their stools, their identical ties askew as their lives, and their marriages and drinks on the rocks. A place that cried out for social worker triage.

A solid three maybe four, hell, maybe five Cosmos in, she went, "Sibella, when did you perform shock therapy on Myron? Because sweetheart would never realize on his own I was queer." And I'm thinking: girl's two fucking sheets.

"What?" I said, because I had done no such thing. And, Officer, this onetime junior editor was also not going to pass a field sobriety test tonight. Honestly, I had never, and it was none of my business. But oh, the truth-telling properties of vodka plasma drip. And yet, sexual orientation on that order supposedly applies often to porn stars, or so I had heard. The wholesale X-rated exposure of the male world and all those male bodies, depilated for the most part as they may have been, might make such a switch attractive, if not inevitable. Then again, what do I know? But as to her statement, I had not drawn any such conclusion, mainly because the question never occurred to somebody as self-involved as me or I and I'm not going to go through that troubling grammar exercise again, and I had other problems I needed to deal with.

"Do you have a partner?" I stupidly asked, not because I was curious but because I was at a loss for polite conversation topics in this context. If she had a partner, I had never heard. Was there a chance she wanted to keep that part of her life private? Considering her public profile in her previous life, that would have been mildly astonishing.

That's when we noticed a man sporting a short-sleeve dress shirt two sizes too small for his button-busting gut and a fat tie big as a flag because he had materialized and was standing over us at our table in the ghost town of this bar.

"My buddy and I would like to buy you two dolls a drink." How you can sneer and offer to buy a drink at the same time must have been tough, and must have required experience and practice as a salesman exiled from some Glengarry or Glenn Ross.

"That's okay," said Ashlay. "Thanks for the offer, though, sir."

The yahoo yahooted and raised up his blubbery arms in victory. Evidently he had won his bet.

"I knew they were dykes!" And his belly jiggled drunkenly away from us, with our compliments.

It was my privilege to know the late Jack Crabb—frontiersman, Indian scout, gunfighter, buffalo hunter, adopted Cheyenne—in his final days on earth.

"Where were we again?" said Ashlay. I think she needed me to repeat the question.

"I was asking if you had a partner."

"No, I don't have one now. How about you?"

"How about me what?"

"Do *you* have a partner?"

She went there. I believe I correctly decoded the subtext. After I gathered my rapidly reducing number of wits, I explained that I had a long-term relationship that fizzled and I probably wasn't over it, and then a recent relationship that I had high hopes for had also fizzled. I had drained a few too many beers myself, because then I made a silly mistake.

"Ashlay, I'm not gay." I awarded myself extra credit for not adding *not that there's anything wrong with that*. At the same time, I was kind of flattered. Okay, a little bit turned on. Though not in that way, I would have said. And, yes, I could well have been kidding myself.

She may have been very drunk, and she was a great actor or a great soul or both, because she smiled and said: "You think I am hitting on you, don't you?"

"Well."

Then there was a loud commotion involving those guys at the bar. Their voices elevated to shouting.

"Is too!"

"Is not!"

"Fuck, bet you your commission!"

"You're on!"

And the intrepid portly fellow bounded back like an overfed Labrador to our table to commingle with Ashlay.

"I am slorry," he slurred, attempting to pull himself together and failing, and hitching up his pants over his paunch in a futile effort at presentability. "My colleeb and I got 'nother bet going."

"Gamblers Anonymous's meeting next door," I suggested.

He was speaking to Ashlay: "I made a bet with that dick at the bar, see um there? I said you're Suzi Generous."

"The actress? Do you like her movies?"

"Man, what a gorgeous piece of..."

"I get confused with her all the time. Sorry, you're a loser tonight."

"You sure?" He looked deflated, as if somebody had stuck a pin into his blow-up life-size sex toy doll.

"I have no doubt whatsoever you're a loser. My name's Ashlay Commingle, and I'm a writer, published my first book, and we're in town..."

"Writers're mosely losers, aren't they?"

"Have a nice night and give my best to the wife and kiddies."

I wished she hadn't put it that way, because he was either going to take umbrage or the family pictures out of his wallet. But nothing of the kind happened. Like us, he was about as drunk as he looked. Inebriation may have accounted for his fulfilling every writer's fond dream when he said, "Think my wife'd like your book?"

That's when I took control of the situation and told him of course any spouse in the world would love it. In fact, he could buy a copy right now, which I conveniently had in my gym bag. He happily threw down the cash and asked Ashlay to sign it "To Patty," which the author did with a happy flourish. He stumbled off.

"Hey," I called out, "you forgot your bedtime reading."

He returned shyly and thanked us again. He almost inspired me to confirm he was right about Suzi Generous, but then again, he was actually wrong.

"As I was saying," I tried to start over with Ashlay, which sounded to me like a brilliant improvisation.

She sipped her drink and spoke over me, I think to be considerate. "Sibella, sweetie, I like you, I do, but not like that. Have I hurt your feelings? Didn't mean to. Like you, before I came out, I would say to women I was attracted to, 'I am not a lesbian,' but that was my way of handling my ambivalence, by trying to deny myself and hoping I had it wrong. Nowadays, I don't feel ambivalent on the subject. One day it could be the same for you."

I downed the rest of my beer. Would that be unfathomable, for her to hit on me? Wasn't I appealing enough for a slow night in a bar like this? Yes, I myself was surprised to be asking myself such questions and making such connections, which weren't serious questions or connections, or were they?

"Are you hitting on *me*, Sibella?"

Not as far as I knew. I went with, "We both drank too much and we can laugh this off tomorrow, whaddaya say?"

But I kind of knew what subtle Ashlay was implying. That I wasn't finished yet, that my life had many phases left to go, with any luck whatsoever. I didn't expect I would ever be gay, because aren't you supposed to feel this in your bones early on in life? Something told me I was completely wrong about that, that people come out when they do and in all shapes and sizes and ages and let the fuck fall where it may. I'd spent many years as a jock in girls' showers and locker rooms and there was no possible mistaking in college there was plenty of experimentation, a patronizing concept although I could see the point of defensively phrasing it that way, to inoculate yourself from the consequences and the risks. I never went that route, for whatever reason. Then again, stranger things have happened to me. And I wasn't done living. This was but one of a hundred more good ideas that my friend, Ashlay Commingle, the original slippery girl, would come to share with me.

"Another round, one for the road?" she asked, in the spirit of let's not let this conversation end on a weird note.

"I've had enough for one night," I said to her, yet another thing I wasn't sure of. But then I reconsidered. "Sure, why not?"

Good thing Myron wasn't at our table. He'd insist upon hearing an answer to my rhetorical question, which wasn't rhetorical at all.

Wolf? I got nothing left to report to you, Wolf, absolutely nothing...

PART FOUR

FOR WHOM THE SIBELLA TOLLS

M Y FRIEND MEL MCGINNIS was talking. Mel McGinnis is a cardiologist, and sometimes that gives him the right.

Like a cowboy on a horse, an astronaut in his space station, a swimmer in the Olympic-size pool, Myron Beam died at his publisher's desk. He was alone in the office after everybody went home, and around midnight the custodian found him slumped in his Aeron chair, and almost suffered a heart attack himself when he came in to remove the trash. Nobody was present, therefore, for the grand exit pursued by a bear, and no last words of Myron's were recorded for posterity. I doubt that there would have been any, as this time the heart attack was anything but fake. It was real and it was massive, so I was told, and his death was instantaneous and painless.

The obits were churlish and few in number. The *Times* chose not to run one, but the trades posted tiny mostly semi-respectful notices in which, of course, they felt obliged to cite the Fontana misfortune, which added color that was, to me, gratuitous if not immaterial and inappropriate. Other than that, not much notice was made of his passing. In this way, the powers that be conveyed the message that Myron Beam's Fifteen Minutes were up Fourteen Minutes Ago.

As you would have expected, the memorial service was sparsely attended, seven of us. You're thinking *The Great Gatsby*, as was I, but let's not push the collusion too hard. Not to give too much away, but nobody should expect a green light at the end of this particular dock. His ex didn't show in the banquet room at the back of Carmine's, and neither did any other family. Maybe in the end we were the closest thing he had to family. The proprietor and the host of Avenue along with Carmine and one of the waiters did pay their gracious respects, which was very kind. YGB and Kelly did not fly out, no surprise. As for the stable of house authors Myron had published and promoted, the less said the better. Don't get me started about the Fontanas. No shows, as was the case with all of his authors but one.

Ashlay was indeed present, and she was broken up like me. We sat together, holding hands, nothing erotic about it whatsoever, but I was still wondering ever since the night at the stupid bar. Sometimes holding a friend's hand seems to be the thing to do, right? Hand-holding is a rare and underrated talent. Some people possess no aptitude for hand-holding, and before long you feel like you're intruding upon their physical space, and other people's hands eventually feel clammy and you pity them and look for the first opportunity to unclench and go to your corner and cut man. None of that applied to Ashlay. Good hand-holding is brave, is humble, is clean, is open, is free, is gentle, is affirming, is comforting. Ashlay was very, very good at it.

Of course, there were a few eulogies, all variations on the theme of Myron's visionary nature and Hard Rain's long run of successes—and nobody touched upon the recent missteps. All were variations on the notion that Myron was a loveably unlovable eccentric and a paradoxically hidebound risk-taking fellow who lived and died for Hard Rain. In other words, he was a man who was hard to pin down.

Memorial services, like wedding ceremonies, usually feature a bombshell or two, and for similar reasons. Such occasions call for taking a risk, because what is the point of holding back now? No exception on this occasion. For one thing, out of nowhere, Caprice delivered a knee-buckler of a gorgeous eulogy—touching, deft, droll, heartbreaking. I did not see that one coming. And Murmechka more than held her own, too—Murmechka! And not one wise beast made a cameo in her stately address. "I loved Myron," she said.

"We all did. If you didn't love Myron, in the end there was one possible explanation: something was wrong with you."

I myself said my piece, and there was plenty wrong with me, but I think nobody could tell who didn't know before. I would insert here an outline of my remarks, but that is impossible because I spoke off the cuff with no notes. And if I possessed a copy of the script, why bother? If this book ever sees the light of day and if it is nestled in your hands, it is, among other things, my eulogy for Myron Beam.

✳✳✳

AS WE FILED OUT, company counsel pulled me aside. He had personally overseen Myron's final disposition.

"How can I help?" I asked. "Everybody's packing up their stuff, and we can clear out as soon as you like." I knew that winding down Hard Rain was not a simple matter, what with contracts to be fulfilled, the backlist to manage—theoretically, the company could run by itself or with very minimal staffing indefinitely. Under the best of circumstances, it would take a while to reorganize and institute corporate or management changes.

"Hold your horses, Sibella. One thing I don't want anybody to do is clear out. We can get into this when we sit down to talk, but I want you to know Myron took measures to help assure the company would go on."

Counsel doubled as Myron's estate lawyer, he said, and he asked me to come to his office tomorrow first thing, and I agreed, and that was a night I didn't sleep a wink.

✳✳✳

MYRON'S LAWYER HAD A neatly topiaried moustache, which reminded me of cute photos of my dad when he was in college, and he had a law degree diploma from Stanford prominently displayed on the wall. Obviously unconcerned about his billable hours, he didn't waste a minute.

"The house is yours, Sibella."

Myron left me Hard Rain Publishing. He had no other heirs. He had hardly any other assets outside the company. What there were would be liquidated and proceeds plowed back in my direction. That was the gist of the lawyer's message, conveyed in the cashmeriest of voices. Myron's wishes were recorded for posterity and his voice rang out from beyond the grave.

"What fuck the fuck?" my voice rang out.

"Myron told me about your Tourette's, but he kind of liked it. Want some water?"

I did not and he went on. Hard Rain, Inc., was a privately held corporation, all the stock owned by Myron, and he was bequeathing all his shares to me, to employ at my sole discretion. Looking back, I might have imagined this development had I been half as smart as I thought I was, but as you determined for yourself starting on page one, I wasn't and I didn't.

"He went against my advice to give you a heads up, didn't want you to know about the bequest, because like most people he thought he was going to live forever. Besides, Myron was Myron and he did things his own way. Everything's spelled out in the last will and testament, and I'll give you a copy to look over."

I asked when Myron wrote his will. No surprise: the week after the fake heart attack.

"But there is something he wanted you to understand in no uncertain terms. You can cash out the stock, or you can sell the company, or parts of the company, or you can keep it and run it, as you choose."

I said it couldn't be that simple, knowing Myron as I did, which was not as well as I might have, but certainly better than most.

"You're right, Sibella, it's not that simple. It's going to be complicated, whichever way you go. You need to know that the company is underwater, the debts are serious."

He told me how serious. I stood up and walked around his office, the place where Myron and his lawyer devised the will. He told me the number attached to the indebtedness. It was a stomach-churning number.

"I'll take that water now." I sat back down and the bottle trembled as I drank.

"This is an estimate, I need to advise you. You will want to hire a forensic accountant, and you need to dig into all the files, to figure out what the true figure is."

"Whatever it is, we're swimming in fucking red ink, right?"

"Afraid so. This is a lot for you to take in."

"Should we sell the *company?* Should we declare *bankruptcy?*"

If my uptalking retained a stressor of any kind, this would qualify.

"This is where I am obliged to go the full legal, and I must advise you that you should retain your own counsel."

"All along I thought Myron was *rolling?* in it, and he was taking in big *money?* season after best-selling *season?*" Uptalk was running fucking *amok*, which is a Malaysian word, like *chimpanzee*, "man of the jungle," and as you can tell, I was decompensating like mad in plain sight. *Glug glug glug* went the water.

"Off the record, Sibella?"

"Off the record, please."

"He spent money like a drunken sailor, he never listened to me, and his revenue streams were never as strong as he wished or as he implied to everybody else. A few big hits early on got him going, and he thought he was never going to lose a dime, so why not take bigger and bigger risks? The divorce settlement was expensive, and that didn't help. That's around the time he started borrowing money left and right, stealing from Peter to pay Paul, and slow-paid when he had the cash to square up. And then he really got slammed. Here was the clincher. His investment portfolio went south. He'd made a lot of good bets in the past and he was fat and happy, and then he made a lot of bad ones and he wasn't. Bears and bulls—most of us get gobbled up or trampled eventually by the market. But Myron? Myron thought he could outrun the beasts. For years he was sustaining the company out of his own pocket with his stock proceeds, but then his luck ran out. He never listened to me. Again, off the record."

"But he did sell lots of books."

"He sold tons of units, but he didn't manage his money, his business. Whenever I got into it with him, tried to rein him in, you know what he told me? He'd say things like, 'You think book publishing is a business? You might be a pretty good lawyer but you're dead wrong about that. Publishing's a magic carpet ride. It's a horse race. It's mud wrestling. It's a fight club—which was the title of a pretty good book, wish I'd published it. Publishing's a fairy tale, and the best fairy tales are messy and violent and unpredictable, and some of them come true. None of that is revealed on income statements and the P&L.' Which is when I told him, 'You could be right, Myron, but what *is* revealed is the income and the profit and the loss.'"

I didn't think mentioning the Venetian gypsy would be advisable at this juncture, because counsel was on a roll.

"Look, Sibella, Myron was a character, like somebody out of one of his books. I loved the guy. You did, too, I know, and he loved and trusted you to the end, and as now you know, beyond the end."

"Myron died broke with his company deep in debt."

"To cut to the chase, uh-huh. But you know, Sibella, you can take a pass on the whole thing, get out from under. I can recommend a good BK lawyer who can help you do a workout."

"The Hard Rain brand name has value, right?"

"But the value has an expiration date, and it won't keep indefinitely. In the meantime, the name is your best asset—along with the backlist."

Sometimes in a basketball game, you get down big in the first half, but you keep playing hard, and if you get lucky your shots start to fall and you find yourself in a position where you can take a shot at the final buzzer and win. To tell the truth, I never had that experience of being the hero, pulling a game out at the last second, but there had to be a first time for everything, and I learned a lot from those losses. Thanks, Dad, for reminding me that time, I never forgot it.

I don't know why or exactly when, but sometime during the course of the hour with Myron's attorney, I impetuously decided I would live up to Myron's doubtlessly misplaced faith in me. At the same time, I would have to come to terms with my misplaced faith in him, too. I knew it was going to take me a while to piece together everything, to gain a realistic sense of the financial state of Hard Rain.

If I didn't hate narrative flashbacks (fucking corny or what?), here's where I would stick them, tugging on my own if not your heartstrings, and what is a heartstring anyway? The dark side would come out, too, if I had a shred of integrity left. I would play back my memories of Myron saying X and realizing in retrospect he should have said Y.

All the multiple takes on the central theme of Myron the Pretender. Myron playing me.

Myron playing everybody.

Myron being the con man.

I thought Porphyry Fontana was a con? He had nothing on Myron, and perhaps that's why Pork struck a sympathetic cord in him. Myron was the best kind of confidence man you would never want to run across in the world. And you know why? Myron believed his own bullshit, and the one he deceived the most was himself.

At the same time, I missed him and mourned him. Explain that one to me when you figure it out.

I asked for a little time, though I knew what I was going to do.

"Absolutely, you're the boss, Sibella."

Like it or not, I guessed somebody had to be.

BRIGHT LIGHTS, BIG SIBELLA

BEFORE I KNEW IT, I was inundated by the invoices and the demands and the summary judgments and the right-to-cure letters from unpaid authors. Our legal bills were mounting by the day, too. Every time I opened a new drawer or looked behind a shelf in Myron's office, there was more trouble, more creditors lurking. It was going to take a lot of work, and a lot of luck, to keep the business afloat. We had a few months, tops, to get a grip. It was going to take a lot of cash, too, and where was that going to come from? Sure, units had been moving, but the distributors and the book stores soon smelled blood in the water and began to make their returns. And we were having trouble with our warehouse, and the printer needed to be paid. Yes, we had turned a big profit on *Slippery Girl*, and the movie option and foreign rights cash were helpful, but the money only trickled in, dribs and drabs. And the tide of debts was rising by the day, by the hour, sending the next late royalty statement and uncovered bill onto our shore.

I stopped paying myself and I couldn't keep paying the senior editors or anybody else on staff, so I gave them the choice: hang in there if you can and I promise that if we survive I will start paying you again. Otherwise, thanks for your dedicated service. Most of them packed it in. I could not blame them. Honestly, I was almost relieved to clear the decks, but it was sad to see Murmechka go. She appeared upset when she said she had no alternative, she had to support her sickly aged mother and she needed to make money. I wished her luck finding a new job. After she cleared out her desk, she said she was going to come back later, she had something she wanted to give me.

"That's not necessary," I said, assuming she meant a farewell gift. Then I got paranoid, and feared she was going to serve papers on me. Take a number, you and Mr. Coyote, I bitterly said to myself.

Caprice was the only one who stayed on, which, after her eulogy, I was hoping, and she was a steadying, clear-eyed influence. And when she talked about using social media to work for us in these trying times, she suddenly made sense, and I allowed her carte blanche. She was going to do all she could to build public support to keep Hard Rain alive. Her personal financial circumstances were such that, well... Caprice, baby, just so you know, I don't think every single person or publicist with a trust fund should be consigned to a dungeon. As they drawl in Alabama, bless her heart.

Ashlay was coming in every day to lend moral support and she was applying her considerable entrepreneurial smarts in addressing the problems and coming up with ingenious solutions. But I feared that between us we didn't have enough will power and enough cash and never would.

Word got out on the street that we were sinking fast, and then the creditors started screaming louder, and the lawyers started sending new demands to pay up or face a lawsuit. We desperately needed a white knight. Unfortunately, that was what we did not get. In fact, we got the opposite. The darkest hour took place when Cable and Caitlin sauntered in without an appointment.

"Sibella, you got problems," saith the jerkoff.

"You fucking *think*?"

"I'd like to help, because I'm your man."

"I must have missed when you became my man. Say, been wondering, is Pork out of jail yet?"

"Long time ago, he is on probation."

"How did you keep your sorry ass out of jail?"

"I couldn't believe it when he made a claim on the life insurance, my dumb uncle. I could say I know what I am doing, but that must be obvious to you, so let's change the subject to something more pressing."

"Caitlin got you some penicillin for your newest STD?"

"How'd you…wait, listen to me. You should sell me Hard Rain Publishing."

I wasn't surprised. He was one with the guys who specialize in foreclosures and fire sales, buzzards in spread-collar shirts and sporting surreptitious spanx.

"For a dollar," he said, expansively.

"High roller."

"But I'll assume all the debt, which, if what I hear is accurate, amounts to being a great deal for you. You can lose all the headaches and"—big buildup—"I would have you stay on as my editor in chief."

"Because you would be the publisher?"

"Yes, *moi*. I think that would be fun."

"*Toi* have no idea."

"You can teach me the ropes around here, and we can publish books together, and before long it'll be like old times with my dad at Hard Rain. I know the first book we'll bring out, too."

"Of course you do."

"*The Life and Times of Calypso O'Kelly*."

Cable and his three-way fucking fantasies.

"You read Caitlin's book?"

That's when she piped up: "He couldn't put it down. All he changed was the title."

"Yes, great, because that's essentially all a publisher does. He sits around changing titles and eating bon bons."

We talked for a while, and I hoped somebody would put Cable, if not the book, down, but I heard him out, and took notes for my Royal Canadian Mounting billable-hours lawyer.

Don't be upset with me, Myron, wherever you are, because if anybody knew what deep shit we were in, you would appreciate what I said to Cable.

"I'll get back to you."

"You may not know this, Sibella, but somebody can also theoretically organize creditors to sue to force an involuntary bankruptcy. *Theoretically*."

"Good to know." Al ass, I resisted: this guy could be my boss someday.

"Take your time. How's forty-eight hours sound?"

"Thanks, Caleb."

✳✳✳

NOTE TO THE HOLLYWOOD sharpster who lunches daily at the Chateau Marmont and who is considering taking out the movie option on this book of mine, or who is contemplating buying the rights to fictionalize the story:

Here's your big chance to spice things up. This is the moment where you plug in Sibella's vampires, who grant her the very sexy eternity she has always deserved, and please let those vampires be gorgeous, and not Chippenclydesdale cartoon handsome steroidilized bodybuilders. Keep away any zombies, however, which have a tendency to creep me the fuck out. Or you could go in a whole other direction—and take your lunch at the Ivy instead. But what I am driving at is this: here's where Sibella finally acquires her supernatural powers. Now she can break down LeBron. Now she can acquire and market great books in her dreams. Now she can make her washing machine and dryer function. Now she can straighten her hair and wear the page boy cut. Now she can permanently vanquish her uptalk. Most of all, now she can ride to the rescue of Hard Rain Publishing, which, as was becoming all too obvious, would require nothing less than powers that were superfuckingnatural.

In Xanadu did Kubla Khan a stately pleasure dome decree: where Ralph, the sacred river, ran through caverns measureless to man.

✳✳✳

AS I HAVE SAID more than once, publishing brings out the asshole in everybody, and in would-be publishers like Cable Fontana, although as anybody could tell he was an asshole well before he contemplated becoming a publisher and hiring me as editor in chief, where I would probably survive a few weeks till he determined he could run the house without me. I may be naïve, but I instinctively knew the subway lines and the exhibitionists to avoid.

I wasn't concerned about the two-day deadline. For one thing, Cable was going to have to generate a binding Letter of Intent that I would have to sign off on and that would entitle him to do all the due dillydallygence, to get into the spreadsheets and nose around in everything and agree to a nondisclosure, so even if I despaired and finally had no alternative but to do a deal with that sluggola, nothing was going to happen overnight.

Meanwhile, I had another piece of business, personal business, to clean up.

✳✳✳

I CALLED JUNIOR AND said, yes, you can stay with me for a while till the dust settles in your life. Was I fantasizing reconsillyiation? Not consciously, and I am being as honest with you as I am capable. Taking over the oars of this seemingly ruined publishing house had wearied me, and I—TMI alert—desired some affection, some human attention, some person who cared for and about me, even as the sharks were circling my little skiff taking on water. Was Junior throwing me a lifeline, saving me and sending my way a little bit of salvation, or was he another anchor taking me down? I didn't know, but I was prepared to temporarily risk my apartment key and self-esteem with him. I understood saying yes to him amounted almost certainly to a doomed idea, that once a snake always a snake, but sometimes hopeless ideas are the only kind you have at your disposal. He told me he was very happy to hear my acceptance of his self-invitation, and that he would get back to me with travel dates, and in the process I thereby squandered the last vestigilations of any respect you ever tentatively held for yours truly. But I did hold the line on one matter.

"You're not divorced," I reminded him.

"It's merely a matter of time," he said, maybe a little too quickly.

"That means we're not sleeping together. We clear?"

I myself wasn't so clear about that last part, but it felt empowering to set a boundary. Hey, a self-respecting girl needs to stand on principles, and so do I.

Click, click, bye-bye, and you'll never guess who called a minute later.

Try, because you can.

YGB, you're right.

All my exes are from Plexedupus. His was destined to be a truncated call. In the whirlwind, I wasn't feeling warm and frizzy today. Besides, a girl can only take so much of nostalgia and bubble bathing, neither of which I ever liked much. I don't know why I phrase it like that, but the two notions connected in my mind, perhaps memories of childhood, like those Monsieur Proust should have written about instead of all that French pastry architecture, which is supposedly a grand achievement of his. Anyway, YGB told me he was getting out of the publishing business. He didn't have the stomach for it, not after *The Dream Calculus* fiasco, for which he took all the heat, and he couldn't walk down an office hallway without getting stared down by Mal Occhio and the rest of the higher-ups. He was going to go into…he told me the color of his new parachute.

I didn't care.

I had used up all my caring resources after Myron died and left me this mess. And then there was this bit of news: YGB left Kelly, too. He was moving back to San Francisco, he hated New York… And what, and what were the chances he and I could…

There was none chance, I indicated.

YGB was clueless and only in passing did he mention Myron's demise. And therefore I didn't let on what was happening now with Hard Rain and self-involved me. I don't know how Myron grasped this truth, Ruth, from the jump, but from the time he christened his editor in chief Young Goodman Brown, he envisioned how the boy's life would play out, like it did in Hawthorne's story of Young Goodman Brown, who took that late night walk into the dark woods and saw or imagined terrible things and would never be the same and would die miserable and alone without Faith, which was the name of his wife, and without faith, as well. Man, if you are testosterone- or faith-deficient, the publishing business is not for you. For the first condition, you can take some pills, but for the other, there is no course of treatment that will do.

You won't believe this, but Cruella DeSibella chillingly materialized, and she said, "Just before you called, I was talking to your once-upon-a-time star author. Weird, huh? Anyway, he's gonna be staying with me in my studio apartment—remember my little place? the one bed?—when he comes into town. Any messages you want me to relay on your behalf?"

YGB did, he really did. To tell the truth, Kelly left *him* after the company fired her. Many heads had to roll after Junior's crash and burn, and hers was a particularly pretty candidate. You'll never surmise this about Kelly. Of course you will. After YGB, she had already hooked up with…

"Eat pray tell," I said, and he did.

I heard him out, hung up, and immediately dialed Junior.

"Harry," I said.

"Hey, Sib, good to hear your voice again, what's it been, like ten minutes? We don't talk for years, and then all of a sudden, we—"

"Been thinking about your visiting me."

"Me too, looking forward. It'll be our chance to—"

"Hold on. Are you listening very, very carefully, Harry?"

"I hang on your every word, baby."

"Great. Here's two you can hang yourself on: ____ ___."

If you cannot correctly fill in the spaces accommodatingly provided above with the two soul-satisfying words I uttered, my work has been in vain. I am aware that it may have been in vain, but as any two-bit juniorish editor would tell you, that's the risk every self-lacerating writer or editor must take.

Best worst click in my life. Here's when I should drop the mic, turn my back to the crowd, and walk offstage to thunderous applause. Some complications: no mic, no stage, no applause, just me, alone, head in my hands.

Wolf, I quit.

＊＊＊

WHO'S THERE?

Note to Kelly, in case you're reading my book because you stole an Advanced Review Copy and temporarily have a lot of time on your hands, what with your professional high ate us. Too bad you lost your job—no, truly, I am sort of kind of almost sorry. I don't take an inordinate amount of pleasure in your misery, though I could, given that you hooked up with both of the heightist giraffe girl's exes, one on the sheets and one on the other kind of sheets, and then the other one on the real sheets, too. In the interests of good sportsgirlship, you should know that *Who's there?* is not the beginning of that famous old Abbot and Costello baseball routine (which is very funny and you could probably use a good chuckle). No, that's the very first line in *Hamlet*, which was written by a certain Mister William Shakespeare a long time ago, like before you started kindergarten, and it's the overriding question that informs the entire play, my favorite Shakespeare. If you ever go to a *Hamlet* performance with your two-faced boyfriend on-the-double-rebound with whom you can share a Tale of Sibella or two, if, that is, he hasn't yet scampered back to his wife, which is what he will do when you least expect it, may I make a recommendation? I hope you'll enjoy the play, which concludes with a fucking blood bath, like your New York publishing experience. And keep in mind, in the theater, no photos, no phones, no gum chewing allowed.

Maybe I am being harsh. Whoever you may be, you have to be a better person than I am. What I'd say to you is, don't bother worrying about Kelly. If history has taught me and Michael Corleone in *The Godfather* anything, you can kill anybody. History has also taught us that the Kellys of the world always manage to survive. She would pull up her pant suits one leg at a time and find another and better job, I had no doubt.

Like Michael in *The Godfather*, that was the day I took care of all the family business.

All that was left was taking care of the business business.

As for *Hamlet* and Hard Rain Publishing, *I* was there, that's
who. And Gentle Penal Reader, I married the company.

If we want things to stay as they are, things will have to change.

Like a number of marriages, this one started out rocky.

✳✳✳

OF WHICH I AM more than confident, unless your reading
comprehension parallels that of a certain senior editor, you have
some inkling.

Then out of nowhere and when I had all but lost hope,
auspicious things started to happen. First off, I discovered an
unopened bottle of Midleton's Irish Very Rare Whiskey tucked
away in a file drawer. I'm usually not one for the hard stuff, and
I prefer my beer, but once on my way out the door at the end
of work, on Myron's last day on earth as it happened, he poured
me a shot, in no time making this bottle one battle-scarred dead
soldier. "Try some, Sibella. Alcohol has been the ruination of lots
of writers, but trust me, this great Irish whiskey is the editor in
chief and publisher's best friend." He had a point. The Midleton's
was a revelation. It was velvety and lilting, as if you could drink the
pipes, the pipes are calling strains resounding far off in a distant
green glade. It was the last valuable lesson he ever taught me.
"Confusion to our enemies," he toasted, words to live by, and our
glasses clicked, and I left, and a few hours later he would be gone.

Then, I found some cash, though not in any file drawer, and
I searched and destroyed, believe me. My folks offered to lend
me some money, that is, to tide me and the company over for a
while. Amazing how useful an influx of cash and Irish whiskey
can be. It wasn't a lot of money in absolute terms, considering the
company debts, but it was real money with five zeroes.

"That's your retirement stash, Dad."

"What good is having bread if you can't help who you love?
It's only money, baby. Another day, another dolor."

God, I hoped not. The offer broke my heart, however, because
it meant I had let him and Mom down once more, as I had all my

life, and I didn't want to accept a loan from them, and I had enough money socked away to pay my escalating rent—for a few months.

"What are you talking about? You've never let us down. Except for maybe that unfortunate high-heel sneaker phase you went through."

"If I had to be tall I might as well have been really fucking tall."

"Point taken. But don't think of the money as a loan, think of it as a gift. We love you, and this is your dream job, books."

I said I loved him and Mom but let's hold off, and if I came to have no choice someday, I would humbly accept the money.

***

As for Ashlay, she had heard that I was grimly negotiating with the ever-grumly Remnant of Fontana. But I told her I was merely buying some time. To what end? No idea.

"Don't do business with Cable, you'll regret it for the rest of your life. He's a bloodsucker."

I knew that, but I was running out of options and time. And Cable had the operating capital, which had to be the money Myron made for his dad. This connection depressed me as much as it would have depressed Myron, who I hope was cutting his own deals in the afterlife and not watching too close.

"What else can I do?"

"Nobody would ever suggest to you, be Zen about it," said Ashlay.

"I am more like Nez, opposite of Zen."

"All right then. I always fantasized doing something with you, Sibella."

She wasn't talking about...? No, she wasn't, so that was good. Maybe.

Truth is, I had mulled over asking her to come financially onboard the company. I knew she had the wherewithal, but I was wary, for all sorts of irrational reasons. For one thing, we were friends, and you weren't supposed to do business with friends, and maybe that was normally prudent, but these were not normal times.

And then, *boom*: Ashlay announced she wanted to invest in the house. She said she had plenty of money from her movie days and a whole lot more from the incredibly flourishing Ashlay Commingle Scrunchie LLC, and she was looking for something new to invest in. Myron may have thought her movie career would be a sound platform for her book, but entrepreneurial Ashlay flipped that around, and she made the book serve as a platform for her other business ventures. And now she wanted to invest her hard-earned cash in Hard Rain, she said. Then she knocked me over when she proposed a number that came near to seven figures. I may have been a bust in math, but I could readily appreciate that serious amount of money now that I had learned how to crunch numbers ever since assuming control of the house. And you may be questioning me, asking me why I myself never approached her to buy in before. That's yet one more place where my inexperience showed and where she had a lot to teach me.

"Had another idea," she said. "Would you ever consider appointing me, I don't know, junior editor? We could work together and you can teach me everything I don't know."

"You already know a lot more than I'll ever know, Ashlay."

I wanted to cry, but I controlled myself because if I wasn't careful I was going to establish a behavior pattern I could not break. There's no crying in baseball, as somebody once famously said in a lightweight but diverting movie, and there's also no crying in publishing, which nobody ever bothered to say, because it was too fucking obvious.

It was going to be tight, and we were going to have a rough go reestablishing the company, even factoring in the serious liquidity Ashlay was willing to provide Hard Rain. We could however pay down a significant portion of the debt, and someday hire a senior editor and some office staff, and take on an intern or two—which I never was for a minute, get it? And hire a junior editor, maybe, who would have a job description and wouldn't be relegated to answering the fucking phone, and have enough money to push the next season of books—as long as the backlist kept generating revenue. And Caprice's work was destined to pay huge dividends via social media. She had no question that Hard Rain would fast become a publishing feel-good story, a back-from-the-dead tale. And who doesn't love one of those?

There were books I was itching to publish that had come in over the transom. Thanks, Myron, for the *transom* concept. I'll never forget it or you and I'll never understand either. That's what we were in the book business for, right? Not negotiating debts and financial complexities, but publishing new and good books, and you're right, it's all connected.

You know what was more valuable than Ashlay's money? Her trust, her belief in what we were doing. We might make it out of this pit. I wouldn't bet against us.

Then Ashlay stunned me all over again.

"Sibella, I need to tell you something else. I'd been contemplating investing for a while, but for some reason I kept holding off, and I think this minute I figured out why I hesitated. You're going to think I'm being ridiculous. It's one thing for someone with my history to write a book or get a doctorate, as I did, which are both pretty unlikely, and which anybody would say who never knew me. In real life, stranger things happen all the time, like I need to tell you. But if somebody like me appeared in a book of fiction, the reader who didn't know any better would say come on. Books are not life, but they are the next best thing to me, and to you, too. Tell me. What's the oldest cliché in the world? Right. The whore with a heart of gold. The image nauseates me. And that's why I hesitated, because I didn't want you, Sibella, to think I was some cliché. Pretty dumb, I realized finally, and that's when I decided I would do what I wanted in my heart, to help out you and the house that gave me and my book a break. And also you'll consider taking me on as a junior editor."

Ashlay was the original slippery girl, and she had given me the slip once more. Over time, she had become anything but a cliché to me.

"If you're a cliché, so was Myron and so was Figgy and Cable and Caitlin and all my exes and so was everybody and so was I."

"Promise me you won't ever think of me as a whore with a heart of gold, because I am neither one of those dumb things. Plus, I'll fucking kill you. Lovingly, but I will still fucking kill you."

***

ASHLAY UNDERSTOOD WHAT MYRON wrought in the company, and I didn't have to do much to get her up to speed—she was a fast study. Her lawyer was in touch with mine and we would work out the details. She did want to know more about the Fontana debacle and the Calypso near miss, and I tried my best to explain all I knew and all my doubts. She listened intently.

"Funny, Sibella, all this multiple identity stuff. Fig and Pork, that's extreme, but I get it—though there's a good chance it was a scam Cable cooked up. But then there were two Myrons, too. And Caitlin who was Calypso. And your old boyfriend, the editor in chief and your college boyfriend, both two-faced. And I guess multiple identity applies to me as well—I mean, how transparent can it be? Suzi Generous and Ashlay Commingle. Maybe all of us are two people, if not more. Identity may be a very fluid construct. Maybe multiple identities are all we are."

"What about me?"

"*You*, Sibella? Isn't it obvious?"

So many selves, so many sensuous worlds, as if the air, the midday air, was swarming with the metaphysical changes that occur, merely in living as and where we live.

SIBELLA'S WEB

ASHLAY AND I WOULD have a lot to work out with the lawyers and we'd need to define her role and her financial share in the company, but I was optimistic. Between us titans of industry, my mind probably never completely changed from day one with regard to women and pornography, but that's an abstraction, and Ashlay may have been lots of things, but she was anything but an abstraction. My views may have never wavered, but my heart did. One other thing. Because this was a privately held company, there was no need to disclose publicly who invested and who our white knight turned out to be, which is what she insisted upon.

Then she reached into her briefcase and handed over what she said was her new novel.

I was stunned. "When did you have the chance to write this?"

"Does a writer ever know how to answer a question like that?"

"I bet it's good. I can't wait."

"Best thing I ever wrote. Then again, I am biased."

With Ashlay's new book and with Murmechka's...

Oh, I forgot to tell you what my old colleague brought back to the office the day she departed. It wasn't a fish wrapped in a newspaper as I had feared. She handed over two manuscripts, which she hoped I would consider one day when Hard Rain was back on its feet. One turned out to be a fabulous children's book based on her Mr. Coyote sayings, illustrations by her, and the other was a mystically beautiful, erotic novel. I craved them both, they were great. Who knew? If I had my way, she was going to be the next Murmechka Sendak Slash Kundera.

Look at that. I came this close to saying Murmechka Fucking Kundera, but I restrained myself. My Tourette's, though it was only my potty mouth, seemed to have begun to recede, slowly, reluctantly. Unlike with Junior, this was one abandonment issue I had no trouble with. Not only that. My uptalk had also apparently gone into Witness Protection on the mean streets of The OC. I kind of missed them both, and I couldn't wait to tell my fucking *mother?* Just kidding. My mom, period.

I also couldn't wait to work with Ashlay and to publish books and keep Hard Rain going—from now on. I recalled when Myron asked me that time, nonrhetorically, "Why in the world would somebody become a publisher?" He must have believed that I had a glimmering, because he left me the company, but I was continuing to work on the answer. I did discover a few things ever since the company turned over to me.

Number one, a publisher has to be certifiably crazy—and no wonder Myron qualified. And B, a publisher is somebody who sees no alternative to the certifiably loony life that is publishing books. Downtown Myron Beam. It's similar to the life of a writer in this way: it's such a demanding and often unrewarding existence, and writers should write if and only if they can imagine no other life to lead. Publishing, same same. And another thing. If publishing brings out the asshole in somebody, it might also bring out the opposite, whatever that is, and I will let you know when I figure it out.

"Hard Rain is coming back," I said to Ashlay.

"Sibella, what shall we do to celebrate?"

Were Ashlay and I going to reprise our awkward conversation in that bar? Well, we could if she desired.

You heard me right.

She pointed to the Midleton on the desk.

Oh.

"It's no Cosmo, but let's drink to Myron," she said.

"He'd also want us to drink to us."

I poured. Confusion to our enemies, indeed.

✳✳✳

NOWADAYS I GET INTO the office early, earlier than I ever did as a junior editor. I still go for the white shirt and black tie. It seems right, and if I ever come across a men's retro blue blazer in my size in a consignment shop I will grab it. Myron turned out to have been a disappointment in some ways, but then again, we all do sometimes, and I missed him every single day. He had done something inexcusably wonderful when he dreamed up Hard Rain and was reckless enough to give somebody like me a job in the first place along with the material for his book. *My* book, too: this one.

As I was walking down the hall this morning to the office, I noticed that the periodontist next door had evidently moved out. I have been busy, and in all the excitement I must have missed the movers. The new tenant was a Dr. Handy, which is a pretty good name for a dermatologist specializing in cosmetic surgery, or so the plaque identified him, and he would be seeing patients by appointment. I didn't have an excuse anymore to delay getting the *Muse* 86'd. But then the issue got complicated in my head, as most issues ultimately do for me, as you have noticed over and over again to your periodic if not unflagging chagrin. On the other doctor hand, you can laser erase a tat, and that would be painful on its own terms, but you cannot laser erase your past, which would be more painful, and that tattoo was my past and my past was mine the way Myron's past was his and your past will always be yours.

Had I changed? There was a chance. That's when I determined I could live with the ink after all. Our penultimate plot twist. That means, Kelly, there's one more little twist to come. We'd been through a lot together, that tat and I, hadn't we? It would provide visual material for a good story to spin for somebody's grandchildren or even my own should they require a cautionary tale, and they always do, not that any kid would listen. I didn't expect any prospective future mate of mine noticing the ink would care—or ever exist. I filed away the laser removal idea at the bottom of the ever expandable slush pile of my brain.

You know what the strangest aspect was? For the first time that I had ever thought about the tat, I did not visualize the image of Junior flowering in my imagination. It wasn't *his* tat on me anymore. It was mine. I claimed possession of it. Maturation or denial? You be my judge. Or my therapist, but if you hang up a shingle down the hall, and if by your misfortune I wander in and hunker down in your chair near a box of tissues, think twice before you utter a "Say more" to me if you know what's good for you. I might hand you this book of mine.

To be clear, by saying I took possession of the Muse, I was laboring under no illusion that was in fact who or what I was. Then again, people often miss that's one of the Muse's neatest tricks, to pretend to exist. Artists plead for the intervention of the Muse when they are stuck, or drink to the Muse when they get lucky, or castigate the Muse when she lets them down. The very notion of the Muse implies that the power for great art, for the creation of something beautiful, is external to the artist. I couldn't confirm that, but I also couldn't assert with conviction that was a wrongheaded point of view. For me, though, the Muse did her best work when nobody was noticing, not even the artist. But you could look at the whole thing in a different way. If you ask me, each of us, artist or no, has our own Muse. Maybe each of us *is* our own Muse. In any case, that's how my tattoo was now speaking to me.

Mr. Zuckerman took fine care of Wilbur all the rest of his days, and the pig was often visited by friends and admirers, for nobody ever forgot the year of his triumph and the miracle of the web.

✳✳✳

THAT EARLY MORNING, AFTER taking my place at Myron's old desk that was now my desk, the phone started ringing. Nobody was picking up, of course, because no junior editor or anybody else was around. But it was different now. Though we were gradually, tentatively becoming more stable as a company, I was not quite fully accustomed to thinking of myself in my new role. I considered letting the call go to voice mail, though not for long, to be honest. After all, it was merely the phone ringing, and what could be more normal than a phone ringing in a publishing house? It might have been a bill collector, it might have been a lawyer, it might have been an A-List movie star looking to take an option. Anything in the world could have been happening around here and anybody could be calling. I decided to take my chances. I picked up the phone.

"Hard Rain Publishing."

"May I speak to the publisher?"

"Yes," I said. "This is Sibella Cassidy."

ACKNOWLEDGMENTS

THE AUTHOR IS DEEPLY grateful to:

Regan McMahon
Kristin McCloy
Briah Skelly

Rare Bird Books:
Tyson Cornell, Publisher
Guy Intoci, Editorial Director
Julia Callahan, Director of Sales and Marketing
Hailie Johnson, Editorial and Design Manager
Jake Levens, Marketing and Publicity Manager
Sydney Lopez, Marketing and Publicity Manager

Elizabeth Trupin-Pulli, JET Literary Associates
Kim-from-LA: Kim Dower; Kristin Spillers
Beth Needel, Lafayette Library and Learning Center
Vickie Sciacca, Lafayette Library
Kathleen Caldwell, A Great Good Place for Books

Ava and Raylan James
Patricia James, as ever and always

JOSEPH DI PRISCO WAS born in Brooklyn and lives today in Northern California, with his wife, photographer Patti James. He's the author of the novels *All for Now*, *The Alzhammer*, *The Confessions of Brother Eli*, and *Sun City*, prize-winning books of poems, and books about childhood and adolescence. His memoirs *The Pope of Brooklyn* and *Subway to California* came out from Rare Bird Books. He is the founding chair of the Simpson Family Literary Project, which promotes literacy and literature, writers and writing across the generations.